THE YEAR THAT ROCKED

THE YEAR THAT ROCKED

KATHY O. SULLIVAN

The contents of this work, including, but not limited to, the accuracy of events, people, and places depicted; opinions expressed; permission to use previously published materials included; and any advice given or actions advocated are solely the responsibility of the author, who assumes all liability for said work and indemnifies the publisher against any claims stemming from publication of the work.

All Rights Reserved
Copyright © 2020 by Kathy O. Sullivan

No part of this book may be reproduced or transmitted, downloaded, distributed, reverse engineered, or stored in or introduced into any information storage and retrieval system, in any form or by any means, including photocopying and recording, whether electronic or mechanical, now known or hereinafter invented without permission in writing from the publisher.

Dorrance Publishing Co
585 Alpha Drive
Suite 103
Pittsburgh, PA 15238
Visit our website at *www.dorrancebookstore.com*

ISBN: 978-1-6470-2217-4
eISBN: 978-1-6470-2918-0

*For my brother Kerby O'Connor and
my husband Greg Sullivan*

AUTHOR'S NOTE

This book is about a time when there were no cell phones, Internet, social media or texting. People in business offices were still using IBM Selectric typewriters.

There were payphones on every corner. And people were listening to Album-Oriented Rock on FM radio stations.

This time was the end of the seventies. The end of a decade of 60s and 70s rock music explosion. The people were a bastion of hippies turned media professionals who kept their philosophies alive.

THE YEAR THAT ROCKED is a work of faction: You don't know where the facts end and the fiction begins. All the concerts really happened. And so did the pop culture events surrounding the narrative.

So, get ready for a rock-and-roll ride through a year that distinguished an era and a lifestyle.

*"Because I believe that cocaine
is God's way of saying
you're making too much money."*

– ROBIN WILLIAMS

CONTENTS

CHICAGO

JANUARY 3

FEBRUARY. 19

MARCH 37

APRIL 55

MAY 75

JUNE 95

JULY 113

AUGUST 131

SEPTEMBER 149

OCTOBER 169

NOVEMBER 187

DECEMBER 205

THE YEAR THAT ROCKED

CHICAGO

1979

JANUARY

THE MIGHTY WIND ROARED DOWN the side streets east of Michigan Avenue as the blizzard dumped piles and piles of heavy snow on the city's most famous street. It was nine o'clock in the morning and it looked like midnight. The snowstorm picked up speed as it stalled and stopped cars turning the Avenue into a parking lot. A few adventurous souls walked in the downpour trying to make it to their offices.

A cab appeared in the distance, windshield wipers turned up to full blast. Inside the cozy vehicle, Flynn sat in relative comfort. He wore a ski parka with a hood and a watchcap. Suddenly, the cab came to a complete stop. The drifts were blocking the way. The mounds of snow were already at least a foot high.

"No go. Out," said the cabbie.

"C'mon, man. We're almost there," said Flynn.

"No go. Out."

Flynn paid and reluctantly got out. His first blast of artic cold was a shock after the warm cab. He flipped his hood over his head and took his first steps. With head bowed he walked toward Wacker Drive. He could barely see his hand in front of him. His cowboy boots slipped on the now dangerously icy street. There was nobody else left on the street. He was a lone figure trudging through what seemed like the end of the earth. The wind picked up and he almost fell down. But he kept on going.

When he reached the bridge going over the Chicago River to Wacker a double whammy of artic air slammed into his face from the Chicago River on his right and Lake Michigan to his left. There was no escaping it if you wanted to get across the bridge. He finally reached the intersection. The traffic light glowed an eerie green and he slowly crossed the street. His building looked like a lighthouse beacon welcoming all travelers. He reached the entrance door and the security guard opened it from his side and Flynn entered.

He took the elevator up the 8th floor and the double doors opened to WSL, a broadcast studio and adjoining offices. Flynn went down the hall to his office. He took off his coat and all his gear and sat down at the desk. His office had framed posters of rock-and-roll stars Jimi Hendrix, Tom Petty, The Doors. And movie posters of *Casablanca*, *The Maltese Falcon* and *The Last Waltz*.

Madison Elliot appeared at his office door. She wore jeans tucked into cowboy boots and a huge cowl-necked sweater. She carried two sets of clipboards and handed one to Flynn.

"You made it in," said Madison.

"Cab stopped down Michigan. Walked the rest of the way," said Flynn. "How'd you get in?"

"I live in the 'burbs, remember? I took the train. So did everybody else. The camera guys, floor director and Brett. We all made it in."

"Perish the thought of the 'burbs. Who's on today?"

"Dr. Weinberg, Head of Psychiatry at Northwestern Hospital."

"I hate shrinks."

"Flynn, tell me something I didn't know."

They walked down the hall to the broadcast booth. Out in the studio the usual bustling live audience consisted only of a handful of people instead of a hundred. The two cameramen, Jeremy and Isaac, stood behind their cameras and the floor director Zeke stood between them adjusting his headset.

On the stage, Brett Adams sat in his wing chair with the one across from him empty.

In the booth, Flynn and Madison donned headsets. Flynn addressed Jeremy.

"Hey, Jerz. Nice of you to make it here. No sweeping audience shot today. Looks like a ghost town out there."

"Roger, wilco," Jeremy answered.

"Nobody says that anymore," quipped Flynn. "Where's the guest shrink?"

"Stage left. Waiting for Brett to call him out," Zeke chimed in.

Two board techs worked the audio for the show. Above them, a line of monitors showed what was going on in the studio and on the stage. On one monitor sat Brett Adams.

"Cue the opening theme music," said Flynn. An upbeat jingle poured through the speakers in the upper corners of the booth.

Flynn talked to Zeke. "Start the countdown."

Zeke used his fingers. "Okay, ready in five, four, three, two…." The last number was silent as he pointed to Brett.

"Good morning, welcome to *The Brett Adams Show*. Today's guest is Dr. Carl Weinberg, head of psychiatry at Northwestern Hospital. Come on out, Doctor."

Dr. Weinberg entered from stage left. Brett stood up to greet him and shake hands. Then he gestured to the chair next to his.

The show was underway.Later, back in his office Flynn toyed with his notes. Foreigner's "Juke Box Hero" poured out of his office radio through the wall speakers.

Madison knocked on the open door. "Good show today," Madison offered.

"I hate shrinks."

"Yes, Flynn. We know."

"N.B.D. Same, same," Flynn said as he cranked up the volume on his radio.

They stared out the window at the turbulent snowstorm. But they couldn't see anything but white.

The news came up on WQXA. "Mayor Bilandic has declared a state of emergency for all of Chicago. The plows are held up. He's advising motorists off the roads. And to stay in if you don't have to go anywhere…."

Flynn turned off the radio. "I'm going to the Wrigley Bar."

Madison frowned. "You're crazy."

The lanky Flynn dressed in black Levi's, cowboy boots, t-shirt and wool blazer brushed his blondish shoulder-length hair back. His trimmed mustache was the only thing that showed once he put the watchcap on. Then he did the ritual that all Chicagoans did when in winter mode: Putting on all the winter paraphernalia: coat, scarf, gloves. He looked like a bundled snowman when he was finished.

When Flynn got outside the snow was coming down with a vengeance. The famous, iconic Wrigley Building, across the Chicago River Bridge, looked like a snow castle complete with spires and turret-like flourishes. He bowed his head and crossed Wacker over to Michigan and made it to the front entrance of the building. He struggled like a wrestler trying to beat the door down to the mat. The door kept blowing shut in the wind. Finally, he out does the door and entered the building. He took a moment to shake off all the snow before heading to the right into the bar.

The cozy room with mahogany bar and tables looked like an oasis in the middle of the desert. The leather barstools added just the right accent. The place was empty. Flynn bellied up to the bar and started taking off his gear.

Hector, the bartender, wiped a glass before coming over to Flynn.

"Hi, Flynn. You're the only barfly who would show up today."

"Hey, man, Hector! Bring me a Johnnie Walker Black with…"

"…one ice cube. You think I'd forget that. You're the only one who orders it." Hector turned around to get the drink.

Flynn eyed the entrance to the bar and saw a man covered with snow from head to toe. He started taking off a ton of layers including a ski mask with holes in it for eyes and mouth. J.J. Watts was under all that gear.

"Nanook of the North!" Flynn said.

"Isn't that a dog?" J.J. inquired.

"Oh, you've seen that old movie."

"I walked from the radio station. I was supposed to die from the cold and wind, but I'm here."

Hector came over with Flynn's scotch and placed it on a coaster. He looked at J.J. "What's your pleasure?"

"I'll have an Old Style. In a bottle."

"How come you're so tan in the middle of the storm of the century?" asked Flynn.

"I went to L.A. over the holidays, remember? Got my warm-weather fix so I could tolerate another Chicago winter. Have you seen Michigan Avenue? No cars, no buses. It's a ghost town out there," said J.J.

"I walked it earlier today. I almost blew off the bridge," said Flynn. "Your radio station up and running?"

"Yeah, rain or shine or sleet or hail, WQXA broadcasts." Hector placed his beer bottle on a coaster. "Thanks, Hector. You're a sane person like Flynn here. When are we all going to smarten up and move to California?"

"Never leave Chicago. You'd have to drag me out there."

"Come on, Flynn, you know you'd like it once you got there."

Flynn sipped his drink. "L.A. is a hundred suburbs in search of a city. Chicago is the real deal. A real city."

"I can't take this weather." J.J. gulped some beer. "It's fucking freezing and you're always inside."

"Drink up, J.J. It'll get you through it. We partying tonight? Or is it canceled?"

"Crazy Miles still wants to have the party. It's on the 95th restaurant on top of the John Hancock Building. You know, the station always has a party in January for good luck for the beginning of the first-quarter ratings. Are we gonna venture out in this later to get there?"

"The only way to go is walk. We'll just warm up here a while, then head down the Avenue to the Hancock. I wouldn't miss the January party cause of a little snow," Flynn declared.

"I have to check back into my office first. We can hang at the station to kill time before the party."

"Whatever. Snow don't keep me down," said Flynn.

Outside, the two snowmen forged through white-out conditions across the bridge and down Wacker Drive in the direction of the Merchandise Mart. They passed a few brave souls who tried to get through the storm. The drifts were two feet high now and the wind had taken on a life of its own. After a long walk, they reached the behemoth Mart and made it to the front door.

Inside the warm building they brushed off the snow and headed for the elevators. They landed on the 19th floor and arrived at WQXA. The lobby was bathed in soft track-lighting and a receptionist sat at a big desk with several phones on it. J.J. waved hello and they went in a door and entered the inner sanctum.

J.J.'s office looked a lot like Flynn's with rock star posters and several awards atop the credenza. Flynn sat down in the visitor's chair. At the desk, J.J. picked up a shoulder bag from the floor and took out a little amber bottle full of cocaine. Out of his desk drawer he pulled out a mirror and dumped a pile of coke on it. Using a business card he started making lines. He then grabbed a wrapped straw out of his pencil holder and cut it in half with a scissors. After taking the paper off, he handed the straw to Flynn, who helped himself to a snort. J.J. took one and then got up.

"I've got to go down the hall to the booth and see if Skye is there. I know he'll want some of this," said J.J.

Flynn turned up the monitor on J.J.'s speakers and the strains of AC/DC's "Gimme a Bullet" poured into the room.

Down the hall J.J. peered into the broadcast booth and saw Skye Matthews, the WQXA morning deejay, as he listened to AC/DC on the monitor. J.J. went into the studio and greeted Skye. He tilted his head to the afternoon deejay Mitch. He waved to him and then checked the board. J.J. led Skye out of the booth and down the hall to his office.

Flynn and Skye shook hands. J.J. shut the door and handed Skye the straw.

"Better not to announce what we're doing to the whole office. Although Miles and everybody else is doing it, too," said J.J.

Skye took a snort in one nostril. Then the other.

"Thanks, J.J. I needed that. My morning show was all about the storm. I hardly got a record in," said Skye.

"What's the latest?" asked Flynn.

"Two feet already with more to come. Predicting five-foot drifts. They're calling it the 'storm of the century.' The whole city is shut down," answered Skye.

"I called it the 'storm of the century' back at the Wrigley Bar. I was just kidding, but it seems that I was right on the money," said Flynn.

"Has Miles called off tonight's shindig?" asked J.J.

"No. He says it's on. People can walk there. He's not calling it off," said Skye.

Flynn piped up, "There's two kinds of snow, man. The one you snort and the one you live through."

"Is that a new Flynnism? Or are you just being profound?" asked J.J.

"N.B.D. No Big Deal," said Flynn.

Later, Flynn and J.J. walked through the white-out conditions. Snow swirled and stung as they faced front into the wind. The arctic blast was relentless. The streets abandoned. When they reached the John Hancock on Michigan Avenue, they noticed that ropes had been attached across the tarmac to literally be used for pulling yourself up to the front door. They grabbed on to the ropes as if they were lifelines. They struggled like mountain climbers on Mt. Everest. Hand over hand until they reached the revolving door. It was frozen and they had to push it back and forth until it finally opened.

In the lobby, they took off their head and face gear.

"Jesus, I'm losing my mind. I think my tan peeled off," shrieked J.J.

"Could you believe those ropes? That's a first in all my days in Chicago. Ropes. Like climbing a mountain," said Flynn.

"This is not N.B.D.," said J.J.

"Uncle. You win. No Big Deal does not apply in this case," said Flynn.

They brushed snow off and headed over to the elevators. When they reached the 95th floor, the doors opened onto a huge room with a bar and tables that surrounded a 360-degree view of the city of Chicago, which was invisible because of the snow.

Miles Lester, the General Manager of WQXA, dressed as usual in his three-piece business suit and red tie, raced over to them as they took off their layers of clothes. The clean-shaven, short-haired man in his thirties stuck out his hand to Flynn and popped J.J. on the back.

"You made it. Way to go. The whole city is shut down and we decided to have a party. I guess that's what happens when you plan a party in January in Chicago," said Miles.

"How about those ropes? Nice to see you, Miles. I'm headed to the bar. You want something?" asked Flynn.

Miles held up a glass full of something. Flynn approached the bar and ordered a scotch. When he got the drink, he saw J.J.'s wife over by a window and walked over to her. Tiffany Watts was petite and pretty with long red hair and a slim figure. She had a tan to match J.J.'s.

"Hi, Flynn. How's *The Brett Adams Show*? Did you make it in today?" asked Tiffany.

"I was in a cab on Michigan heading toward the station when the driver said, 'No go.' Or something like that. I walked the rest of the way. The show must go on and all that. J.J. and I have been doing a lot of walking," answered Flynn.

"I walked over, too. But we're just down a couple of blocks on Superior Street in that high-rise, so it wasn't too far. Did I tell you about my new boobs?" Tiffany straightened up a bit and stuck out her chest.

"Your what?"

"I'm getting new boobs next week. Two of them."

"I don't know what to say. I really don't...I...congratulations?"

"I've always been small breasted. And now I'll have something to show off."

Flynn quickly changed the subject. "Can I get you something to drink?"

"Oh, Flynn. You're embarrassed. How cute. White wine will do."

Flynn walked over to the bar while J.J. grabbed Tiffany and lead her over to a table where a group from the station was sitting. Miles was holding forth with some of his troops. He launched into a rah-rah mode of station talk.

"We're number two in the market. Neck in neck with WLUP. Of course, we're both album-oriented rock stations, but we're the better one." He raised his glass. "Here's to beating them first quarter in the ratings."

Flynn joined them and handed Tiffany her wine.

She smoothed down her dress. "Thanks, Flynn. White. Just what I wanted."

Flynn wandered around the circular room. He kept trying to see through the snow, knowing he was missing a fantastic view of Chicago and the lake. When he circled back to the station table somebody new had joined the group. She was a striking blonde, tall and thin like a model with piercing blue eyes.

J.J. introduced her as Stephanie Lloyd. Flynn shook her hand.

"You work in radio or TV?"

"No."

"Good."

"I work at *Playboy*. The magazine. Assistant to the Editor."

"How refreshing."

"Glad it meets your approval."

"No need to get sarcastic. I rarely meet someone who doesn't work in radio or TV."

"Where do you work?"

"I'm the Director of *The Brett Adams Show*."

"You mean the talk-show with all the shrinks on it?"

"I hate shrinks," moaned Flynn.

"I love them. I've been going for a while now. I love exploring my bad side."

"You have a bad side? I like that."

"It gives me something to talk about in therapy."

"Where are you from?"

"L.A."

"Is anybody not from California? And don't tell me you like wine."

"Of course. Could you get me some white French Bordeaux?" Stephanie held up her empty wine glass.

They walked over to the bar together. The small TV set above the bar had the local news on the screen. The announcer talked about the storm and how the streets weren't getting plowed. A record fourteen inches had already fallen.

Stephanie took her wine and turned to Flynn.

"This is my first blizzard."

"Now I know you're not from Chicago." Flynn got his second scotch and led Stephanie back to Miles' table.

Miles was holding forth again. Among the men seated there were two Sales Associates and a couple of wives.

"Hey, Flynn. How's *The Brett Adams Show*? You still the director or did they can your ass?" asked Miles.

"My ass is still in place. Thank you very much. Everybody, this is Stephanie Lloyd."

The group shouted in unison, "We've met her."

The party continued. A buffet dinner was set up near the windows that displayed only the snow that was coming down with a vengeance.

Around midnight, Flynn, Stephanie, J.J. and Tiffany stood waiting for the elevator. When the doors opened, they went in and rode down to the first floor. They reluctantly walked over to the revolving doors and stared out at the Armageddon scene.

"Let's go to Butch's," Flynn ventured.

"Are you crazy?" yelled Tiffany and Stephanie.

"I'm game," answered J.J.

They donned their head gear. Stephanie had a fur-style Russian hat and Tiffany had a ski mask to match J.J.'s. Flynn had his watchcap. They went through the revolving doors and headed into the blizzard. The ropes were still there and they grabbed them with relief as the wind was at their backs now and fierce as ever. Hand over hand they walked down the tarmac to the invisible Michigan Avenue. Nobody was on the snow covered streets. And nobody was plowing. The drifting was a couple of feet high. They were all flabbergasted to see how much snow had fallen since they were at the top of the Hancock. The group of four trudged forward.

After a few minutes they hadn't gone very far and Flynn looked around for anything the color of yellow. No luck. They kept walking.

They had formed a line and were walking together toward Division Street. It took them more than a half an hour to get there, but they finally reached Butch McGuire's pub. The front door, like all the others, was hard to open because of the wind. Someone from inside finally helped with the door. When they got in the bar was practically empty. Only a handful of adventurous souls had ventured out in the "storm of the century." Flynn and the gang peeled off their layers, dumping everything on an empty couple of barstools. They stood in front of the bartender.

"Hey, man, Joco! How's it going? Line up the 12-year-old scotch. These fools want some kind of wine," said Flynn.

Joco started working behind the bar. "Red or white? California or France? Name your brand."

"California white," answered Tiffany.

"White French Bordeaux. Anything expensive," added Stephanie.

"Wine. Wine. N.B.D. Isn't it all the same?" quipped Flynn.

"What's N.B.D.?" asked Stephanie.

"'No Big Deal,'" J.J. answered. He asked Joco for an Old Style in a bottle as he was serving the scotch and wine. "It's a Flynnism. He's got his own language. You'll see if you hang around him enough."

The front door opened to a rush of snow and freezing wind. In came Miles Lester and the sales team from the John Hancock party.

"Humans are still alive in this blizzard! I had a feeling I'd find you people here. No other idiots would walk from the John Hancock to Butch's. But then of course we did it, too. Let's all take a table in the other room," said Miles.

The other room was deserted except for one person. He sat at the biggest round table in the middle of the room. It was Don Bennett, a Butch's regular, who always dressed in black and always seemed to dwell in the shadows. No remarkable feature stood out. He was just Don and he always had coke.

"Anybody want to go to the bathroom?" Don asked the group. The universal question of the day for anybody wanting a few hits of coke.

Stephanie and J.J. followed Don to the back of the bar and into the men's room. Don pulled out a small amber vial and a gold, tiny coke spoon. He dipped the spoon into the vial and offered up a snort for Stephanie. She took a toot in both nostrils. Then it was J.J.'s turn, followed by Don.

"Thanks. As if we don't have enough snow. But I like this kind better," said Stephanie as she sniffed.

"A hundred bucks a gram," Don said as he pulled a snowseal out of his pocket.

"I'll take one," said J.J. "Let me get some change from Joco."

When they came back to the table it was obvious to everyone they'd been snorting coke. J.J. headed off to the bar to get his change. Tiffany, who had missed her chance, grabbed Don's arm and led him back to the bathroom.

Stephanie sat down next to Flynn. "So, this is your bar?"

"I have many bars. Some are on the Street of Dreams, some aren't," said Flynn.

"Division Street is the Street of Dreams? It's just another street in Chicago," said Stephanie.

"This street is just a metaphor. You go after your dreams and you see what happens." Flynn sipped his scotch.

"Nobody gets their dreams. They always end up compromising."

"Stick with me. You'll see. You'll start believing. You gotta have dreams. That's what this street is all about. Like in *The Maltese Falcon*, Bogart at the end of the movie telling the cop Ward Bond what all the fuss was about. 'The stuff that dreams are made of.'"

J.J. returned from the bar with his cash. He overheard what Flynn said. "Quotation King. You always have one handy."

"You've never seen *The Maltese Falcon*?"

"Missed it."

"Catch it on TV sometime."

Don and Tiffany returned from the bathroom. The snow didn't let up and neither did the consumption of alcohol. The group took turns going up to the bar and ordering from Joco. There were no waitresses on duty tonight.

Flynn and Stephanie flirted at a corner of the table. She kept raising her head and laughing. They were getting pretty cozy. At about 2 A.M. everybody decided to venture back out into the winter wonderland and go home. The ritual of getting dressed in snow gear took a couple of minutes. Then they all went out. Braced for the wind and said their goodnights.

Outside the door, Flynn took Stephanie's hand and whispered to her, "I'm just around the corner on Elm."

The snow had drifted into five-foot mounds. They bowed their heads and walked into the wind. It was a short walk to Flynn's high-rise apartment building. The doorman, Billy, tried to open the door for them. He struggled on his side and the wind kept closing it in his face. After many tries, the three of them finally got the door open and Flynn and Stephanie stepped into the vestibule. They brushed off as much of the snow as they could.

Billy spoke first, "Flynn, are you crazy being out in this? And you dragged this pretty girl with you. The news says there's more snow coming. And there are no plows clearing. It's a nightmare."

"N.B.D.," said Flynn.

"No, it is a big deal. I'm used to surfing in January," said Stephanie.

"California. It's not even real. Let's go upstairs and get warm. I've got a fireplace," promised Flynn.

They walked through the ultra-modern lobby. Billy stepped ahead to push the elevator button. Flynn and Stephanie stepped in and he pushed number 18. They stepped out into a hallway plush with carpeting and low lighting. When they reached 1812, Flynn unlocked the door and let Stephanie go in first. He switched on the light and the track-lighting bathed the room in softness. The living room was a leather couch and club chairs and a big oak coffee table. The bedroom was off to the left. Dining room two steps up in its own area with another big oak table and four chairs. The kitchen was just to the right of that. The huge fireplace with a marble mantle dominated the entire apartment. Next to it were double French doors leading to a balcony that was invisible with several feet of snow on it. His entertainment center had a turntable on top of a receiver and huge KLH speakers on either side of the fireplace. His record collection was massive and took up one whole wall.

Flynn took some kindling out of one wicker basket and newspaper out of another and started to light a fire. The room took on a new perspective as flames started to build.

Stephanie had taken off all her gear and was planted on the couch watching the fire take off. Flynn added one of the bigger, perfectly round logs from his wicker basket filled with urban wood.

They both waited for the fire to take hold of the log as Flynn looked through his record collection for just the right album to suit the mood.

Stephanie pulled out a small amber vial of cocaine from her purse. "I bought this from Don. He gave me the bottle 'cause he was out of snowseals. But it doesn't matter as long as it's coke. You gotta mirror?"

Flynn went into the bedroom and brought back a small hand mirror. "This is about the best I can do."

"That's fine." She poured some of the coke out onto the mirror and made lines with her business card. Then she rolled up a hundred-dollar bill and made a snorting tool. She went first and snorted up a line in one nostril. Then the other. She handed the bill to Flynn, who took a line.

"That's all for me. I'd rather smoke a joint. I'm into a mellow buzz." He reached into a cigarette box on the coffee table and pulled out a rolled joint. The box was full of joints. As he lit up, the room filled with the unmistakable scent of fresh marijuana.

Stephanie did two more lines. She handed him the bill. "Come on, Flynn, let's keep partying."

He waved off the bill. "Let me pick out some music. You want ORGs or something more current?"

"What are ORGs?"

"Original Rock Gods. Like Jimi Hendrix, Eric Clapton, The Stones. Then there's the brilliant Crosby, Stills and Nash. Dylan. Many others. I've also got Neil Young. I've actually got just about everybody."

"How old are you, anyway? That's a lot of music from the past."

"Classic rock. The best of times. I'm twenty-nine. How 'bout you?"

"Twenty-two."

"You were twelve when some of this came out. God, I'm robbing the cradle."

"I've been on my own for a couple of years. I met my boss at *Playboy* when he came to San Diego State to give a lecture on publishing. Later we reconnected and he offered me a job here in Chicago. I hated to leave California, but assistant to the editor was something I couldn't pass up."

Stephanie took another line of coke. Flynn smoked his joint, then placed it gingerly into the ashtray.

"I'm going to put on some music. How about Fleetwood Mac's *Rumours*? I think Led Zeppelin and Foreigner are always good. But let's go with Fleetwood Mac."

He got up and searched through his alphabetized record collection until he came up with the Fleetwood Mac album. He put it on the turntable. Music wailed through his mega speakers.

"Want a drink?"

"Whaddaya have?"

"Scotch or beer."

"No wine?"

"Sorry, I wasn't expecting company."

"I'll have a beer."

Flynn walked up the two steps and turned into the sizable kitchen with granite counters. He came out with two bottles of Old Style.

Stephanie looked aghast at the bottle of beer. "No glass?"

"What? Are you high-maintenance?"

"A glass is high-maintenance?"

"In my book."

Stephanie sipped her beer. Flynn gulped his. He lit some candles and then they started kissing. It became hot and heavy petting quickly and the next thing they're on the floor on the Oriental rug making love. Flynn rolled her over so she landed on top of him. They finished that way and fell back on the rug laughing. Flynn got up to change the record to Jimi Hendrix's *Are You Experienced?* When he got back to the floor they started in again with round two.

Sometime during the night they switched from the floor to the bedroom. In the morning, Stephanie wore one of Flynn's robes and wandered around the apartment. She looked at the framed artwork on the walls. Two Monet prints and several rock star posters including Eric Clapton and Tom Petty with the Heartbreakers behind him. She walked over to the French doors that led out to the balcony. The snow drifts were higher than the railing and it was still snowing. There was no visible view except a white blur.

Suddenly, Flynn stood behind her. "Hey, you. Not a good day for sitting out and enjoying the view."

"I've never seen so much snow in my life," said Stephanie.

"Let's see what the local news says."

Flynn turned on the TV to WSL news. The announcer was outside reporting from the bridge over the Chicago River. The Wrigley Building was in the background. "... breaking all records for snowfall. 18.8 inches dumped on us so far. As you can see, it's still snowing. Some cabs and buses have managed to break out onto the streets. Right here, Michigan Avenue is passable...."

"Want coffee?" asked Flynn. "How about tea?" answered Stephanie.

"High-maintenance!" laughed Flynn.

He went into the kitchen to get the drinks. There was a small TV on the kitchen counter and he turned it on. The big news on the snowstorm continued.

"...all Chicago public schools are closed today...."

Stephanie joined him in the kitchen. "You have a TV in here, too? And all that record-playing equipment. You're like a multi-media man."

"That's me!"

"I guess the magazine will be up and running today," whined Stephanie.

"I haven't heard anything from the show, which means we're definitely broadcasting today. There won't be much of an audience. If anybody." He listened to the news again. "Bilandic really blew it. He's never going to get elected again after this."

Stephanie tightened the belt around the robe. "I'm gonna have to go home and change clothes. I can't show up at work in the same thing I had on yesterday."

"Oh, God forbid. Get dressed. We'll venture out. Maybe I can find a cab and we'll drop you at your place so you can change."

Flynn and Stephanie went down in the elevator. When they got out, Steve, the daytime doorman, was there to help.

"Any cabs at all?" Flynn asked.

Steve went out the front door and looked for a cab. Elm Street was one of the lucky ones that got plowed. Dim headlights came toward him. A cab. Empty. He flagged it down.

Back at the front door, he waved Flynn and Stephanie outside and helped them into the cab. Inside, the heat poured out. They sat in the backseat and just stared out the window at the world of white.

"Where to?" the cabbie barked.

"Sandberg Village," Stephanie said.

"Then on to Michigan and Wacker," said Flynn. "How'd you make it out?"

The cab driver grunted an answer, but it was beyond understanding. The cab moved along slowly and slipped frequently on the icy streets.

When they got to Sandberg Village, Stephanie told the driver which building in the multi-building complex. When she got out, she almost fell but caught her footing.

Flynn rolled down the window. "You should get yourself some proper boots for Chicago weather."

"Flynn, I'm okay. Thanks for the night. I had a great time."

"I'll call you. *Playboy*, right?"

Stephanie waved as she walked toward the entrance to the building. "Sure thing."

The cab turned around and headed into a thin stream of traffic. Parts of the city were coming back alive on North Avenue. When they reached Wacker and Michigan, Flynn paid the driver and got out.

Upstairs in the studio things seemed normal. The staff of the show ran around doing prep for the taping. Flynn went into his office to get his clipboard and notes. He noticed that today's guest was another shrink, Dr. Rosenfeldt. Suddenly, Madison sauntered into his office.

"You ready for Rosen what's it? I know how you love your daily dose of shrinkdom."

"I'm as ready as I'll ever be," countered Flynn. "Hey, did everybody make it in?"

"Yeah, remember most of our staff live in the 'burbs. We've got the Chicago Northwestern and the Milwaukee Road. Trains always going. Along with the L we've got the best mass transit in the country."

"Okay, I believe you. You're a walking train schedule, for God's sake. When are you going to move into the city, anyway?"

"Spring or summer. I told you I'm saving up for a studio apartment. Can't wait."

"Then you'll have to suffer the weather like the rest of us." Flynn gathered up his notes and clipboard and headed to the broadcast booth. Madison at his heels.

Another day of *The Brett Adams Show* was about to begin.

FEBRUARY

FLYNN SAT AT HIS DESK with his feet up. He was listening to WQXA out of his office stereo speakers. Foreigner's "Cold as Ice" segued to Led Zeppelin's "Stairway to Heaven." Line one on his multi-lined phone lit up. At the office door was Madison.

"J.J. on line one," she said.

"Put him through." Flynn punched the line and greeted his friend. "Hey, what's happening, man?"

J.J. talked for a minute.

Flynn jumped in. "Tickets to The Police at Park West? I'm in. Can I bring a date?" Another pause. "Backstage access. Tickets at Will Call window. This gets better and better."

Flynn and Stephanie got out of a cab in front of Park West, a small, intimate venue near Lincoln Park for rock shows and comedians. They went up to the Will Call window, got their tickets and went inside. A bar stood to their right, and down some stairs was the main room filled with tables and chairs. Behind the tables and chairs were leatherette booths forming a semicircle. Every vantage point faced the darkened stage. There wasn't a bad seat in the house.

J.J. and Tiffany had already taken over a booth and they waved Flynn and Stephanie over. They slid into the booth on the opposite side of J.J. and Tiffany. Suddenly, Don stood at the booth. He pushed in next to Flynn.

"Don, you keep turning up," said Flynn.

"I invited him," said J.J. He reached into his canvas case and pulled out a bunch of laminated badges attached to string-like necklaces. He started passing them around the table.

Flynn picked his up and stuck it around his neck. Stephanie just stared at hers as Tiffany and Don put theirs on.

"All-Access Passes are getting pretty fancy," said Flynn.

"What is it?" asked Stephanie.

"Embellish that in your bird dog," said Flynn.

"Who? What?"

"Embellish that in your bird dog."

"That's Flynnspeak for put that thing around your neck," said J.J.

"Okay, okay. I'm not going to lose it. But embellish…." Stephanie placed the necklace around her neck. "Everybody happy?"

"I just don't want you to lose it. When the show is over it gets pretty crazy," said Flynn.

Don spoke. "Anybody want to go to the bathroom before the show starts?"

Stephanie and J.J. were out of their seats in a flash. They followed Don over to the bathrooms.

"I guess that just leaves you and me, Tiff," Flynn broke into the silence. "How's it going?"

"Not that great. I'm getting my boob job this week and J.J. isn't being very supportive."

"He'll come around."

Stephanie, J.J. and Don slid back into the booth just as the stage lights went on. The stage was transformed into a rock set. The clapping started as Sting, Stewart Copeland and Andy Summers took to the stage. Copeland went behind the drums. Sting and Summers tuned their guitars. Sting's bass boomed into action and they broke into "Can't Stand Losing You" followed by "Message in a Bottle." They went through their entire repertoire as the booth gang clapped and boogied along.

When they left the stage there was such a round of applause from the now packed room that they came back on for an encore. "Roxanne" led the ecstatic audience to its feet. Everybody was rocking the house down.

You could feel the let down in the room as The Police left the stage. J.J. motioned to his gang to follow him. They walked to the side of the venue, down a hall and up to the backstage door. Two security guards awaited them. They showed their necklace badges and were let in.

They could hear noise coming from one of the rooms down the hall. When they got to the room people were pouring in and out of the hospitality suite. They went in pushing and shoving through the crowd. Inside, The Police were having drinks by the bar. There was some coke on a table and a bunch of groupies snorting it. Stephanie went straight for it. Flynn went to the bar and got a scotch. J.J. and Tiffany somehow found wine. They were right next to Sting. J.J., who had met him before, introduced Flynn and Tiff. Flynn shook his hand and they started having a conversation. J.J. led Tiffany over to the coke pile.

Flynn had a long conversation with Sting and they seemed to hit it off. Then one of the groupies handed Flynn a snorting tool and pointed to the coke table. She wanted her time with Sting and wasn't going to let it go. So Flynn left and found Stephanie snorting a line off the table.

"I'm so psyched. First hearing The Police. Now this!" She sniffed a couple of times. Then her jaw moved back and forth on its own. The coke was probably cut with speed of some kind.

"Slow down, kid. Your jaw's doing a dance of its own."

"Sometimes that happens with coke. I'm so psyched."

"I'm so psyched out after my week with psyches."

"Maybe you should listen to some of their advice. Become your own best friend."

"I already am my own best friend. The problem is there aren't enough true friends. I'm always looking for one."

"Get over it. It won't kill you."

"You're delightful when you do coke."

In response Stephanie did another line of coke. The crowd in the courtesy-suite grew. Hangers-on, groupies, friends of the band were among them. A tall, bearded man named Walt told the room that he had an announcement.

"I'm having an afterparty at 10 Lake Shore Drive. Everybody is invited," he shouted.

After about another hour backstage, Flynn, Stephanie, J.J. and Tiffany walked out of the club. There were five-foot mountains of stacked snow and it was below zero with the wind chill factor. They had their choice of cabs on the freshly paved street. Three of them huddled in the back seat. Flynn got in and sat next to the driver. They took off toward Lake

Shore Drive. When they got to the address, Flynn paid the cabbie and they all jumped out. Number 10 was a beautiful, old, classic brownstone tucked in between newer buildings. They quickly marveled at its uniqueness and they rushed to get out of the cold.

When they reached the front door, Walt swung it open and welcomed them in. "Bar's on this floor. The white stuff is up on three. Two is free to roam."

Stephanie took to the stairs and headed up. Flynn, J.J. and Tiffany found the bar and ordered drinks from a long-haired hippie type behind the bar.

J.J. spoke up. "Did I tell you Flynn that Tiffany is going for her boob job on Monday? The revealing party will be two weeks later. You've got to come."

"Wouldn't miss it."

"Oh, good, Flynn. I wouldn't want you to miss it. Let's go upstairs and find Stephanie," said Tiffany.

They climbed up the heavily carpeted stairs. The landing on the second floor was overflowing with people. They kept climbing. On the third floor the landing was clear and they went into a cozy den with a big round table full of coke. Stephanie snorted a line with a gold-plated snorter.

Flynn said to Stephanie, "You really like your coke."

"Perfect for shaking off the winter blues. I always get depressed in Chicago in the winter. Of course, this is only my second winter here, but still. Have some Flynn," Stephanie said. She handed him the snorter. Flynn waved her off.

Suddenly, Walt came in. He turned on the TV set in the corner. *Saturday Night Live* was almost over. They had just enough time to watch Dan Aykroyd and John Belushi finish a skit.

"I love this show," said Walt. "Did you know that Belushi has a bar off North Avenue? Called the Blues Bar. It's really a dive, but he hangs out there sometimes. Has a good jukebox, of course."

J.J. chimed in, "We missed M*A*S*H."

"It was never the same after Frank Burns left the show. His best line ever: 'I wouldn't mind being a doctor if I didn't have to be around sick people all the time.' That could encompass a lot of general things," Flynn laughed.

"Is that a Flynnism?" J.J. laughed, too.

"Could be."

Later, Flynn couldn't find Stephanie. He looked around the third floor and saw a study off the main room. There she was on a couch next to J.J. Tiffany was not around. They both looked up when Flynn entered. A group, including WQXA DJ Skye Matthews, were passing around the infamous gold snorter.

Skye offered the snorter to Flynn. "Have a bump of blow."

"I'm bumped out."

"Not your favorite drug, hey, buddy."

Stephanie got up and went to Flynn. She handed him a joint that someone had given her.

"Weed. Now we're talking," said Flynn. He grabbed some matches from the table and lit up.

Suddenly, Don was next to Flynn. He took the joint and toked. As usual, he seemed to come out of nowhere. Stephanie saw him and gestured for him to join the table. He came over and snorted a line. Then he tapped her on the shoulder and the two of them disappeared into the bathroom adjoining the room. Flynn sat down and enjoyed some more of his joint.

Around three in the morning, the party finally wound down. They all made their way down the stairs and out into the freezing-cold Chicago night. They walked over to the Drive and looked for cabs. Tiffany and J.J. flagged down the first one. Flynn and Stephanie caught the next one.

They arrived at Flynn's apartment and Billy let them in the door. They quickly headed to the elevators. When they got to the apartment, Flynn let them in and turned on the lights. He quickly lit a fire before even taking off all his gear. Stephanie was already at the table laying out lines from a snowseal. She rolled up a hundred-dollar bill and snorted up a line.

"Flynn, have a line," said Stephanie.

"No thanks. I'm gonna get a beer. Want one?"

"Sure."

Flynn went into the kitchen and brought back two beers. He attended to the fire that was just starting to kick in with some warmth. The room took on a firelight glow. Very soothing and mellow.

"Nice fire. You're lucky to have a real wood-burning fireplace. That's really a luxury in Chicago apartments," said Stephanie.

"That's why I bought this place. That and the balcony and the track lighting and wood floors. I just fell in love with it. And of course, you can't beat the location."

Stephanie snorted up another line of cocaine. She handed the bill to Flynn, who declined. He reached for a half-joint that was in the ashtray.

"Let's have your first music lesson. Since you were only seven when the Beatles hit America you missed the mid-to-late sixties and early seventies," said Flynn.

"I want to know everything," said Stephanie.

Flynn walked over to his huge collection of albums. They were all alphabetized so he went quickly to the Y's. He pulled out Neil Young's *Everybody Knows This Is Nowhere*. He turned on the receiver and put the album on the turntable.

Flynn handed the album cover to Stephanie as the music started with "Cinnamon Girl."

"Think 1969. That was the Year of the Guitar. Somebody dubbed it that. But it was a time of an entire music explosion that went into the early 70's. There was Cream with Eric Clapton, Jimi Hendrix, The Rolling Stones with the great Keith Richards."

"I was only twelve. But my sisters were into the Stones and the Beach Boys, of course, coming from California. I remember an album called *Pet Sounds*."

"That was their answer to the Beatles' *Sgt. Pepper's Lonely Hearts Club Band* that came out in 1967. They wanted to do a concept album like the Beatles and it came out great."

Stephanie took a credit card out of her purse and made some more lines. She snorted one up in each nostril. Flynn took a hit off his joint as the Neil Young record played in the background. At one point, Flynn turned up the sound on the stereo and it boomed out of his huge KLH speakers.

When the record got to the last song, "Cowgirl in The Sand," Flynn had started kissing Stephanie. They had a long make-out session on the couch and then they moved to the floor. The thick Oriental rug kept them cozy and warm as the fire light filled the room. They made love for a long time and eventually collapsed together on their backs laughing. Flynn put his boxer shorts on and got up to put a new album on the turntable. He picked The Rolling Stones *Let it Bleed*. The first song up was "Gimme Shelter." Stephanie put on her blouse and nothing else and began to dance around to the music.

"1969, The Stones. I saw them on their tour that year when I was at the University of Michigan. It was a small venue. It was so cool. J.J. and

I were friends then and he was the head of the entertainment committee at Sigma Chi so we had great seats."

"Were you in a frat, too?" asked Stephanie.

"No. I was the head of the Students for a Democratic Society. SDS. I was part of that whole political movement against the Vietnam War."

"So you really were a hippie!"

"Yeah, I was. It was a really turbulent time with lots of music and politics."

Flynn pulled Stephanie back down on the rug and they made love again. This time with much more passion. When they were finished, Stephanie put on her blouse and sat on the couch in front of the coke. She did another two lines. Flynn didn't move off the floor. He was listening to the Stones.

★ ★ ★

J.J. lived in a high-rise on Superior Street. Flynn jumped out of a cab in front carrying a bottle of expensive white wine. He made his way into the lobby and the doorman asked him who he was there to see. The doorman called up to J.J.'s apartment, got the okay, and pointed Flynn in the direction of the elevator. Flynn got off on the 20th floor and went to J.J.'s front door and suddenly the door flew open.

"Flynn, my man, you're here for the unveiling!"

They went into the apartment where a crowd of men including Miles Lester, Skye Matthews, Don Bennett and a few unfamiliar faces waved at him in greeting.

J.J. took the bottle of wine and put it on the table. "We're all here. Let's all kneel down on the floor to partake in the white powder elixir."

They all knelt down. It looked like a come-to-Jesus meeting. J.J. leaned over at each person's place and presented a small amount of coke on a small gold spoon. He went around the circle and gave each person a snort. Then he knocked on the bedroom door.

"Okay, Tiff. We're ready."

She bounded out the door topless like a hooker coming out of a birthday cake.

"Ta, da. Ta, da. Look at my new breasts." She held them up to the men. They were perfect specimens. Gorgeous and full.

The crowd of men remained mute. They had no idea what to say. One murmur of "nice" squeaked out.

They all continued to stare until Tiffany went back in the bedroom. J.J. was at the ready with another snort for everybody. He got a corkscrew and opened up the wine. Some of the men including Flynn went for a scotch.

Tiffany returned from the bedroom with a very tight sweater on.

Flynn asked J.J., "Is this a California thing?"

"No. It's a Tiffany thing. She always wanted boobs. Now she's got them. And proud of it."

Flynn laughed. "This is too weird. Even for me."

"She picked the guest list personally. She definitely wanted you. You should be honored."

"I am. I am. Honest."

J.J. slapped him on the back.

"I'm heading over to the Blues Bar after this shindig is over. Valentine's Day and all that. Come along and bring all the guys. We can jump in a couple of cabs."

The Blues Bar was just off North Avenue down a short alleyway. The nondescript building was big, black and boxy. Stephanie was waiting outside the entrance door.

"They wouldn't let me in without being with a regular. Somebody who knows the people who work here."

Flynn opened the door and found a bouncer-type checking people in.

"Hey, Flynn. How goes it? Didn't let your girlfriend here in 'cause I didn't know her. But if she's with you, okay."

Flynn talked to the bouncer as they stepped into the bar. "A couple of other people are coming over. They'll ask for me. Let them in."

"No problemo, Flynn."

"Thanks, man."

The inside of the bar was old, seedy and no-nonsense. Bar and stools on one side. A big, open space by the jukebox across from it. And an old-fashioned pinball machine in the corner. AC/DC's "You Shook Me All Night Long" was blasting from the speakers inside the jukebox. Two people were dancing.

Flynn and Stephanie bellied up to the bar. Wally, the bartender, an oldish hippie type with a ponytail, asked them what they wanted.

"Hey, Wally. How's it going, man?"

"Not bad. You want your usual scotch?" asked Wally.

"Yeah. And white wine for the lady," said Flynn.

They grabbed two stools and took off their coats and gear. Flynn noticed that Stephanie was wearing dressy sandal-type shoes.

"Where are your boots? It's eighteen degrees outside. Are you crazy?'

"All I am doing is getting in and out of cabs. So what's the difference? I like my shoes. Boots are so clunky and heavy," said Stephanie.

"We got to get you over to Marshall Field's and get you some real Chicago boots," said Flynn.

"Saks, not Field's. And I do have boots. I'm just not wearing them."

"Whatever."

"So how was the viewing?" asked Stephanie.

"Really weird. I've never seen anyone quite that excited."

"Did she let you touch them?"

"No. Ick. That would have been too much."

"What's so special about this place?"

"John Belushi owns it."

At the entrance door a crowd barged into the bar. There was J.J., Tiffany, Miles, Don and some others from the viewing party. They walked over and joined Flynn and Stephanie at the bar. Tiffany took off her coat and revealed her very tight sweater.

"You look great, Tiffany," squeaked Stephanie.

"Thanks. I feel great. On top of the world."

Wally took drink orders. On the jukebox AC/DC segued to Led Zeppelin's "Stairway to Heaven."

J.J. piped in, "Who programs that jukebox? If I hear 'Stairway to Heaven' one more time I'm going to scream."

"Who are you kidding? Your station plays it all the time," said Flynn.

"That's why I'm so sick of it. I'm going over to see what else they have on that machine." He walked across the room to the jukebox.

Don tapped Stephanie on the shoulder, whispered something to her, and they headed to the restrooms in the back of the bar. Flynn looked annoyed as they left the bar.

Stephanie came back to her stool with a little white powder under her nose. Don took Tiffany next.

Flynn addressed Stephanie. "Do you always have to do that?"

"What?"

"Hide out in bathrooms?"

"That's the way people do coke in this world. It's just a thing. I like it."
"I think you like it too much."
"What about you and your scotch?"
"Nobody talks to me about what I drink or when."
"I'm not nobody. I thought we were together."
"We're together when I say we are."
"Get a grip."
"Whatever."

J.J. returned from the jukebox as the music segued again, this time to Foreigner's "Urgent."

He took his drink off the bar and said to the crowd, "I've got a bunch of Foreigner plugged in now. We can all breathe easier."

"What about the Stones?" asked Flynn. "I seem to remember that jukebox having a lot of Stones."

"I plugged them in, too. We'll have to wait around until it gets to those songs."

Tiffany came back from the bathroom. Don looked at J.J. and they communicated coke, bathroom. And they were headed toward the back.

When everybody was back at the bar, the front door opened and John Belushi came into his bar. He brought a bunch of hangers-on with him. They headed straight for the bar and greeted everybody sitting there. He took out a snowseal full of cocaine, put the whole thing on his hand near the thumb and snorted it off.

The group all clapped at his extravagant gesture. Then Don took his coke and dumped it onto the top of the bar. Everybody was rolling up bills and taking a snort. Even Flynn took a hit.

The Blues Bar party lasted until after 3 A.M. John Belushi had gone home. But Don, Tiffany, Stephanie and Flynn and J.J. were still there. Don put the rest of the coke on the bar. Only he and Stephanie snorted. Everybody was really high and really drunk.

Finally, Flynn said, "I think it's time to leave. Let's go get cabs. Call it a night."

They put on their coats and forged out into the frozen tundra that was Chicago in February.

★ ★ ★

The next morning in his apartment, Flynn nursed a terrible hangover with spicy tomato juice. Then he grabbed his coat and hat and headed out the door. When he got downstairs, Steve went outside to flag down a cab. Outside it was below zero with the windchill. There were weird frozen pellets dropping from the sky. Flynn tried to ignore them, but was bombarded in the face. He got into the cab as fast as he could.

"Michigan and Wacker," he told the cab driver.

Flynn arrived on the set of *The Brett Adams Show*. He ducked into his office and checked out his notes before the taping. He smiled when he saw that the guest today was an author instead of a shrink.

Madison stood in the doorway to his office. She was wearing over-the-knee black boots and a dress. Flynn looked up.

"Wow. You look great," he said.

"Thanks. We're having William Styron on the show so I thought I'd dress up for an author. Also, I've got a date tonight."

"Cool. Whatever. Let's head to the set and get this show on the road."

They walked down the hall to the booth. Out on the stage, Brett was already seated in his chair. The studio audience was pouring in. Jeremy and Isaac were ready behind cameras one and two. Zeke stood in the middle of the cameras and waited for his cues from Flynn in the booth.

Flynn and Madison entered the booth and immediately grabbed headsets. They looked out at the stage. The audience had settled in.

"Jeremy, camera one, you ready?" asked Flynn.

"Roger, wilco," said Jeremy.

"Not that again," said Flynn.

Isaac spoke into Flynn's headset. "I'm ready."

"Zeke, get ready to start the countdown. Cue the theme music." The music blared through the speakers. "Okay, we're ready in five…"

"Four, three, two…." Zeke finished it off with a silent one.

Brett started his introduction and William Styron came on the stage from the right wing. They shook hands and Brett pointed him to his seat in the chair next to his.

"Please welcome William Styron. Author of the best-selling *Sophie's Choice*. Tell us about it."

"It's a story of the Holocaust. A woman has to choose between her two children as the Nazis tell her that she can only save one. The other one has to go to the gas chamber."

"Sounds like a very important piece of history."

Flynn looked intently on the set to make sure that everyone was doing what they should be doing. William kept talking.

"It is. Nobody should ever forget the Holocaust. It happened. It's real. And my story is about what happens to one woman. There are thousands of stories from that time. Sophie is just one of them."

"Why do you think people will want to read this book?" asked Brett.

"Because a lot of people care about what happened to people like Sophie."

"You're very brave to write such a story. Tell us a little bit about your writing process."

Later, Flynn sat in his office with Madison in the visitor's chair. They looked at the schedule for the upcoming week of shows.

"Looking good. Only two shrinks on this week. We've got a couple more writers and shock of all shocks, an actress. This is going to be a great week."

Madison clapped her hands together, then gave Flynn the peace sign. He laughed and gave it back to her.

"Just a couple of old hippies doing a TV show. What are the odds?"

"They're in our favor, Flynn. They're in our favor," added Madison.

★ ★ ★

The Palm restaurant was on a side street facing Lake Michigan. Flynn got out of a cab and went inside. The decor was very masculine. Lots of wood. Leather booths. A wraparound mahogany bar with matching barstools that had backs. Instead of photos on the walls there were caricatures of the Chicago famous and well known. As well as the celebrities that had been there. A tank with live lobsters was up against one wall. The post-lunch crowd had dissipated and the bar was empty waiting for the media people of Chicago to claim their hangout.

Flynn took off his gear and grabbed a barstool. The bartender was there in seconds.

"Hey, man, Frank! How's it going?"

"I got bombarded by frozen pellets on my way here. When are we all going to pack it in and move to California?" said Frank.

"Not me, man. I'm stickin' here. Winter is just part of the whole Chicago thing," said Flynn.

"If you say so. You want a good scotch, right? With one ice cube. I know these things."

"You've got my number."

Frank brought the drink and Flynn sipped. Suddenly, there was movement behind him. He turned around and saw Don creeping around the bar.

"Isn't it a little early for your services, Don?"

"I know where the action is. It's late afternoon, you're in media, you're at The Palm," said Don.

The front door of the restaurant opened with a swish of arctic air and a few frozen pellets. J.J., in his ridiculous ski mask entered. He walked over to Flynn and Don before he started taking off his gear.

"Don, I'm glad you're here. I'll meet you in the bathroom," said J.J.

"Did you tell him to meet you here? I've never seen him in The Palm before," said Flynn.

"He's everywhere you want him to be," said J.J. He headed off to the bathroom.

Flynn just sat there. "Hey, man, Frank, how 'bout another scotch?"

A few minutes later, Don and J.J. returned from the bathroom. J.J. asked Frank for an Old Style in a bottle. Don ordered the same thing.

"How'd your taping go today?" asked J.J.

"It wasn't bad. We had the author Willian Styron on."

"*Sophie's Choice*. I read it. Pretty depressing."

"I don't care. It wasn't a shrink."

The front door to the restaurant opened followed by a burst of arctic air. In walked Stephanie with Miles on her heels. They strolled over to where the gang hung out at the bar. Stephanie immediately kissed Flynn and ordered a white wine from Frank. Miles noticed Don and the two were off in a flash.

J.J. asked Frank if he could turn on the receiver behind him on the bar.

"Put on WQXA," said J.J. The music of Fleetwood Mac blasted out of the two speakers on opposite ends of the bar.

"'Second Hand News' is a great song," said Flynn.

"Fleetwood Mac is going to be at the station tomorrow. You're invited to meet them for a cocktail party at around five. We're having a caterer bring in some food and drink," said J.J.

"Can I bring Stephanie?" asked Flynn.

"I think I can get her on the list," said J.J.

Don stood behind them and touched Stephanie on the shoulder. She knew what it meant and got up and followed Don to the bathroom.

"Where's Tiffany?" asked Flynn.

"We had a fight," answered J.J.

"Bummer. Is everything okay?"

"Not really. Ever since she got those new boobs she's been acting strange. And you know how much she hates Chicago in the winter."

"Not much you can do about that."

Stephanie and Don returned from the bathroom. She tucked a little white snowseal into her purse.

The Palm filled up as it got close to the five o'clock hour. The gang at the bar kept ordering drinks and taking trips to the bathroom.

At some point, Flynn asked Stephanie if she wanted dinner. And she declined saying she was at the point where the coke cut her appetite. Flynn wanted a steak, so they took a booth and he ordered. J.J. slid into the booth next to Stephanie. He didn't want any food either.

"You guys are crazy turning down a steak from The Palm. That's the thing about coke. It makes you not want to eat. Just the opposite of weed. But you guys can just keep drinking while I eat," said Flynn.

Flynn ate. More media types hung around the booth and the bar. Don was unmoving at the end of the bar. Always in the shadows.

★ ★ ★

Flynn and Stephanie got out of a cab at his apartment building. Billy opened the door for them and they rushed in with the wind pushing at their backs.

"Fucking freezing," shouted Stephanie.

Billy spoke up. "Get in here. It's toasty. We always blast the heat in the lobby so folks like you can warm up immediately."

"What is it out there, anyway?" asked Flynn.

"Two below. Without the wind chill factor," said Billy.

"My God," squeaked Stephanie.

Upstairs in Flynn's apartment he lit a fire and the kindling caught right away. While they waited for the logs to catch, he went to the kitchen to get a beer and a wine. When he came back to the living room, Stephanie was laying out lines of coke on his coffee table.

"Have a line, Flynn." She handed him the little gold snorter she had picked up somewhere.

"I'll have one." He snorted up a line. Then he reached for his joint case on the coffee table. And stoked up some pot.

"More on your music lessons of the sixties and early seventies. You familiar with The Byrds? You've got to at least have heard 'Mr. Tambourine Man.'"

"Yeah, of course I've heard that. I'm not that lame."

Flynn got up off the couch and moved to his huge stereo setup. His one-hundred-plus record collection took up one side of the wall. He thumbed through the collection and pulled out The Byrds' *Turn! Turn! Turn!* He carefully took the album out of its cover and placed it on the turntable. Then he came back to the couch and took another hit off his joint. He offered it to Stephanie and she took a toke.

"I smoked pot in high school. But it was never my drug of choice. Now coke, that is definitely my thing." She snorted up another line. Her jaw started moving involuntarily from all the coke she had already had.

The Byrds music filled the space. His KLH speakers picked up every nuance.

Stephanie sang along, "To everything there is a season...."

"David Crosby started with the Byrds. That was way before Crosby, Stills & Nash." He got up and went through the collection until he came across the first CS&N album. He showed it to Stephanie.

"The 'Couch Album.' That's what I call it. There's a story here. The group was driving around L.A. and they saw an old couch outside an abandoned building. They decided to take a picture. Then when they saw it they realized they were out of order to match the names. They were lined up Nash, Stills and Crosby. So, they went back to do it right and the building had been torn down, couch gone. Thus the album cover didn't match. Who cares? It is a great album."

"How do you know all this stuff?"

"I read a lot. You can find out a lot of stuff from *Rolling Stone* magazine. But I've just been following bands since college."

Stephanie snorted up another line. Flynn smoked his joint.

"What was your favorite concert, back in the 'old days'?"

"I remember it well. The Rolling Stones on their 1969 Tour. Saw them in a small venue, only about three thousand people, on the campus of the University of Michigan."

"So that's what you did when you weren't organizing protests for the SDS."

"I was doing both. Protesting the Vietnam War and seeing the latest groups. Also saw Jimi Hendrix, Janis Joplin and The Doors. Just to name a few."

"How'd you end up in TV instead of radio like J.J.?"

"I met Brett right out of college at a broadcaster's seminar I was invited to. We liked each other and he asked me if I wanted a job as an intern on his show."

"So of course you said yes."

"I did. I was right out of college trying to break into something. So, I went to work for WSL and Brett. I stayed and kept getting promoted till I worked my way up to Director."

"And the rest is history…."

"Something like that. I like directing live TV for now, but I have some ideas for something else down the road."

Flynn got up to put the CS&N album on the turntable. He carefully placed the needle on the record, not using the automatic setting.

"What do you want to do when you grow up?" asked Flynn.

"I don't know. *Playboy* is okay. But it's really an old boy organization. And of course, the content. But my boss, Bobby Marin, sort of holds me back."

"You can do whatever you want to do. I'm a firm believer in that," Flynn said as he moved over to Stephanie on the couch. They started a passionate kiss and it led to heavy petting. Suddenly, they were on the rug making love. They took a long time with it as the music segued to "Suite: Judy Blue Eyes." When they finally finished Stephanie rolled off of Flynn and grabbed some pieces of clothes. Then she was back on the couch snorting another line off the coffee table. Flynn just stayed on the floor listening to the music.

★ ★ ★

The next afternoon, the WQXA studios were jumping. Employees milled around outside the broadcast booth. Inside was Mitch, the afternoon DJ, J.J., Miles and Flynn talking to each other. Mitch was playing "Second Hand News" from Fleetwood Mac's *Rumours* album. The door to the booth opened and in walked Stevie Nicks, Lindsay Buckingham,

Christine McVie, Mic Fleetwood and John McVie. Everybody shook hands and introduced themselves.

J.J. asked Stevie, "What's this new album you've got?"

"It's called *Tusk*. It won't be out till October. We've got some great songs we're recording for it," answered Stevie.

"We'll be playing it. I always put you guys at the top of the playlist."

Flynn joined them. "How'd you hold up with the success of *Rumours*? Didn't it win album of the year last year, 1978?"

"It did. It was a huge success beyond our wildest dreams. We've got a whole new confidence in the studio. We're really cooking," said Stevie.

J.J. broke in, "Why don't we retire to my office for a little treat?"

Stevie motioned to the other band members and they all filed out of the booth. Mitch segued to "Go Your Own Way." So when they reached J.J.'s office it was blasting through his speakers. He offered Stevie and Christine seats by the window where they could see snow coming down fast. He opened his desk drawer and brought out a tiny, amber vial full of cocaine. He dumped the devil's dandruff out on the desktop. Then he made lines with a credit card. He offered a gold-plated snorter to the women first. They took a line and passed the snorter to the guys. Flynn was the last to snort. Almost a gram was gone.

"How do you like the Windy City?" Flynn asked Christine.

"It's fucking freezing," she said.

John joined the conversation. "How do you people live here? Ever think about California?"

"As little as possible," quipped Flynn. "I don't care how cold it is here. I love the city."

J.J. announced, "Let's hop in a couple of cabs and hit Butch McGuire's. It's on Division Street, for those of you new to the city. Our friend Don will be there with more of the white stuff."

Late afternoon in Butch's was quiet. The tone changed drastically when J.J., Flynn and Fleetwood Mac entered and took up residence at the bar. Joco was star struck when he saw the band. He quickly took orders.

"Hey, man, Joco! How 'bout a Johnnie Walker Black with one ice cube?" Flynn asked.

"Sure thing, Flynn. Where'd you pick up this fantastic lineup of people?" queried Joco.

"At the radio station. They're doing a promotion," said Flynn.

Suddenly Don came through the back room into the bar. He was acting like he was a rock star as J.J. introduced him.

"I come with Bolivian Marching Powder," announced Don.

"I'm game," announced Stevie and Christine as Don escorted them to the bathrooms in the back.

The music coming through the speakers up near the ceiling was Queen's "Bohemian Rhapsody."

"Joco, turn on that receiver to WQXA, you'll find some Fleetwood Mac music."

He adjusted the tuner to the station and "Don't Stop" blasted through the speakers.

The women returned with Don and it was the men's turn. Flynn sipped his scotch while they went to the back.

When everybody was back at the bar, Fleetwood Mac finished their drinks and suddenly said goodbye. There was no explanation, just a hurried putting on of their coats.

"Sorry, we've got to go. We've got another promo thing with WLUP," said Christine. "Thanks for playing our music at your station."

The wind roared in the door mixed with snow as they left the bar.

MARCH

THE CHICAGO RIVER WAS DYED green for St. Patrick's Day and looked pretty weird as people crossed the bridge from Michigan Avenue to Wacker Drive. Already the city was in celebratory mode. Some people wore green mad-hatter-type hats, green coats, green gloves, green scarves. Anything or everything that was green was being used to be a part of Chicago's infamous day.

Flynn, dressed normally, crossed the bridge and stopped in the middle and stared at the green water. It was a balmy 30 degrees and the wind from both river and lake bombarded him as he stood there. After a while, he moved along to his corner at Wacker and Michigan. The traffic light turned green and he walked across the street to the studio.

Upstairs the studio was jumping. Some of the crew sported green ties. Others wore buttons that said, "Kiss Me, I'm Irish." Everybody was really excited because the king of horror novels, Stephen King, was on the show today. Flynn checked out the studio audience before heading to his office. Once there, he took off his big, ski parka and watchcap. Under his blazer he was wearing a green t-shirt with Chicago printed across the top.

Madison entered his office wearing a short green dress with her knee-high black boots.

"Happy St. Patrick's Day," she sang.

"Nice getup. How did you actually own a green dress?" asked Flynn.

"You never know what a girl has in her closet."

"I'm glad I don't know. Too much information."

"Grab your clipboard. We're due in the booth."

They left his office and made their way down the hall to the broadcast booth. When they entered, they could see Brett on stage and the studio audience getting situated in their seats. They donned their headsets. Flynn spoke.

"Everybody ready? Cue the opening music. Cue Brett."

On the floor the camera guys did their preparations. Zeke counted down and pointed to Brett.

"Welcome to *The Brett Adams Show*. Let me introduce today's guest, the inimitable writer Stephen King."

Stephen King came out from the wings and Brett stood up and they shook hands. Stephen sat down in the chair opposite Brett's.

Brett held up a book and said, "*The Dead Zone* Stephen, your latest horror novel. Tell us about it."

Stephen was shy. A bit reticent. "A guy came out of a coma after years and has special powers to see what's going to happen in the future. The dead zone refers to the part of his brain where all the action is happening. He just has to touch somebody and he can see into the future."

"Sounds pretty scary."

After the show was over, Stephen sat in Flynn's office with a big, mug of coffee. They were talking about the book.

"I loved *The Dead Zone* a lot. I like all your books, especially *Salem's Lot*. That is really spooky. And *FireStarter*, too," gushed Flynn.

Stephen came alive at the mention of these two books. "I scare myself sometimes when I'm writing. I really get into my material. I actually believe some of my stuff."

"You want to experience something scary, Chicago-style? Meet me and some others at Butch McGuire's and see what a St. Patrick's Day is really like."

Stephen was tentative when he answered, "Okay."

"It's on Division Street. Any cab will get you there. I'll be there after seven. Just meet me at the main bar in the front room."

Division Street overflowed with people going in and out of bars. Flynn got out of a cab in front of Butch's. There was a three-piece walk-around band ensemble headed into the bar to play Irish songs. They were dressed in some kind of kilt outfits under their heavy coats. One of them had a bagpipe. They tried to enter the bar along with Flynn and got stuck in the crowd. The only way to get in was to push. So they did. The band turned left off the main bar to the tables and a bigger space. Flynn saw Stephanie, J.J., Tiffany and Miles three deep from the bar. Flynn greeted them and then tried to get up to the bar.

"Hey, man, Joco! Twelve-year-old scotch. One ice cube," yelled Flynn.

Somehow Joco heard him and went to get the drink. The strains of "Greensleeves" could be heard from the other room fighting against the music of Jimi Hendrix's "All Along the Watchtower" pouring through the speakers.

Stephanie was wearing a low-cut, very revealing green sleeveless dress and opened-toed sandals.

Flynn looked down at her shoes with horror. "How can you be wearing sandals when it's 30 degrees and snow coming?" asked Flynn.

"They went with my dress. What's it to ya?" said Stephanie.

"You can't walk back to my place in those."

"Then we'll take a cab."

"For five blocks?"

"Oh, come on, Flynn, lighten up. I'll be fine. Just let it be."

Joco realized the St. Patrick's Day band in the other room was trying to be heard above the music coming out of the speakers, so he turned the music down and gave them their full chance to play their music.

"I had a cool day today, I got to meet Stephen King," said Flynn.

"The writer? He's too scary for me. I get freaked out when I try to read his stuff," said Stephanie.

"Has anybody seen him? He said he was going to come, but I doubt we could even find him in this mass of humanity," said Flynn.

Don Bennett suddenly materialized. He whispered into Stephanie's ear and they turned around and headed for the bathroom.

"Coke. It's always in bathrooms. And it's always with Don. Where'd he come from anyway, J.J.?"

"Who knows? He's always around when you need him."

"I'm going to join them if I can get back there," shouted Tiffany.

"It's too much trouble to get back there," said J.J. "I'll just drink."

"Yeah, man. It's just us boozers out here," said Flynn.

The little band segued into another Irish tune and the bar got more and more crowded. People were waiting at the door to get in. Flynn and J.J. sipped their drinks and waited for the "bathroom gang" to come back.

Around 2 A.M. the Street of Dreams was crowded outside Butch's. People in their St. Patrick's Day getups were still partying like it was early in the night. Out the door came Flynn, Stephanie, Tiffany, J.J. and Don. Right in front of them was a big puddle of slush and a man down on all fours puking his guts out. When he finally was able to stand up the group saw that it was Miles Lester. It was a very embarrassing moment for everyone. But they helped him up, steadied him and led him in the direction of Flynn's apartment building.

They walked in a freezing sleet that was trying to turn to snow. J.J. and Flynn were on either side of Miles. Stephanie's sandals were completely soaked and ruined. She was whining the whole way. When they reached Elm Street they were almost to Flynn's apartment. Miles had to throw up again, so they waited while he did it in the street.

When they arrived at Flynn's building, Billy the doorman saw the distress and helped the guys with Miles. They all went in and headed to the elevators. Billy helped them pour Miles into it.

Upstairs at Flynn's, J.J. and Flynn took Miles into the bedroom and flung him on the bed. He quickly curled up in the fetal position and went to sleep. The guys went back into the living room to join the girls. Stephanie was already lining up coke on the coffee table. She used her hundred-dollar bill to snort up a big hit of coke. Then Tiffany took her turn.

"Hey, don't leave me out," said J.J. He joined the girls on the couch and snorted a line.

The house phone rang on the wall. Flynn picked it up and said, "Yeah, yeah. I guess so. Send them up." He then turned to the group and asked, "Did I invite people from the bar to my apartment? I can't remember."

Stephanie took another line. "You told Joco to tell everybody there was a party at 18 E. Elm. That everybody was welcome for an after St. Patrick's party at your place."

"I must be out of my mind. Some people have taken me up on it 'cause they're downstairs and coming up."

The doorbell rang like the sound of doom. Flynn opened the door and there were five drunk people waiting to get in. One of the men held paper St. Patrick's Day hats and handed one to Flynn, who immediately put it on. Don was sitting at the dining room table just taking it all in. When the newcomers were inside the apartment he approached them.

"Coke for sale. Grams of coke for sale," he held up some snowseals. One of the women who came in asked how much. "One hundred dollars a gram." She opened her purse and took out the money. Then she saw the girls on the couch doing coke and sat down next to them and laid out some of her recently purchased blow.

Flynn started a fire and the room took on a mellow glow. The Jimi Hendrix song "Foxy Lady" was on the stereo. Flynn picked up a joint from his stash and somebody lit it for him. He began to pass it around. Some of the newcomers took a toke, the gang on the couch ignored it.

"Okay, now's the time to bring it up," Flynn said. "We're going to take a vote on who is the best guitar player of all time. Either Jimi Hendrix or Eric Clapton. I'm a Hendrix."

J.J. vehemently disagreed, "I'm a Clapton. You know that, Flynn. We've had this discussion before."

He asked the newcomers now sitting at the dining room table. Two were Hendrix and two were Clapton.

"Seems were at a standstill, we've got three Claptons and three Hendrix types. Girls, you gonna give your vote?"

Tiffany said, "Clapton."

Stephanie said, "I don't know. I'll go with Flynn. Hendrix."

The other girl said, "Fuck it. I don't go with either. I like Pete Townshend."

"Ah, a music person. Come over here, little lady, and talk to me," said Flynn.

She got up from the couch and took her coke with her. Flynn motioned her into the kitchen.

They did drugs and listened to music into the wee hours. Miles appeared in the doorway of the bedroom. He was up and feeling better. When he saw all the coke on the table he asked for the bill so he could snort a line.

"Nothing like a toot of coke to get rid of drunkenness," said Miles.

Flynn came out of the kitchen and put some more wood on the fire. When he saw Miles he came over to greet him.

"You're among the living. We rescued you from a slush puddle. Right in front of Butch's."

"Don't remind me. Too much St. Patrick's Day. I feel all right now. And the coke I just did helped wake me up."

The party continued. Nobody wanted to face the freezing cold that was outside waiting for them. But eventually people started leaving. The newcomers went first, then Miles and Don. J.J. asked Flynn to call down to Billy for a cab.

Stephanie was the only one left on the couch. There was still a lot of coke left. She offered Flynn the bill and he declined. He was smoking a joint instead.

"There's no way I'm gonna be able to sleep," said Stephanie.

"This should help." He handed her the joint. She took a toke and sipped her wine.

Flynn took a pillow off the couch and put it on the rug facing the fire.

"I'll just hang out here. You can join me when you stop zippity-zooing."

"It's gonna be a while. I'm really stoked. I'm pouring myself some more wine." The bottle was empty.

"Kitchen. Wine in the kitchen. I'm just gonna rest here for a minute.," added Flynn.

"Can I keep the stereo on?" asked Stephanie.

"I'll turn on FM radio. WLUP. Don't tell J.J. I listen to it sometimes," said Flynn. He got up and took the record off the turntable and turned on the radio. "This way you don't have to mess with my records."

"Oh, heaven forbid. I'd never do that!"

The next day was Saturday. No work. No reason to get up early. Flynn and Stephanie were asleep on the rug covered with a quilt from the bed. It was already noon when Flynn groaned and got up. The apartment looked like a hurricane hit it. Glasses and bottles adorned all surfaces.

"I have a terrible hangover. I need a line of coke. Sort of like 'hair of the snort' or something like that," said Stephanie.

"I've got just the antidote. Let's go to the Billy Goat for cheeseburgers and fries. Nothing like it for a hangover. Don't do any coke. We eat first," said Flynn.

"Okay, I'll give it a try."

"First thing, though, we're taking you to Saks, not Marshall Field's, for a new pair of boots."

Stephanie picked up her ruined sandals from the floor and held them up. They were matted down and completely wrecked.

"I hope I can get there in these. What a mess."

"Come on, get dressed. We'll take a cab."

Stephanie and Flynn were in the shoe department at Saks. A saleslady brought out several boxes full of boots. The first pair they looked at had high-heels.

"No way," said Flynn. "Don't you have L.L. Bean with the waterproof bottom?"

The saleslady kept bringing out boots that either Stephanie didn't like or were not walkable. Finally, she reached the L.L. Bean in the bottom box. Stephanie tried them on and they fit perfectly. They were navy blue cloth on the top and rubberized on the bottom. She tucked her jeans into them and they came up to almost knee length.

"These will do. They're not very sexy, but I have to admit they are cozy and comfortable." Stephanie stood up and went over to the mirror for the final test. "Okay."

Flynn handed the saleslady his credit card. Stephanie handed over her wrecked sandals to the woman.

"You can throw these away, if you don't mind."

She picked them up like they were diseased and took them to the back of the store. Stephanie danced around in her new boots. Flynn smiled his approval.

Back on Michigan Avenue they walked south toward the Billy Goat. Stephanie deliberately stepped in puddles and pranced around the sidewalk like a little girl. When they got to the stairs off Michigan that went underground to the restaurant, Stephanie practically flew down the stairs. Flynn followed quickly behind her.

Right around the stairs, under Michigan Avenue stood the Billy Goat, the iconic Chicago hangout for newspaper reporters and everyday Chicagoans alike. The man behind the counter was shouting, "Cheeseburger, cheeseburger." They ordered their food and sat down at a table to wait. The room was adorned with photos of Chicago's past and newspaper stories framed into history.

"I've never been here before," ventured Stephanie.

"It's one of the most famous places in Chicago. Reporters come here a lot. And the ad crowd off the Avenue. Don't you love the framed photos and stories?"

Their food was ready and Flynn got up and brought it to the table. They immediately dug in.

"Like I said, best thing for a hangover."

"It's all that grease. Absorbs all the alcohol," Stephanie said as she ate French fries and cheeseburger.

When they finished, they left and walked back up the stairs to Michigan Avenue and Flynn flagged down a yellow limo.

"Art Institute," he told the cab driver when they got in.

"Another first for me," said Stephanie.

A light snow began to fall and the driver turned on the windshield wipers. They drove up across the street from the Institute and the driver made a U-turn to let them off in front of it.

"Check out these lions," Flynn said as they stood on the stairs in the middle of two huge stone lions.

"Cool," said Stephanie.

Inside was a hushed world filled with the beauty of art. They got their tickets and started to walk around. They were looking at some Picassos when Stephanie started complaining.

"I need a line of coke."

"Well, you can't do it here."

"I'll go to the bathroom."

"High-maintenance!"

Flynn sat on a bench while Stephanie went to the bathroom. She came back stoked and sat down next to Flynn.

He was annoyed. "This isn't even a party."

"Don't need one. And speaking of parties, *Playboy* is having one next Saturday night at the Mansion. Can you make it?"

"I've never been to the Mansion. Probably the only place in Chicago I haven't been. What's the occasion?"

"Hugh Heffner's birthday. The sky's the limit. Can't wait," said Stephanie. "By the way, these boots are hot."

"N.B.D."

★ ★ ★

Another freezing cold below zero night in Chicago. Flynn picked up Stephanie in a cab and she was not wearing her boots. She had on black pumps to match her fancy black dress. Her coat wasn't buttoned, so you could see her outfit.

"Where are your boots?" Flynn asked as she got in the cab.

"Not with this dress. We're gonna get in and out of a cab."

"It's below zero with the windchill. You're gonna freeze in that outfit."

"Flynn, let me just dress the way I want to. You like the way I look, don't you?"

"Of course I do. I like it a lot."

"Then don't complain. Let's just have a fun party at the Mansion."

They pulled up at the Playboy Mansion. It was a huge stone structure that looked like a glamorous early century house or a European castle. A group of people stood by the front door. Several limos were at the curb with people getting out. Everybody was dressed to the nines. Flynn and Stephanie opened a tall metal gate and walked up the sidewalk leading to the entrance. Snow was piled high on both sides of the sidewalk.

They made their way through the front door among a throng of partygoers. A mob scene was in the living room surrounding Hugh Heffner. Tall, statuesque Playboy Bunnies were interspersed throughout the room. These women were gorgeous and very revealing in their push-up-bra-style outfits. A waiter hoisted a tray full of glasses of champagne. Stephanie reached for two glasses and handed one to Flynn.

"There's a downstairs. Let's go. I want you to meet my boss," said Stephanie.

"Show me the way," Flynn quipped as he sipped his champagne.

The stairs down were steep. They held the handrail and wound their way down. More people and more Playboy Bunnies partied on both sides of a huge tropical fish tank that was the divider between the two big rooms. There was a bar on the back wall. Flynn made his way over, left his champagne glass on the bar and ordered a scotch. Stephanie scanned the crowd for her boss and finally located him in the middle of the craziness. She grabbed his hand and led him over to Flynn.

"This is Bobby Marin. Bobby, this is Flynn."

"I didn't catch the last name," Bobby said as he stuck out his hand.

"It's just Flynn."

"Sorta like Cher."

"No, sorta like Flynn."

"Okay, Flynn. Your first visit to the Mansion?" asked Bobby.

"Very first."

"What do you think?"

"I like the Bunnies!"

"Everybody likes the Bunnies and the fish."

"Well, I guess I'm everybody."

Stephanie broke in. "Bobby is the editor of the arts section of the magazine."

"Pretty cool job," said Flynn.

"What do you do?" Bobby inquired.

"I'm a Director on *The Brett Adams Show*."

"Oh, the one with all the shrinks."

"The very same."

Out of nowhere appeared J.J., Tiffany and Don. Stephanie introduced them all to Bobby. Then she was off with Don to find a bathroom. Flynn frowned.

J.J. spoke up, "Stephanie got to invite up to ten people. I guess we're considered the elite or we wouldn't be here."

"I like the Bunnies," Flynn repeated.

"I could be one with my new adjustments. Those outfits are pretty sexy. I can see why you like them, Flynn," Tiffany gushed.

They all drank their champagne, Flynn his scotch. Then there was a fluttering of noise at the bottom of the stairs. It was Hugh Hefner surrounded by Bunnies. He shouted to the crowd.

"For those of you who don't know me, I'm Hugh Heffner. Welcome to our annual Mansion party. And thank you for supporting *Playboy Magazine*. We want you to keep on reading and keep on advertising."

The whole room laughed. At the same time, Stephanie and Don returned from the bathroom. They grabbed glasses of bubbly from one of the waiters. Bobby spotted someone across the room and left the group.

Stephanie was virtually twitching. "Champagne and cocaine. The perfect combination."

"I'll take scotch, thank you very much," said Flynn.

The waitresses were circulating with trays of canapes and whole shrimp. Flynn took a shrimp, dipped it in red, hot sauce and took a bite. Then took his place again staring at the Bunnies.

"Let's check out the upstairs. We've been holed up down here with the fish and the Bunnies," said Tiffany.

"Lead the way," said Flynn.

The group climbed up the stairs and landed in the main room. Just as many Bunnies up here but they managed to grab the couch near the roaring wood-burning fireplace. Don squeezed in next to Stephanie.

"Your drug dealer keeps showing up," complained Flynn.

"What is your problem? I like coke. And he always has coke. You should do more of it. It really helps you perk up," said Stephanie.

"I don't need to perk up. If anything, I need to calm down. We should go soon. The crowds are getting to me," said Flynn.

"I didn't know you were claustrophobic. How come you don't get it at Butch's?"

"I'm used to it there. Butch's is one of my hangs. It only hits me sometimes, and now is one of those times," said Flynn.

They spent another half-hour enjoying the fire and the champagne. By then, Flynn had had enough.

"Let's all go over to my place."

"We'll meet you over there," said J.J.

"Am I invited?" asked Don.

"Of course you are," Stephanie quickly answered.

Outside the Mansion a freezing sleet was covering the sidewalk. The temperature had dropped way below zero. Stephanie's pumps became immediately soaked.

"I need a cab. My feet are getting wet," she said.

"Where are your new boots?" Flynn asked.

"Those aren't the kind of boots you wear to a party. Don't kid yourself."

"We'll have to walk to the corner. I don't see any cabs right here."

They walked up to the corner and were lucky enough to catch a cab right away. They got in and asked the driver to turn up the heat. He did it. His windshield wipers were working overtime against the freezing sleet.

When they got to Flynn's apartment, Billy opened the door for them.

"Hey, Flynn. Another beautiful night in downtown Chicago, right?"

"Hey, man, Billy! Yeah, a great night it is. Every night in Chicago is great."

"Who made that up? It's another freezing, fucking night in Chicago," complained Stephanie.

Billy pushed the elevator button for them. And they stepped in. When they got to Flynn's apartment the first thing he did was light a fire. The room began to glow and throw off heat.

Stephanie was already at the table laying out lines. She snorted two really fast. Flynn went to get a scotch from the kitchen. Just when he sat down the buzzer from downstairs rang.

"Billy, yeah. Send them up," said Flynn.

Moments later, there was a knock at the door. Flynn opened it and found J.J., Tiffany and Don. He invited them in. After they removed their coats they immediately joined Stephanie at the coffee table. Flynn went over to the stereo and picked out an album. He chose *Who's Next*, a classic by The Who.

"Good pick, Flynn. Did we decide who has more albums. You or me?" asked J.J.

"I win, hands down. You can't count the records at the station, man," said Flynn.

"I wasn't. I've been collecting as long as you," J.J. said as he took his turn with the straw they were using for a snorter.

Stephanie and Tiffany were going back and forth doing line for line now with each other.

Flynn sat down in the club chair across from the coffee table. He grabbed a joint out of the stash box and lit it up. When he offered it around there were no takers. Don slithered in the background by the dining room table.

"Hey, man, Don! You wanna toke?" asked Flynn.

"Don't do pot, man. You know that. But I can always get you some when you want it," said Don.

"Thanks, but I don't need any right now. Hey, guys, you want some beers?"

"I'll have one. I know Tiff will too," said J.J.

"I'll have white wine. I know you still have some of that expensive French stuff you got for me," said Stephanie.

Flynn went to the kitchen to get the drinks. Don followed him in. He took a snowseal out of his pocket and held it in front of Flynn.

"No thanks, Don."

"Don't you want it for your girlfriend out there? She might want some and you don't want to disappoint her."

"Okay, man." Flynn took out his wallet and counted out five twenties.

"Just one?" asked Don.

"Just one." Flynn pocketed the little package.

Back in the living room the threesome were still doing lines. Flynn handed them the beer and wine. Then he sat back in his chair to watch as they got really high on coke. Don came over to the table and did a line, then went back to the dining room. The Who music poured through the speakers into the room.

"Do you guys know where the expression 'Sex and drugs and rock-and-roll' came from?" Flynn asked.

"Ian somebody with the somebodies," said J.J.

"Not bad. It's Ian Dury and the Blockheads. Everybody thinks it started in like the late sixties, but this guy came out with it in 1977. Just two years ago. The song was a huge hit, but they never put it on an album. Now it's part of the vernacular. Everybody uses it like it's been around for years. Maybe somebody said it in the sixties, but it was never really around for real until '77," said Flynn.

Stephanie sang it out, "'Sex and drugs and rock-and-roll.' It's perfect no matter when it came out."

J.J. chimed in, "Flynn, you beat me. I would never have gotten the name of that group. But I like the meaning of the line. Speaking of lines." He took his turn with the straw.

The Who's "Won't Get Fooled Again" blared out of the speakers. The coke snorters on the couch blabbed and blabbed. Didn't matter what they were saying as long as they kept talking.

Flynn went to change the album. Stephanie got up and went over to where Don was lurking. J.J. and Tiffany were starting to have a fight.

"That was my line. You stole it," said Tiffany.

"Don't be ridiculous, I already had one. I didn't take yours."

"People, be cool," interjected Flynn. "I'm putting Cream on the stereo."

"Oh, good. *Disraeli Gears*?" asked J.J. as he snorted another line. "Remember when this came out in 1967 and we were just freshman. It was a revelation. I can see us in our dorm rooms blowing smoke out the window so nobody would know we were smoking joints."

"I remember. 'Strange Brew' was an anthem. Not to mention 'Sunshine of Your Love' even more so," added Flynn.

"Goes back to why I'm a Clapton instead of a Hendrix," said J.J.

"I still think Hendrix was the best guitar player ever," said Flynn.

"We can agree to disagree. Mostly we agree when it comes to music, Flynn, going all the way back to college and the late sixties."

Flynn took a toke off his joint. "We were psychedelic. We were hippies and activists. It was a great time. Nothing like it since. The explosion of music then was incomparable."

Stephanie jumped in from the corner with Don. "Did you ever drop acid?"

Flynn answered first. "A few times. But pot was always my drug of choice."

J.J. took a snort, sniffed and answered, "Flynn and I dropped acid a couple of times together and got on the roof of my fraternity house to watch the sun come up. Talk about psychedelic. The sun was alive. Bursting above the horizon. That was unbelievably cool."

"One of my fondest memories of college," said Flynn.

Around 4 A.M., Tiffany, J.J. and Don put on all their winter gear and prepared to leave. Flynn walked them to the front door. Stephanie waved goodbye from the couch. When they were gone, Flynn placed another log on the fire. He sat down next to Stephanie and took her in his arms. They kissed very passionately for a long time. Then Flynn went into the bedroom for the quilt and they got down on the rug and covered up.

"How come we never make love in the bedroom?" asked Stephanie.

"I like the rug. Nice and thick. Perfect for doing the wild thing."

"The wild thing?"

"Yeah, the wild thing. No more talking."

They started in again kissing and it turned into a passionate love-making session on the rug with the fire roaring.

★ ★ ★

Flynn walked into the booth on the set of *The Brett Adams Show*. He donned his headset and started checking with the two cameramen Jeremy and Isaac.

"You guys ready out there?" asked Flynn. "And don't say 'Roger, wilco.'"

"Roger, wilco," they said in unison cracking up the booth and the floor.

"Cue the opening music," said Flynn. The theme music filled the space. Zeke got ready with the countdown on the floor.

"And we're ready in 5, 4…"

Back in the booth Flynn counted with Zeke. "3, 2…."

Zeke pointed at Brett and the show was going. "Welcome to *The Brett Adams Show*. Today's guest is Dr. Oppenstein of St. Joseph's Hospital."

Dr. Oppenstein entered from stage right. Jeremy's camera turned around to take in a sweeping shot of the clapping studio audience. Stephanie, J.J. and Tiffany were right up in the front row center.

Isaac's camera was on Brett, who held up Dr. Oppenstein's book. "*How to Survive a Dysfunctional Family Childhood,* that's made it to *The*

New York Times Bestseller List. Tell us, Doctor, what gave you the impetus for this book?"

Flynn silently groaned in the booth. Madison laughed to herself and adjusted her headset. The show continued. When it was over, Stephanie poked her head into the booth.

"Can I come in?"

"Yeah, the show's over. Come in."

"I've got J.J. and Tiffany behind me."

"Everyone come in. We'll have a booth party," said Flynn.

The threesome bounded through the door. Flynn and J.J. shared a brief "man hug." Stephanie checked out Madison who looked great in tight jeans and boots. Tiffany lingered.

"How did you get my shrink on the show?" asked Stephanie.

"You told me his name. The casting people looked him up. And he was here."

"I felt like he was talking about my family. A family of four, alcoholic father. Maybe I'm in the book. Oh, this is all so exciting."

"Everybody's got a dysfunctional family. Doesn't matter who you are. This guy just chose to write about it."

"But he's my shrink. He had to get his material from somewhere."

J.J. talked to the tech people at the board. Tiffany was talking to Madison. Up on the monitors was the regular WSL programming and a promo came on for *Charlie's Angels*.

Stephanie couldn't contain herself. "I love *Charlie's Angels*," she said.

"I love the girls on the show," quipped Flynn.

"Should I be jealous?"

"If you want to."

At the end of his workday, Flynn walked out of the office building and crossed over the river at Wacker. He quickly put on his hood and wrapped his scarf tighter around his neck. It was still in the teens in late March and a light, fluffy snow was falling. He headed north on Michigan Avenue and passed the famous Water Tower that survived the history-making Chicago Fire, the modern Water Tower Center, the John Hancock, The Playboy building. He turned east toward The Palm restaurant. The wind whipped off the lake across the street. He was glad when he reached the building. The door was hard to open as it fought against the wind. Finally, he got inside and immediately put his hood down. He hung his coat on a hook hear the door. He took a few steps over to the bar. J.J., Miles and a new face Ernie Mendez were already drinking. Frank, the bartender, approached Flynn.

"Johnnie Walker Black, one ice cube. Right?"

"Hey, man, Frank! You've got my number," said Flynn.

"Your face is red. Did you walk here in this cold?" asked J.J. Not waiting for an answer he introduced Ernie. "Flynn, this is Ernie Mendez. Creative Director at Leo Burnett. Ernie, Flynn."

They shook hands.

"How's it going, man?"

"It's going," said Ernie.

A blast of arctic-like air swooshed through the door and hit the guys at the bar. They shivered a little as they saw Stephanie on the other side trying to get in. Flynn went over and held the door open enough so she could get inside. He stared down at her feet.

"What are you wearing? Those couldn't be high-heels when it's snowing and freezing," said Flynn.

"They're new. Aren't they cool? I went out at lunch to Saks and got them," said Stephanie. "It's only a short walk to here from the Playboy building. You know that. And I figured we'd take a cab back to your place," said Stephanie.

"What would we do without cabs!" hailed Flynn. "This is Ernie Mendez, Stephanie. Stephanie, Ernie."

"Hi. Nice to meet you. Are you in media?"

"He's a Creative Director at Leo Burnett. I think he's definitely in media," said J.J.

"Well, at The Palm almost everybody is in media of some kind. I work at *Playboy*," added Stephanie.

She took off her coat and threw it over a barstool. Frank approached her and she ordered a white wine. The group sat on stools and talked as the bar filled up and then the dinner crowd started to arrive.

"Heard you were an eyewitness to the famous *Brett Adams Show* today," said Ernie.

"It was so cool. I've never seen my therapist out of his office. Actually, it was sort of weird. To think he's written a book and everything. I kept waiting for him to divulge one of my secrets," said Stephanie.

"How long you been in therapy?"

"A year or so. Since I moved to Chicago from California."

"How's it going, then?"

"He says I'm making progress."

"What's your big problem?"

"I like men too much."

Flynn snorted out a laugh as he sipped his scotch. Suddenly, out of nowhere, Don appeared. Everyone except Flynn was glad to see him. He kept his coat on and gestured for Stephanie to come with him to the bathroom. It only took her seconds to accompany him.

A little later, she returned and then Ernie and J.J. went with him.

Miles, who remained quiet up to now, said, "I can take it or leave it." He followed this with a big sip of his martini. "I do like my Stoli. Vodka is where it's at. At least for this minute."

The others returned from the bathroom. J.J. was the first to talk. "Foreigner is in town first week in April. I've got primo seats and a stretch limo to take us to the Auditorium. And All-Access Passes for everyone."

"I'll drink to that," said Flynn. "Something good in April. It's one of the worst weather months in the year. You think it's going to be spring and it's always freezing and raining. Even those frozen pellets are still around. Don't put away your winter coat yet."

"Can't wait for that," said Stephanie.

"Chicago is Chicago," said Ernie.

"That toddlin' town," added Flynn.

APRIL

A SHINY, BLACK STRETCH LIMOUSINE pulled up to the front entrance of the Merchandise Mart. The driver got out to open up the back door. Out of the building came Flynn, Stephanie, Tiffany, Miles and Ernie. J.J. went directly over and introduced himself to the driver.

"Are you the WQXA party?" asked the driver.

"That's us," said J.J.

"Pile in. There's room for everybody."

Inside the limo was a backseat facing front, two bench-type seats on the side and an entire other seat facing the backseat. Everyone got in and found a place to sit. The interior looked like a little sitting room, very cozy and good for talking. Just as the driver was about to close the door, Don slinked in and sat in the one empty space.

"Thought you might have gotten the wrong memo," said J.J.

"I'm here. Not to worry," said Don.

The limousine headed toward Michigan Avenue and turned south. A light snow began to fall as they were off to the Auditorium. Tiffany passed around some paper cups and then pulled out of her bag a bottle of champagne. The cork popped and they all cheered. She started pouring the bubbly into the cups.

Don spoke up, "Have you guys seen this new Bullet Coke Tool? You turn the little handle on the side, tip the bottle so the coke goes in and then snort. It screws on the top of any vial. You can take it anywhere. Completely portable." He demonstrated how to use it, took a snort and started passing it around the limo. Everybody took a hit off the new tool, even Flynn.

"Anybody got any reefer?" asked Flynn. "I know nobody does. It's all coke, all the time."

Don whipped out a joint from his inner pocket. "I was thinking about you, Flynn," said Don. "You really should order it from me."

"I thought you only had coke."

"I'm full of surprises." He pulled out a lighter next and lit Flynn's joint.

"This is a rock concert, for God's sake. What is a rock concert without pot?" He passed the joint around, only Ernie took some. When the joint came back to him he stubbed it out in the ashtray in the door. He pocketed it for later.

"It's 1979 and cocaine rules," said J.J.

"I'm ready for Foreigner, champagne and cocaine. There outta be a song about it," said Tiffany as she snorted out of the new Bullet tool.

"Did you know that Mick Jones of Foreigner used to be with a band called Spooky Tooth. He's a Brit. The band is half American, half British. They're a pretty cool outfit," said Flynn.

"The drummer, Dennis Elliott, is also a Brit. No matter where they're from, they put on a good show. So I hear. I've never seen them in concert," said J.J.

The limousine inched forward the last couple of miles as the snow picked up its pace. When they got to the Auditorium, the driver got them as close to the entrance as possible. The venue was a three-thousand seat amphitheater. Just big enough for a large sound, but still intimate.

The whole gang poured out of the limo and J.J. led them to the Will Call Window, where he picked up tickets. He gave everybody their All-Access Passes, laminated necklaces, and they all put them on. Then they entered sacred ground: a rock concert.

The Auditorium was packed. They walked down an aisle that led them to the very first row of VIP seats. They were front and center. So close they could touch the stage. The opening act was just leaving the stage and they settled in. Don snuck out his Bullet Tool and took a snort. Then passed it to Stephanie, who did a toot in each nostril.

The stage went dark. There was a lot of murmuring and excited voices in the audience. Then suddenly Foreigner appeared on stage as the lights went into action circling the stage. They strapped on their guitars and began playing "Hot Blooded" to clapping and shouting from the audience. They segued into "Cold As Ice" and everybody was on their feet. J.J.'s group was mesmerized. A joint was passed to Flynn from some stranger and he took a toke and passed it on. Stephanie had the Bullet again. Foreigner played their third song, "Feels Like the First Time."

The concert continued for an hour with Foreigner playing all of their hits and some new songs as well. When they left the stage, the crowd cheered for an encore. After a few minutes the group came back out and went right into "Double Vision." The song brought the house down.

When the band had cleared the stage, J.J. pointed the gang in the direction of the backstage entrance. They showed the guard the plastic necklaces that allowed them access. Inside was a hallway already full of people. They were all trying to reach the hospitality suite to connect with Foreigner.

The room had a makeshift bar with bottles of every kind of booze. And there was coke everywhere. Mick Jones of Foreigner shook hands with J.J.

"J.J., am I right? WQXA? I remember you from our last trip to the radio station. Thanks for putting us on your playlist," said Mick.

"Wouldn't have it any other way. We're a rock station. You're a rock band. Makes sense," said J.J.

Stephanie signaled to J.J. that she wanted to meet Mick. So, he introduced them. She started flirting immediately. He looked like he liked her too.

"How 'bout a drink?" he asked her.

"I'd rather have a snort."

"Well, let's see what we can do about that."

Flynn was not pleased with Stephanie's attention to Mick. He joined a group that was smoking some weed and that pleased him for the moment. Tiffany, J.J. and Don were showing some groupie-types how to use the Bullet. Miles and Ernie had stationed themselves at the bar. The party went on and on until the band finally left the suite. Then the rest of the partygoers trickled out.

When the gang of seven left the Auditorium, the stretch limo was waiting for them curbside. They climbed into the back. Everyone sat in the same seat as on the way to the concert. Don had replenished his Bullet and started to pass it around. Another bottle of champagne was opened. The party continued full force in the limo. The snow had picked up and the driving was slippery.

J.J. spoke up, "Let's have an afterparty!" The limo gang, mostly high on cocaine, was up for it. "Where should we go? Street of Dreams or someplace else?"

"Let's try the Boul-Mich. My buddy Teddy's the late-night bartender. He'll do well by us," said Flynn.

Just then, the limo driver slides the glass open from the driver's seat and spoke to J.J. in the back. "Hey, QXA. Where to now? I hope you're all going to the same place."

"We are," answered J.J. "The Boul-Mich on Michigan Avenue."

Moments later the limo pulled up in front of the Boul-Mich. They all piled out and raced to the door to get out of the snow and cold. J.J. took care of the limo driver, who had also gotten out to get paid and say goodnight.

Inside, the bar was warm and cozy. Only a handful of people were still drinking. Flynn and company bellied up to the bar.

"Hey, man, Teddy! How's it going?" asked Flynn.

"Flynn. What's happenin'? Is it time to line up the twelve-year-old scotch?" asked Teddy.

"Don't forget the one ice cube," said Flynn.

"Never. What do the rest of you want?" asked Teddy.

Stephanie and Don had already gone to the back to the bathrooms. Ernie and Miles ordered beers. Tiffany was waiting by the door for J.J. to finish with the limo driver.

When Stephanie and Don returned from the back, Miles grabbed Don by the arm and led him back again for his time with the blow.

Finally, Tiffany and J.J. approached the bar. They asked Teddy for wine. Everybody was pumped up after the rock concert. Especially Flynn.

"Nothing like a rock concert to make things come alive. There's something kind of magical about a group of musicians getting together and coming up with a dynamite sound. It's pure magic. Nothing like it," said Flynn.

"Let's push some tables together and sit around them so we can all talk," said J.J.

The guys moved away from the bar and turned a couple of tables into one big one. The bar was practically empty. Just a few late-nighters sitting at a table in the corner.

"The Boul-Mich is supposed to be a media hangout. Where are all the media? It's only about 1 A.M.," said Flynn as he sat down at the table.

Ernie and Miles went back up to the bar to get their drinks. J.J. led the girls over to the new table. They sat next to each other, across from Flynn.

"Hey, man, J.J.! Foreigner was pretty cool, but you can't beat the concerts we went to in the late sixties. Remember seeing Jimi Hendrix in that small arena in Ann Arbor?"

"Who could forget it?" said J.J.

"'Purple Haze,' 'Foxy Lady,' 'Fire.' It was far-out," said Flynn.

"Don't forget 'All Along the Watchtower.'"

"And 'Voodoo Child' with the wah-wah pedal."

Miles spoke up, "And 'The Wind Cries Mary.' You guys weren't the only ones into the late-sixties music scene. I was at Syracuse. All the same stuff was happening all over the country."

Flynn jumped in again, "An explosion of music that has never been seen again. Every group back then had something to say. Every album meant something. Every time a new album was released it was a very big deal."

"Do you guys ever talk about anything but music?" asked Stephanie. "Some of us were too young to have experienced the sixties the way you guys did. I was like in 8th grade or something."

Over at the bar, Don was standing by himself drinking his drink.

"Just stick with me, kid, I'll teach you everything you need to know," said Flynn.

"Got it," said Stephanie. Then she got up and went over to the bar and whispered to Don. They were quickly headed back to the bathrooms.

Tiffany and J.J. were holding hands, talking quietly together. Ernie sipped his drink and spoke for the first time.

"I don't know about the sixties. I'm a little young for that, too. But I thought Foreigner was fantastic. That Dennis Elliot on drums. Wow. Jones and Ian McDonald. All the British part of the band. I'd never seen a rock concert so close up. Thanks for the whole evening, J.J."

"You're welcome. I'll be sure to invite you to the next one. Although at this moment I don't know who that's going to be," said J.J.

"So Flynn, you're a musicologist of sorts. Where did the wah-wah pedal come from?" asked Ernie.

"It originated in the 1920s with trumpet and trombone, but it came into use in 1967. In 1966 an actual guy name of Bradley J. Plunkett at an electronics company, was the real creator. Then Hendrix used it and Frank Zappa did, too. They were the first rockers to use it," said Flynn.

"I love that effect. Too bad Foreigner didn't use it. I would have liked to hear it. I think it is one of the coolest techniques," said Ernie.

"Foreigner isn't an ORG. There's only a few of them," said Flynn.

"What's an ORG?" asked Ernie.

"'Original Rock God.' Like Eric Clapton or Hendrix. The Beatles, Bob Dylan, The Who, The Doors. New ones get added all the time. But those are some of the first," said Flynn.

"Don't forget Mick Jagger. And all the Stones," J.J. came out of his hand-holding with Tiffany. "Mick has got to be on any list of Rock Gods."

"The Rolling Stones are my favorite group, Rock God or not," chimed in Tiffany. "We saw them in '75. They were fantastic. We didn't quite have the seats we had tonight."

"The Stones are Rock Gods, for sure," said Flynn.

At the bar, Don and Stephanie were back from the bathroom. They ordered drinks from Teddy. They were both pretty high now. They started flirting. Flynn saw this from his place at the table. He frowned.

Teddy bellowed to the room, "Almost 2 A.M. Last call. Get a drink now or forever hold your peace."

Flynn went up to the bar and ordered a last scotch. Teddy got it for him before he took care of the handful of people from the tables who wanted another drink before closing.

Flynn chugged his drink. Then he stepped into the Don/Stephanie conversation. "We're going home."

"Let me just finish my drink," Stephanie blurted. She was moving her jaw and slurring her words a bit.

"We're going." Flynn went back to the table to thank J.J. for the fantastic evening. Everybody was getting their coats and gear and thanking J.J.

They walked out into the Chicago weather. The snow had stopped but the temperature had dropped. It was frigid and windy.

"It's April, for God's sake. What is it with this cold?" asked Tiffany.

"Life in the Big City," said Flynn. "J.J., Tiffany, you're headed our way. You want to share a cab?"

"Yes, I'm not walking in this," said Tiffany.

Ernie and Miles decided to also share a cab. Don hung back by the entrance door. They all looked at him. "I'm walking. I'm walking."

"Whatever," said Flynn.

They were lucky. Two cabs pulled up as if on cue. The gang said goodnight and got into the two cabs.

Don put up his hood and walked down Michigan Avenue.

When Flynn and Stephanie reached his apartment building, Billy was practically out the door as they stepped out of the cab.

"Hi, guys," he said as he opened the door. "Another cold one. What you guys been up to?"

"We saw Foreigner in concert. Then stopped at the Boul-Mich," said Flynn.

"Pretty cool. You always see the rock shows. Seems to be your thing," Billy said as he pressed the button for the elevator. "Have a nice rest of the night."

Flynn stuck the key in the lock of his apartment and let Stephanie go first. When he got inside, he immediately went to the fireplace and started working on a fire. He pulled small pieces of wood and newspaper out of their baskets. Put them under the grate and placed a big piece of wood on top. He then lit a match and started the fire. The kindling ignited.

Stephanie took off her coat and looked down at her high-heels. They were completely soaked and ruined. She undid the straps and put them on the hearth.

"Well, another pair of shoes ruined because of this stupid Chicago weather."

"Why didn't you wear your boots?"

"They didn't match my dress."

"When are you ever going to learn how to dress for this weather?"

"I'm not going to sacrifice fashion because of it." She sat back on the couch and pulled out a snowseal from her purse. She began to make lines on the coffee table.

"Just what you need, more coke."

"What's it to ya? You have your pot and scotch."

"It doesn't make me move my jaw back and forth and flirt with rock stars and drug dealers."

"Oh, so that's what it's about."

"Yeah, I'm pissed. When I take a girl out, I want to feel that she's with me."

"I'm with you. I'm just a friendly person. Have a line."

"You get as high as you want. I'm going to bed in my bed. I'll get you a quilt. You can sleep out here, if you'll even go to sleep. I've had it."

He went into the bedroom and came back with a quilt. He threw it at her. "Sweet dreams."

Stephanie snorted a line just to spite him. Flynn sighed and went back into his bedroom.

★ ★ ★

In the morning, Flynn came out of the bedroom and found Stephanie asleep on the couch all bundled up under the quilt. He got in with her and she stirred.

"Wanna make up?" Flynn asked.

"Ummmm…."

"Well, do you?"

"Okay."

They cuddled for a while and then Flynn got up from the couch to make coffee. Stephanie crawled out and put the quilt around her. The dress from last night was crumpled on a chair. She grabbed it and went to the bathroom. When she came out she looked great even in last night's clothes.

Flynn slid open the sliding glass door to the balcony. There was a small table and two chairs out there. He placed the two coffee mugs on the table and then sat down. Stephanie saw him out there and joined him. The temperature was in the 40s and it was cold, but they were determined to be out there.

"I can see a small part of the lake from up here. I've never been out here before, it's a beautiful view. But I'm going to get my coat," said Stephanie.

"Bring mine, too. It's on one of the dining room chairs," said Flynn.

Stephanie returned wearing her coat and bringing Flynn's. They sat for a while pretending that it wasn't still freezing.

"Wait till summer. You'll love it out here."

"I'd settle for some nice spring days. Does it get any better in May?"

"Yes. It does. But technically Chicago has three good days of weather. One in May and two in October."

"Very funny."

"I'm not kidding."

"So why does anyone want to live here?"

"'Cause it's Chicago. And there's no place like it."

Stephanie got up and started to go inside. "I'm going in. It's too cold."

"I gotta get ready anyway. I'm meeting J.J. at Wrigley Field for opening day of the Chicago Cubs. I'll be taking a cab. I'll drop you off on the way," said Flynn.

"Baseball today? You really are a little crazy."

The cab pulled up at the entrance to Wrigley Field, the famous ballpark on the North Side of the city. This Chicago landmark sat right in a residential area filled with quaint townhouses and single-family dwellings. A man in a booth was selling pennants, knickknacks, mugs, all bearing the Chicago Cubs logo. At the ticket booth J.J. stood waiting. Flynn jumped out of the cab and waved.

They got their tickets and went to their seats. When they pushed the seat open they had to brush off snow before they sat down. The stadium was not crowded. Only a handful of loyal fans were braving the cold. Flynn and J.J. sat down. They were about ten rows up from first base. Great seats on a miserable day. The Cubs were playing the New York Mets. They watched for a while in silence.

"I'm freezing. I don't know if I can make it through a whole game," said J.J.

A vendor came by with plastic cups full of beer. Flynn asked for two. He handed one to J.J. "This might help."

"Yeah, cold beer. We should be drinking hot chocolate."

"You gotta be tough to come to a Cubs game on opening day. It's always in April and it's always cold," Flynn shivered as he spoke.

"I prefer an indoor rock concert. Wasn't Foreigner great? That was such a blast," said J.J. "We've got concerts coming up all over the place. I do like this city for music. Being in media here is like a dream come true. Limos. Rock stars."

"It's far-out, man. Rock is king. Just like in college," said Flynn.

They watched the game for three innings, had another beer and then J.J. announced, "I can't take it anymore. I'm freezing my ass off. Let's call it a day."

"I wanna see who wins," cried Flynn.

"We can hear it on the radio. WGN broadcasts all Cubs games," said J.J.

"Okay, but I'm not happy about it," whined Flynn.

They got up and walked toward the exit. When they were out front they flagged down a cab.

THE YEAR THAT ROCKED

★ ★ ★

It was a busy day on the set of *The Brett Adams Show* and all of the crew were ready to tape. Flynn was in the booth, headset on, gearing up for another taping of a live talk-show. The guest was author Norman Mailer. He walked onto the set and shook hands with Brett. Then he sat in the guest chair across from him.

"Norman Mailer. Welcome. There's a lot of buzz about your book *The Executioner's Song*. One of the networks has bought it for a made-for-TV movie. Pretty exciting. Tell us about it."

"It's about Gary Gilmore who robbed two men in 1976 and killed them in cold blood. He was tried and convicted and immediately insisted that he be executed right away. Fought a system that seemed intent on keeping him alive after he was sentenced to death," said Norman.

"That fight for the right to die is what made him famous. Right? And the book's about that fight," Brett said.

"Based on that fight. The story has a lot of layers. It was a joy researching. And I hope the book sells like wildfire," Norman added.

"Isn't it up for a Pulitzer Prize?"

"Yes. We'll see what happens."

Brett held up a copy of the book. "Everyone in the audience gets a copy of this. Look under your chair."

The audience clapped like trained monkeys. In the booth, Flynn laughed out loud. The rest of the crew joined him. "At least it's not a shrink," Flynn said.

After the show, Brett came into Flynn's office with Norman. He gestured for them to sit down.

Brett spoke first, "Can you believe our luck getting America's hottest writer-of-the-moment?"

"It's a show to remember," Flynn chimed in.

"Flynn, let's take Norman to The Palm for lunch. You up for it author extraordinaire?"

"I've heard good things about it."

Brett, Flynn and Norman sat at the bar in The Palm nursing their drinks. The entrance door opened with its usual burst of cold air coming off Lake Michigan across the street. Covered in his usual gear, J.J. entered with a good-looking guy with long blond hair. He was only wearing a leather jacket. No hat. They walked over to the bar, where the threesome sat.

"Flynn, Brett, this is Tommy Shaw of Styx," introduced J.J.

"Hey, man, Tommy! This is the author Norman Mailer," said Flynn. Everybody shook hands.

"I've read *The Executioner's Song*. Cool book," said Tommy. He and Norman fell into an easy conversation about it.

The bartender, Frank, came over to take drink orders. When J.J. was sipping his beer he addressed Flynn.

"Norman Mailer, pretty cool. No shrinkdom today?"

"N.B.D.," said Flynn.

"Is anything a big deal for you?" asked J.J.

"Not really. Except for music. But a famous author could be high on the list of big deals."

"How about Tommy Shaw?"

"You've definitely got me there. I can't wait to talk to him after he finishes with the author of the day."

The door opened again and this time it was Stephanie who literally blew in. She had on her winter coat, hat, gloves and scarf. Everything seemed right except the open-toed sandals. She saw the gang at the bar and walked over.

"I thought I'd find you here. I'm on a break and seeing as how we're practically next door, I decided to take a chance," said Stephanie.

Flynn introduced Stephanie to everyone and she was beyond impressed with the famous that were present. She talked to Tommy for a minute and then ordered a glass of white wine. Flynn saw his opportunity to get Tommy alone and started to talk with him. Stephanie sat down next to J.J. and within minutes they were on their way to the bathrooms. Norman Mailer said goodbye to Flynn and Brett and headed out the door. He didn't mention that they hadn't had any lunch. But he was on his way to another interview and had to go.

Flynn and Tommy Shaw were talking up a storm. Flynn gestured to Frank for another round of drinks. Brett declined and then said his goodbyes. Before he left he asked Tommy if he wanted to be on his show and the rock musician agreed.

Stephanie and J.J. returned from the back. She was visibly high moving her jaw back and forth and grinding her teeth. J.J. was as cool as ever. She approached Flynn and Tommy.

"Is your group, Styx, playing around Chicago? J.J. takes us to all the concerts. Would love to see you do a show," gushed Stephanie.

"We're not touring right now. I just came to see J.J. at the station. He always promotes us so heavily we've become buddies," said Tommy.

"You could thrill us right now by hitting some of those high notes on 'Lady,'" laughed Flynn.

"Oh, yeah, do it," pleaded Stephanie.

"Guys, I don't sing unless I'm on stage or in the studio. Unless, of course, you count the shower," said Tommy.

J.J. laughed. "That is something I'd like to hear. Tommy Shaw in the shower. The new album. Speaking of new albums, what are you working on right now?"

"We're recording at Pumpkin Studios in Oak Lawn. The song titles are not being talked about until the record is released. Should be in October. The name of the album can be talked about. It's *Cornerstone*. Last year's *Pieces of Eight* was our second consecutive top-selling Triple Platinum album in a row."

"I loved *Pieces of Eight*. Can't wait until the new one comes out," said Flynn.

"J.J. will get us front-row seats when you do the tour. We just saw Foreigner last week. Front-row seats and backstage passes," added Stephanie.

"J.J.'s the best when it comes to getting backstage. I've seen him there after every concert," said Tommy. "The band loves J.J. Who else would give us all that air time?"

Flynn and Tommy started talking music again in an intense one-on-one. J.J. and Stephanie ordered another drink. They fell into an easy conversation. The front door kept opening as media types were getting off work and coming to The Palm. Stephanie never did make it back to her office.

Later that night, Flynn and Stephanie were sitting on the couch at his apartment eating takeout pizza and pasta. A roaring fire warmed the room and set a tranquil atmosphere. Outside the sliding glass door to the balcony a light snow was coming down.

"It's snowing again," complained Stephanie.

"Just a flurry," said Flynn. He got up and put an album on the turntable. The music of David Crosby and Graham Nash came through the speakers.

"What's this record?" asked Stephanie.

"*Wind on the Water*, Crosby and Nash without Stills and Young. It came out in '75. Just the two of them. It's one of my favorites. The two of them together with their harmonic and melodic style. You can't get any better than this."

"Carry Me" was just ending and "Mama Lion" was starting. Stephanie had finished her food and began listening intently. Flynn was lost in the music. It played on while they just sat there mesmerized by the fire and the music. When the album was over, Flynn turned to Stephanie.

"If we're going to be a couple, you're going to have to cut down on the coke and flirting."

"You do coke."

"Sometimes. But not the way you do."

"I don't flirt. I'm just friendly."

"That's an understatement. Here. Try some weed for a change." He pulled out a joint from the table stash.

"Grass is good sometimes," purred Stephanie as she took a toke.

"Just as good as in 1969."

"Your radical hippie days. Weren't you head of the SDS or something?"

"I organized and marched in a lot of demonstrations against the Vietnam War."

"I missed that whole thing just by a few years. I told you. Remember?"

"It's too bad. It was a really cool time to be in college. Did I ever tell you that I went to Woodstock?"

"You didn't. You did? I can't believe it. I've never known anybody who was actually there."

"Yeah. J.J. was with me. We took off from U of Michigan in a rented Volkswagen van and drove all the way to New York State. We were one of the 500,000 hippies that saw the whole thing. In the mud. In the rain. It was totally worth it. Just to see Jimi Hendrix play the National Anthem was amazing. We stayed for the entire show. Three days of peace and music."

"You didn't follow J.J. into radio and music. That's surprising."

"Just fell out that way. But I have some ambitions toward music in the works. I'll tell you about it sometime."

Flynn took Stephanie in his arms and they began kissing. When it changed to heavy petting he went into the bedroom and got his quilt. They then set up on the thick, Oriental rug.

"Why can't we do it in the bedroom?" asked Stephanie.

"I like it out here."

Flynn got up to put another log on the fire. When he returned they were lost in each other quickly.

★ ★ ★

Flynn walked south on Michigan Avenue toward the studio. There was a freezing, sleety rain pouring from the sky. The temperature was 30 with a windchill of 18. He bowed his head and tried to resist the typical late April weather. He finally reached Wacker and stopped for the light. The wind was doing its double whammy of river wind and lake wind. Flynn crossed the street and headed toward the building. The security guard opened the door for him when he got there.

He took the elevator up to the studio. The audience was streaming in and taking their seats. Flynn went immediately to his office. He saw Tommy Shaw sitting in his visitor chair.

"Hi, Flynn. Thought I'd hang out in here until the show starts taping. I've never done this before. I'm a little nervous," said Tommy.

"Piece of cake, Tommy. Just be yourself. Brett will do the rest."

Madison stuck her head in the door. "We need to get to the booth. We're ready."

"Let's go. I gotta get to the booth. Madison will take you to the backstage area, where you'll wait until they announce you," Flynn encouraged.

They walked out of the office. Madison grabbed Tommy. Flynn went to the booth. Brett was already in his chair on the stage.

Flynn donned his headset. "Cue the opening music. Zeke, Jeremy, Isaac. You ready?"

Zeke began his countdown. "In five, four, three, two…."

"Cue Brett," barked Flynn.

Brett started in, "Welcome to *The Brett Adams Show*. Today's guest is Tommy Shaw, frontman and guitarist for the rock group Styx."

Tommy entered from the stage wings. He took in the scene with the audience, the crew on set and Flynn in the booth. He shook hands with Brett, who then gestured him to his chair.

"Chicago loves Styx, Tommy. Tell us about the song 'Come Sail Away.'"

Tommy looked around before answering. "Our album *Grand Illusion* out in '77, went triple platinum because of that song. It was written by Dennis DeYoung. The album became our breakthrough album."

"When did you join the band?"

"In 1975 I replaced guitarist Curulewski when the members were excited I could hit the high notes on 'Lady.' Been with the band since then."

In the first row of the studio audience, J.J. and Tiffany were sitting there. They were having some kind of argument and she got up and stomped off down the aisle. Tommy noticed from his chair and sort of waved to J.J. Flynn, in the booth, saw the commotion and was extremely irritated. He told Zeke to get ready to cut to a commercial. The tech at the board punched up a commercial for Tide. On the stage Brett and Tommy kept chatting and waiting for the signal that they were back on the air.

★ ★ ★

Down on lower Wacker Drive was a restaurant famous for its artwork and cozy atmosphere. Flynn and J.J. walked down the stairs from Michigan Avenue and fought the sleeting rain to the front door of Ricardo's. Inside was a cavernous room surrounded by famous paintings hanging in every available spot. The bar was directly in front of them and that was where they went. They grabbed two stools.

"What a cool show today," said J.J.

Flynn smiled. "I loved it. More rock guests is what I've been waiting for. Getting back to my music roots. Hopefully, we'll have a lot more band guests."

"I can help you with that. As you well know from all the shows we go to, QXA always has people coming through town."

"Far-out. We could use some help. So, what was the deal with you and Tiffany today?"

"We're not getting along. In fact, she's threatened to go back to her parents' home in San Diego. Says she missed the weather and family."

"Is she really serious? I thought you guys were so tight. And she was so excited about her new boobs."

"Things change. How about you and Stephanie? Are you together?"

"Yeah, we're together. She's the first girl that I've dated in a long time that I'm really serious about."

"Wow. Flynn serious about a girl. You're lucky. She really is a looker."

Suddenly, some people came up behind them. It was Miles and Don and an entourage. They ordered drinks and gathered around the bar.

"We can't go anywhere in Chicago without running into you two," said Miles.

"You're just lucky that way, I guess," responded Flynn. "I know you're just checking up on your Program Director. You don't want him getting into trouble and missing work."

J.J. turned around on his stool to face Miles. "Miles, my man. You checking up on me?" They both laughed.

Don broke in, "I'm going to the bathroom. Anybody coming?"

J.J. jumped off his stool and followed Don toward the back. Flynn talked to Miles.

"We had Tommy Shaw on the show today."

"I heard it went great. You could start coordinating rock guests with people we have coming to town. It could be a regular thing," said Miles.

"I'll get with my guest scheduler and Brett. Maybe we can work something out. But I'm not counting on it. Brett likes his shrinks. It's what the audience expects," said Flynn.

Miles gazed around at the artwork. There were some Picassos and Monets and some local artists, too. The room felt like being in a museum.

"I love Ricardo's. Don't you?" asked Miles.

"It's pretty amazing. Good food, too. Are you guys staying for dinner?" asked Flynn.

"Yeah, why not?"

Don and J.J. returned from the bathroom.

"Let's get a table," Flynn suggested.

J.J. sniffed and said, "I'm not hungry anymore. But I'll sit with you guys and just drink."

"Same here," said Don.

When the group came out of the restaurant later, the sleet had turned to snow as they made their way to the stairs up to Michigan Avenue.

"We're going to Butch's, Flynn, you in?" asked J.J.

"I'm done. I'm just going to flag down a cab and go home. Later, guys!"

Flynn shouted for a cab at the same time his hand went up. One pulled up instantly.

The cab pulled up to Flynn's apartment building and he got out. Billy opened the front door.

"Another nasty night with temperatures in the teens," moaned Billy.

"Thanks for reminding me."

When Flynn got up to his apartment he immediately picked up the phone and called Stephanie.

"Hi, it's me. What are you doing? Why don't you take a cab over and bring some clothes for tomorrow. Yes, I've got wine. Okay, see ya."

A little while later, Stephanie knocked on the door. Flynn opened it and ushered her in. The fire warmed up the room and the stereo was blasting. She had a little overnight bag with her and Flynn took it and her coat. She was wearing the L.L. Bean boots that Flynn had bought for her.

"The end of April and you're finally wearing the boots," he said.

"I wore them just for you. Pretty soon the weather will change and I won't need them," Stephanie said. "Who's that on the stereo?"

"Jimi Hendrix. 'All Along the Watchtower.' One of his best songs."

"You're obsessed with Jimi Hendrix."

"Shrink word."

"Yeah, it is. And you are."

"Well, then it's a good thing.

Stephanie took a Bullet Snorter out of her purse. She turned it upside down and got some coke in the dome. Then she put it up to her nostril and snorted.

"Talk about obsessed," Flynn said.

"Want some?" She did the other nostril.

"No thanks. Not tonight. Hey, do you know who wrote this song?"

"Hendrix, I imagine."

"No, Bob Dylan wrote it. But Jimi's version is far-out."

"It sounds pretty good, whoever wrote it. Can I have a glass of wine?"

Flynn went to get it. He also dropped another log on the fire on his way to the kitchen. He came back with the wine and a beer for himself. They cozied up on the couch and sipped their drinks. Stephanie took the Bullet, opened it up and poured out the contents onto the coffee table. She made lines with a credit card. Then she took a rolled up bill and snorted a line. Then she handed the bill to Flynn.

"The Bullet's good for when you're in a car or somewhere where you can't make lines. But I like it this way much better. You get much more in your toot."

Flynn took the bill and snorted a line. "Okay, you sold me." He sniffed and then did the other nostril.

"Don sold me the Bullet. That guy's got everything."

"He gives me the creeps. He's always just suddenly there. You just look around at any bar and there he is."

"I love it that he's around. That means there's coke."

"As I said earlier, talk about obsessed."

"Shrink word."

Stephanie did another line and Flynn lit a joint. They sat in companionable silence for a minute enjoying the fire and the music. "All Along the Watch Tower" ended and Flynn got up to change the record.

"Who do you want to hear?" asked Flynn.

"Do you have any disco music?" Stephanie asked.

"Don't even say that word. 'Disco.' It's horrible."

"Have you heard Steve Dahl and Gary Meyer on WLUP? They hate disco and talk about it all the time on their morning show."

"Don't tell J.J. you're listening to them. He gets really pissed. But, yes, I've heard them. Their show is high-larious. I hate disco as much as anybody. There are no ORGs in disco."

"Original Rock Gods, I got it. But disco is fun to dance to. I like some of it."

"Just don't talk about it. Gives me the willies."

Flynn stood waiting at the stereo and Stephanie snorted another line. He picked out *Music from Big Pink* and put the needle down on "The Weight."

"This is The Band. You ever heard them?"

"No. I like the beat, though. Who's singing?"

"Levon Helm. He's the drummer. The Band recorded this album in 1968 at a house in Upstate New York that was actually pink. They used to be known as Bob Dylan's backup band. This was their first attempt on their own. It's a classic."

"Weren't they in that movie *The Last Waltz*? I remember it coming out last year but never saw it."

"The best rock movie ever made. It's perfect. Seamless. I saw it twice in one week."

"Enough talk." Stephanie put down her rolled-up bill and leaned into Flynn. They began kissing. Then it turned into heavy petting and they ended up on the thick Oriental rug. She was on top when they finished making love. She rolled off and lay there panting.

"Why don't we make love in your bedroom?" she asked.

"Call it an obsession, if you will. I'm saving it for when I make a commitment."

"And you're not doing that with me?"

"We've never talked about it."

"So, do you only like me for sex?"

"That's ridiculous. You're not that kind of a girl."

"What kind is that?"

"The kind you sleep with once and then forget about it."

"Have you had a lot of experience with that?"

"Sure. But I don't feel that way about you. I think of us as a couple."

"That's good."

Stephanie snorted the rest of the blow on the table. She was instantly awake.

"You want to go again?" she asked.

"Far-out. You took the words right out of my mouth."

MAY

SPRING BLOOMED IN CHICAGO. BIRDS were tweeting, the sun was high in the sky. Lake Michigan glistened. Temperatures had reached into the high 60s. People were out riding bicycles up and down the lakefront. Oak Street Beach was packed with Chicagoans desperate to catch the sun and feel the warmth.

Flynn and Stephanie stepped out of a cab at the Monroe Street Yacht Club, a flat-roofed building that looked like a ranch house. From the outside it didn't look like much, but when you entered you were faced with floor-to-ceiling windows overlooking Lake Michigan. There was a long bar on the left and tables up near the windows. Big, double-glass doors led out to the patio. It stood high above the lake with a railing for protection.

Flynn and Stephanie came in the front door and headed straight for the outside patio. They picked a table near the railing for the best view of the lake. As soon as they sat down, a waiter took their drink order.

"This is fantastic. I've never been here," said Stephanie.

"I've been a member for a while. I keep a speedboat here," said Flynn.

"You didn't tell me you had a boat."

"It never came up."

"You're full of surprises."

J.J. came onto the patio and headed for their table. He was noticeably without Tiffany.

"Join us," said Flynn.

"I've forgotten how great this place is. Looks like some clouds moving in, though," added J.J.

"Don't jinx it," said Flynn. "Where's Tiffany?"

"She took off for San Diego. Said she couldn't stand another minute of Chicago. And she couldn't stand another minute of me either."

Stephanie blurted out, "But she told me... I mean... she ...."

"She talked to you about it? I didn't even know till today when she was headed for the airport. What do you know that I don't know?" asked J.J.

"Nothing, really. Have a drink. Forget about it for a while," soothed Stephanie.

"N.B.D. She'll come back," said Flynn.

The waiter brought the drinks and took J.J.'s order.

"It is a big deal if it's your wife. She was so adamant. She hates it here and she hates me," moaned J.J.

The waiter brought J.J.'s beer and they sat in companionable silence and looked out at Lake Michigan. Suddenly, the wind changed direction and picked up ferociously blowing right over the patio. Then there was a switch of lightning followed by a huge thunderclap. The temperature dropped about ten degrees in ten seconds.

Flynn, Stephanie and J.J. acted fast. They picked up their drinks and rushed for the inside of the Yacht Club. They burst through the double doors just as the rain started a downpour. Some other people on the patio scrambled in behind them and caused a backup of people trying to get in in a hurry. The threesome made it and headed straight for the bar and grabbed stools before the crowd got there.

"The Windy City at its best. I knew it was premature thinking we'd have a nice spring day," said Flynn. He turned on his stool and gazed out at the torrential scene on the patio.

"I'll never get used to this town, the way it changes on a dime. But I sure love the media scene here. Speaking of that, I've got VIP seats and All-Access Passes for Journey on May 16th. They're going to be at the Aragon Ballroom," said J.J.

"Far-out!" cried Flynn.

"Do we get to meet them?" asked Stephanie.

"Of course. That's what backstage access means," said J.J.

"I can't wait," said Stephanie.

Flynn signaled the bartender. "Let's order some food and wait out the rain." When he got there, Flynn asked for menus.

"It's gotten cold," Stephanie complained. "I didn't bring a jacket."

"Never go anywhere in Chicago without a jacket, no matter what time of year it is. Rule number one." The waiter handed Flynn and company menus.

"Another Flynnism. I've got to start writing these things down," said Stephanie.

"No, just embellish it in your bird dog," Flynn laughed.

"What does that mean again?"

"It means put it in your brain and keep it there for when you need it."

J.J. chimed in, "Flynn's bird dog philosophy. He's had it since college. I'm used to it.

Later, Stephanie, Flynn and J.J. stood under the eaves outside the Yacht Club and waited for a cab. The rain was coming down in buckets and they could hardly see as a yellow limo pulled up in front of them. They jumped in. Flynn talked to the cabbie.

"Butch's on Division Street."

"Street of Dreams. I know. It's where all your dreams come true," said Stephanie.

"If we ever get there in this downpour," said J.J.

The cab inched its way north on Lake Shore Drive. The windshield wipers were going full blast and not keeping up with the rain. The three of them in the cab were scared. Nobody said anything for a while. When they finally pulled up at Butch's there was a collective sigh of relief.

They entered the crowded bar and were able to find stools at the far end of the main bar. People were spilling out from the adjacent room.

"Hey, man, Joco!" Flynn managed to get the bartender's attention in the milieu of humanity. "Line up the twelve-year-old scotch."

"Beer, Old Style in a bottle," J.J. shouted.

"White wine. French," Stephanie also shouted.

Suddenly Don was there behind them. Stephanie moved over a little to include him in their little group.

"Don, my good friend Don. Always there when you need him," said J.J.

"Anybody want to go to the bathroom?" he asked.

Stephanie was off her stool in seconds. She headed to the room across from the bar and back to the bathrooms with Don following her.

"Don is Johnny on-the-spot," said J.J.

"He gives me the creeps. He's always in the shadows but always there," said Flynn.

"He's our go-to coke guy. We need him."

"What does he do anyway? When he's not selling coke?"

"No one knows."

"He gives me the creeps."

"You said that."

Stephanie was back and J.J. left with Don. Flynn sipped his scotch and contemplated life for a minute. Stephanie was stoked and gulped a little wine.

"What do you do back there?" asked Flynn.

"Snort coke. What do you think I'm doing?"

"I've never snorted coke in a bathroom. A table or that Bullet tool is one thing, but I won't do the bathroom."

"The men's room has a door that locks. It's perfect."

"Whatever."

J.J. and Don were back. J.J. offered to buy Don a drink and they tried flagging down Joco. After a few minutes, he was there. Don ordered a red wine. The others got a second round.

The bar had thinned out and they were still drinking when Joco yelled, "Last call."

The hangers-on ordered. Joco was busy for a minute and then he returned to Flynn and company. "You guys want to go with us Butch's guys over to the State Street Diner? We're all going for breakfast."

"Let's do it," said Flynn. Stephanie and J.J. were up for it, Don bowed out and left.

A little later, Flynn, Stephanie, J.J., Joco and two waitresses from Butch's stood outside and braced themselves against the wind. The rain had stopped, but the wind had picked up. They all bowed their heads and walked the short distance over to State Street.

The diner was brightly lit with a sign that read "OPEN 24 HOURS." They went in and grabbed a booth. There was only so much room, so Stephanie and J.J. took a separate booth. The diner waitress handed out menus. Joco spoke directly to Flynn.

"You still a TV director?" he asked.

"That would be me," said Flynn.

"Isn't your show the one with all the shrinks?" asked one of Butch's waitresses named Sue.

"I hate shrinks," said Flynn. "But yes, it is."

Peggy, the other Butch's waitress, broke in, "Aren't you the music guy? Somebody told me you were the music guy."

"That would be me, too."

The diner waitress was back and she took their orders of scrambled eggs and omelets. Stephanie and J.J. just ordered coffee and were talking up a storm in their booth.

"What's your favorite live concert that you've ever been to?" Joco asked Flynn.

"The Rolling Stones in 1969. U of Michigan, small venue. I've never seen anything like Mick Jagger performing. That was in their heyday."

"My favorite was The Who. Pete Townsend is too cool," said Joco.

"I've seen The Who. They even did the whole rock opera *Tommy*."

J.J. broke in from the other booth. "I can do you guys one better. I've met The Who. Townshend, Daltry, Entwistle and Keith Moon. Talk about the best drummer ever category. R.I.P., Keith. We'll miss you."

"I've said this before but it's worth repeating: rock-and-roll is not just a musical form, it's a lifestyle. A lifestyle that I really dig," philosophized Flynn.

"You should be in music instead of TV," said Joco.

"I've got some ideas about that. I'm thinking about starting my own music show on WSL," said Flynn.

"That's news to me," J.J. said and turned his attention back to Stephanie in their booth.

The dawn doused State Street with light. The gang was still in the diner as the morning began to come alive. Traffic picked up on the famous late-night street and another day in Chicago started.

Flynn was annoyed by the light and took a pair of sunglasses out of his pocket and put them on. "Come on, Steph, I'll take you home in a cab. Then I've got to go home, take a shower and go to work."

"The only place I'm going is to bed," groaned Joco. "I don't know how you guys do it. Go to work and all. More power to you."

Peggy and Sue yawned at the same time. "Bed…," they mumbled.

Outside the diner, a cab pulled up and Flynn, Stephanie and J.J. got in. The cab dropped them both off. Flynn was left alone in the cab. By the time he got to his apartment, the day was starting out to be warm. He paid the driver and got out and went up to the front entrance. Steve, the daytime doorman, opened the door for him.

"I just came on duty. You just missed Billy going off," said Steve.

"Hey, man, Steve! How's it going?"

"Good. Were you out all night? How can you go to work now with no sleep?"

"Years of practice."

Flynn got in the elevator and went up to his apartment.

★ ★ ★

In his office right on time, Flynn looked at the day's schedule. He laughed out loud when he saw that today's guest was Dr. Wilson, a psychotherapist. He turned on his radio and switched the dial from WQXA to WLUP. Madison entered his office and heard the morning team of Steve Dahl and Gary Meyer.

"…and we hate disco, don't we, Gary?" asked Steve.

"Much hatred, we definitely hate it. Don't give me Donna Summer or Gloria Gaynor," added Gary.

Madison started to laugh. "You better not let J.J. catch you listening to WLUP. That's their biggest competition."

"I know. But they are really funny. And they hate disco as much as I do."

"Back to reality, Flynn. We've got a show to do."

"I know. Dr. Wilson, super shrink. I'll be right there."

After the show, Flynn was back in his office on the phone with Stephanie. He was holding two tickets in his hand.

"I've got two tickets to the Premiere of *Apocalypse Now*, the new Francis Ford Coppola film. Okay. Yeah, Martin Sheen's in it. Oak Street Theater 7:45, so we can get good seats."

Oak Street Theater was smack dab in the middle of Oak Street. A grand old theater with one of the biggest screens in the city. Stephanie waited in front dressed in a sleeveless dress and open-toed sandals. When Flynn pulled up in a cab she rushed over to him.

"I'm freezing. Hurry up."

"Why are you dressed that way? It's May in Chicago, but you still need a jacket or sweater or something. It's not quite the time for sandals."

"I'm tired of boots and heavy coats. This is more my style."

There was a huge crowd waiting outside the theater and Stephanie and Flynn joined the throng. Since they had VIP passes they went right up to the front of the group and showed their tickets at the entrance door. Inside, the lobby was overrun with people. Some just talking, some getting snacks. They went into the main part of the theater and walked down the aisle to a cordoned off area that said "VIP Section." They moved the gold braid and walked down the aisle. They were in the third row center. They waited for all the people to get settled in their seats and then the movie began.

When the movie was over Flynn and Stephanie were back outside looking for a cab. They didn't see one anywhere.

"Let's walk. It's not that far," said Flynn.

"But I'm wearing high-heels," said Stephanie.

"And they're open-toed as well. You'll just have to deal with it."

"I'm waiting for a cab."

Flynn frowned but went along with it. After at least fifteen minutes a cab finally came. They got in and went to Flynn's apartment. Billy, the nighttime doorman, was waiting for them as they pulled up.

"I saw a cab coming so I came out. Guessed that it might be you," said Billy.

They got out of the cab and followed Billy into the apartment building. He went to the elevator and pushed the button for them.

When they got into the apartment, the first thing Stephanie did was take off the shoes. She put them on the hearth near the fireplace. Flynn opened the sliding glass door to the balcony.

"It's a lovely night. Just a little chill in the air."

"Can I borrow a jacket or something?"

Flynn went into the bedroom to get something. He came out with a baseball jacket. Stephanie put it on gratefully and then went on the balcony and sat down. She took a little amber vial out of her pocket along with a small gold coke spoon. She did a toot in each nostril and then handed the vial and spoon to Flynn.

"Tonight I will have some blow. I've been running on empty all day. Closing Butch's then going out to breakfast. I'm getting too old for this. How did you do with no sleep?"

"I ended up taking a sick day. So I slept most of the day."

"Lucky you. There are no sick days in live-TV. The show must go on."

Flynn dipped the spoon in the vial and took a hit. He was immediately awake.

"Take another hit. You'll forget all about no sleep."

They looked up at a sky full of stars and the lights from the other apartment buildings in the Gold Coast area. It was too dark to see the lake, but there was a sense of it from 18 floors up.

"So, what did you think of *Apocalypse Now*?"

"I liked it. But it was too violent."

"Did you know that it was an adaptation of the book *Heart of Darkness* by Joseph Conrad? Only set in the Vietnam War. I thought it was a searing indictment of warfare. And what it does to the people in it. My favorite character was the one played by Robert Duvall. 'I love the smell of napalm in the morning.' It got a little heavy-handed at the end, but it's going to be an important movie."

"I thought it was like two movies. The first part mostly about the war. Then the whole boat thing was like part two."

"Hey, Steph. That's a pretty good observation."

She put the coke vial back in her pocket. Then she leaned into Flynn and they began kissing. He took her hands and led her back into the living room. What followed was a lot of foreplay and kissing before they moved to the rug. She was now on top and moving with sexually charged energy up and down. Flynn rolled her over and now he was on top. When they finished, they lay there gasping for breath. Stephanie was first to get up. She grabbed her dress off the chair and took the little vial out of the pocket. This time she laid lines out on the coffee table and grabbed a bill out of Flynn's wallet. She snorted up a line.

★ ★ ★

A beautiful May evening was enveloping the city. J.J. and Flynn stood on Oak Street Beach as the sun was setting in the west. The reflections lit up Lake Michigan as they watched the daylight disappear. When it was fully dark they walked the short distance to The Palm. The bar was just starting to fill up, but they found two stools and sat down. The bartender, Frank, was there in a flash.

"Hey, man, Frank! How's it going?" asked Flynn.

"I'm cool. I don't have to ask what you want. I already know. Johnnie Walker Black for you, Flynn, one ice cube. And for J.J., an Old Style," said Frank.

"You've got it down," said J.J.

Frank brought the drinks and they took big gulps in unison.

"So did Tiffany come back?" asked Flynn.

"No. She's asked for a legal separation."

"You've got to be kidding me. I thought she was so happy. You guys have been together since we all first came to Chicago."

"She doesn't like the nightlife. She obviously doesn't like me."

"Bummer."

"Bummer? Is that all you have to say?"

"Sorry, J.J. It just came out. It does that when I think something is terrible."

"Flynn, embellish this in *your* bird dog. She's gone."

"I've embellished it. I'm really sorry."

J.J. became almost morose as he sat there drinking his drink.

Miles and Don came through the front door and saw the two of them at the bar. They rushed over.

"Glad I found you guys. I've got two tickets to see *The Warriors* for tonight. It's the new movie directed by Walter Hill. Supposed to be great," said Miles.

J.J. took the two tickets. "Thanks, Miles. Flynn, you want to go?"

"What time does it start?"

J.J. looked at the tickets. "Eight P.M. Oak Street Theater."

Flynn got excited for a minute. "We've got plenty of time to eat, drink and still get over there."

"Hey, J.J. You wanna come to the back with me? I'm holding some really great stuff," said Don.

"The man talks," Flynn said sarcastically.

J.J. and Don took off toward the restrooms.

"How's the TV business, Flynn?" asked Miles.

"Same old, same old. Lots of shrinks. How about you?"

"We're fighting the battle of the ratings with WLUP. That morning show with Steve Dahl and Gary Meyer is killing us. Skye Matthews is a good morning show DJ, but it's hard to compete with those guys," said Miles.

Flynn suppressed a smile. "Yeah, the ratings suck. Brett is holding his own at the moment."

J.J. came back. Don was lingering down at the end of the bar with some media folks.

"What are you guys talking about? You look serious. The rumor around the station is that you're going to replace the Program Director," laughed J.J.

"You should laugh. What else is there to do? And you know it's not true. If anybody gets replaced it would be me," said Miles.

"Guys, guys. Don't look so glum. It's only radio," said Flynn.

J.J. perked up. "Yeah, that's like saying it's only TV."

"Let's have another round. Miles, get a drink. You want to eat with us before the movie?"

"You're on. I'm hungry. Worrying takes a lot out of you."

Don came back to their end of the bar. He stood there saying nothing.

★ ★ ★

The next day, in Flynn's office, he lifted a poster tube off the desk and pulled out a movie-size poster of *The Warriors*. Madison walked in and helped him unfold it.

"Saw this movie last night. It is so cool. Michael Beck, James Remar, a stellar cast and a great story," said Flynn.

"It doesn't open until Friday. Not everybody gets free tickets to everything," said Madison.

Flynn's radio was turned to WLUP again and we hear Steve Dahl and Gary Meyer coming through loud and clear.

"I'll say this again, don't ever tell J.J. I listen to WLUP. He'd kill me," said Flynn.

"Mum's the word," whispered Madison.

Flynn grabbed his notes and started out the door and down the hall to the studio. Before he entered the booth, he went to the set and greeted Isaac and Jeremy, who were steadfast behind their cameras. Zeke stood in the middle of the two and waited. Behind them, the studio audience was settling in. Flynn went back to the booth. Madison was already there. She handed Flynn his headset.

"Cue the theme music," Flynn said to the two techs in front of the interior monitors.

The music came through the speakers. On Flynn's mark, Zeke started the countdown. "Four, three, two...," and the number one was silent. Zeke pointed to Brett on the stage.

"Welcome to *The Brett Adams Show*. Today we have a very special guest. Dr. Wayne W. Dyer. Self-help guru, American philosopher and motivational speaker."

Dr. Dyer entered from stage right. Brett got up and shook his hand. Then they both sat down in the side-by-side chairs.

"Your first book, *The Erroneous Zones*, came out in '75. And it's been a huge hit. Then in '78 you published *Pulling Your Own Strings*. You've been a busy writer," said Brett.

"It's indicative of the times. Everybody needs help. I just feed the need," said Dr. Dyer.

Brett asked, "What's that famous line about karma that's attributed to you?"

"How people treat you is their karma, how you react is yours."

In the booth, Flynn burst out laughing. This set off Jeremy and Isaac and Zeke out on the floor. They were all trying to hold it in.

Madison spoke through her headset. "Guys, get it together. It wasn't that funny." This only set them off again. Finally, she was laughing, too.

Brett said, "I love that. Tell us about your writing process and how you come up with your ideas."

Dr. Dyer cleared his throat, then started talking. "Well...."

★ ★ ★

Flynn and Stephanie came out of her apartment building and were enveloped in a glorious May evening. Temperature in the 70s, a light breeze, sun shining brightly, not a cloud in the sky. Flowers were in full bloom in the courtyard. The air smelled fresh and clean. Everything around them seemed alive.

"Let's walk over to Park West," Flynn said. "It's a long walk, but we don't want to waste this summer-like evening."

"What about my heels?" complained Stephanie.

"Go back in and get some walking shoes. I'll wait here."

Stephanie went back to her apartment to change her shoes. When she came out she was wearing another pair of shoes with smaller heels.

Flynn looked at the footwear. "You're kidding. Don't you have any tennis shoes?"

"These will do. I'm not wearing tennis shoes to Park West."

"Okay. It's your feet. Let's walk by the lakefront first. It's too great not to."

"Isn't that out of the way?"

"We've got plenty of time."

Flynn and Stephanie walked along the lakefront. There were boats out on the lake and bike riders on the path. It seemed like the whole city was out. Flynn took Stephanie's hand and they walked close together. They reached the overpass and took it over toward Lincoln Park. They passed Lincoln Park Zoo, the entrance spilling over with people. In a couple more blocks they had arrived at Park West. A mob waited in front to get in. They went straight to the Will Call ticket line and got their passes. At the entrance door they were immediately admitted.

Inside, the club was just opening up. Bartenders wiped down the bar. Waitresses were standing by to start serving the tables. On the stage, a crew was setting up the mic, amps and equipment. Don and J.J. had secured a booth before the club got too crowded. Stephanie saw them and grabbed Flynn's hand and led him over. She scooted into the booth. Flynn hung back a minute.

"I get the outside, please. I don't like being squished in," said Flynn.

"I'm exhausted. We walked all the way here. And my feet are killing me," said Stephanie. She adjusted her low-cut dress. "Sure could use a pick-me-up."

Don stood up on cue. "Let's go backstage. Get your Access necklace from J.J."

J.J. reached into his carryall and pulled out two All-Access plastic necklaces. He gave one to Stephanie, who immediately put it on, and one to Flynn, who left his on the table.

Don and Stephanie rushed away to go backstage.

"Aren't you going with them?" asked Flynn.

"I've been back there twice already. It's no fun without Tiffany. I really miss her," J.J. replied. "I don't know what happened to us. How I ended up in Chicago alone."

"There are plenty of available women. Just look around. They're starting to come in. Did you meet Robin Williams yet?"

"I met him at the station. Very personable. Very accessible. And of course, super funny."

A waitress came and took their drink orders. They watched the club get ready for Robin. They sat in companionable silence for a while.

Don and Stephanie returned to the booth. Both J.J. and Flynn got up and let them in, so they didn't have to be on the inside.

"This is the first time I've been here when it wasn't music," said Flynn.

"I've been here for everything, even a private party once. It only holds about seven hundred. So it's the coolest place in Chicago to see any act. Of course, it's best when it rocks," said J.J.

Don and Stephanie were sniffing and laughing.

"What's so funny? Let us in on the joke," said Flynn.

"Nothing," said Stephanie.

The waitress came back with scotch and a beer. Don and Stephanie asked for white wine.

The room was filling up fast. All the tables were first come first serve and they were closest to the stage, so people were almost fighting to get one. The area around the bar was standing room only. Not a space in sight.

The lights went on up on the stage and Robin Williams came out from the wings. The crowd went wild with clapping and shouting. Robin grabbed the mic and started his standup act. He was unbelievably funny and so quick you might miss a joke if you weren't paying attention. He was up there for about an hour, all by himself, doing his hilarious best to turn on the audience.

Back at the booth, the gang of four were laughing too hard to even stop for a sip of their drinks.

When the show was over, Flynn, Stephanie, Don and J.J. pushed their way forward to the backstage entrance. It was a mob scene. The hospitality suite was filled to capacity and Robin was in the center of it. One table of people were snorting coke right off the table. To get to the bar was next to impossible. They were just standing there in a throng of people.

J.J. shouted to them, "This is ridiculous. Let's head over to Butch's."

Butch's was crowded too but they found seats at the bar. Joco, the bartender, took their drink order.

Stephanie whispered in Don's ear and they were up headed to the back.

"You better keep an eye on her, Flynn. She likes to flirt," said J.J.

"I think it's more she likes whoever has the coke."

"Same thing, isn't it?" quipped J.J.

When Stephanie returned to her barstool her white wine was waiting on the bar. Don disappeared into the fog of people.

"That guy gives me the creeps," said Flynn.

"He's just Don. The deal guy. You've got to give him credit for always having the good blow," Stephanie shouted above the crowd noise.

"Don't broadcast it," Flynn shouted back.

Stephanie pulled J.J. off of his stool. "Let's dance." She led him to the side room, where the jukebox was blaring the Rolling Stones song "Jumpin' Jack Flash." They pushed their way onto the dance area and began to bounce around. The music segued to Journey's "Wheel in the Sky." They kept dancing while Flynn stared at them from the bar. He was getting angrier and angrier as he drank his scotch.

When they came back to the bar, Flynn laid some money on the bar and grabbed Stephanie by the arm.

"We're outta here. Now."

J.J. gave a little wave and reached for his drink.

Outside the bar, Flynn confronted Stephanie.

"Since when do you dance with J.J. instead of me?"

"He's a good dancer."

"And I'm not? And also, I don't like this thing with Don."

"What thing? He's a drug dealer. He has coke."

"You're a little too buddy-buddy with him."

"Why Flynn, I do believe you're jealous."

"I'm putting you in a cab and then I'm walking home." He flagged down a yellow limo, literally put her in the backseat and shut the door.

Flynn walked away and headed in the direction of Elm Street. It was a beautiful May night, soft and warm. The walk was helping his anger.

★ ★ ★

Back at the bar, Stephanie's cab pulled up and she got out and went into Butch's.

She looked for J.J. and Don and found them at a table in the side room.

"You're back. Where's Flynn?" asked J.J.

"He went home. He put me in a cab, but I came back. I'm not through partying."

"Did I hear the magic word: 'party'? Come back to the men's room with me," said Don.

Stephanie followed him to the back of the bar. They went in and instead of offering her a snort from his Bullet Snorter, he held two grams of cocaine wrapped in snowseals up above his head.

"Two grams of coke for a blow job." He waved the grams in the air.

Stephanie just stared at him for a moment, trying to make a decision. He repeated his offer. "Two grams for a blow job. Right here."

She looked longingly at the packages. She looked at the door to the men's room.

"Lock the door."

★ ★ ★

A black stretch limousine pulled up in front of Flynn's apartment. The chauffeur got out and came around the car to open up the back door. Flynn came down the walk and peered into the back. Seated on cozy leather were J.J., Don and Stephanie. On the other seat facing them were Miles and his date, a Playboy Bunny type, and DJ Skye Matthews. Flynn squeezed in beside Stephanie.

"Thanks for saving me some room," Flynn said sarcastically.

"It's the biggest limo we could get," said J.J.

The limo edged down Elm and headed for Lake Shore Drive. The chauffeur opened the sliding glass panel to talk to them in the back and confirm that they were headed for the Aragon Ballroom. He then closed it and left them alone.

Don brought out his little Bullet Snorter and did some coke. Then he started passing it around. Everybody did a snort. When it came back to him, he put it in his breast pocket and pulled out a joint.

"Flynn, look what I brought just for you," said Don.

"Reefer! Finally, somebody knows how to go to a rock concert."

Don brought out a lighter and lit up the joint. He handed it to Flynn, who took it and inhaled deeply. He offered it around and Skye took a toke. The others were busy with a bottle of champagne that J.J. had opened and was pouring into paper cups.

"Journey's frontman, Steve Perry, was at the station today. He gave me a bunch of backstage All-Access Passes." J.J. started handing them out to everybody. They all put the plastic necklaces on.

Flynn toked on his joint while listening to the coke-infused conversation about the rock group Journey and the Aragon Ballroom.

He broke in. "I know I've already asked this question to death, but Skye hasn't been asked. Who's the best guitarist of all time? Jimi Hendrix or Eric Clapton?"

"I'd have to go with Hendrix. For such a short time he made the greatest impression," said Skye.

J.J. said, "You know the rest of us are Claptons."

The Playboy Bunny type rang in, "I'm a Clapton. Not that anyone asked me."

Skye spoke again. "How 'bout drummers? I always ask this one. Ginger Baker or Keith Moon?"

Flynn quickly answered, "Keith Moon. May he rest in peace."

The others all said Ginger Baker.

Skye said, "We're the same again, Flynn. It's gotta be Keith Moon. The Who, in general, are super fantastic. Pete Townshend might make the guitarist list, too."

"Titans of rock-and-roll! Everybody that isn't an ORG. Original Rock God. All the rest are Titans," Flynn said excitedly.

"Titans of rock-and-roll! Perfect. Gonna use that one on my morning show," chimed in Skye.

"The Aragon Ballroom used to be the home of 'monster rock shows' that lasted six hours or more. And they had a reputation for attracting a rough crowd," said J.J.

"Yeah, didn't I hear somewhere that they used to call it the Aragon 'Brawlroom'?" asked Flynn.

"Yep. And the place dates back as far as 1926," said J.J.

"You guys know everything. All I know is I'm going to see Journey and I'm really excited about it," Stephanie said. "Hey, Don, how 'bout another hit from your Bullet Snorter?"

Skye broke into the conversation. "Journey is our destination tonight. Should be great. They didn't really hit it big until last year with the song 'Lights' from the *Infinity* album."

"Tonight I hope they play 'Lovin', Touchin', Squeezin'' from *Evolution*," said J.J.

The limo pulled up to the front entrance of the Aragon Ballroom. The building resembled a Moorish architectural style. A crowd was waiting outside in the ticket line. The gang of seven jumped out of the vehicle and headed for the VIP entrance.

Inside, it looked like a Spanish village. The ceiling resembled the sky, the clouds moving across the stars.

The Playboy Bunny-type chirped, "Wow!"

J.J. led them in the direction of the stage, where they took their seats fifth row center. The crowd was restless and anticipatory. Stephanie sat down next to Flynn and took this opportunity to talk to him.

"I couldn't talk to you in the limo. Too many people. I'm really sorry for the other night. Please forgive me."

"I'll forgive you if you tell me it won't happen again," said Flynn.

"It won't. I promise."

The stage was dark. The audience started chanting, "Journey, Journey, Journey…."

In a flash, the stage lit up like a Christmas tree. The band came from stage right and took up places by their instruments. They started playing "Lovin' You Is Easy." The smooth voice of Steve Perry boomed through his microphone. Neal Schon on guitar sounded fantastic. Steve Smith kept perfect rhythm on drums.

Don brought out his Bullet Snorter and did a hit in each nostril. Then he handed it to Stephanie, who did the same. The smell of marijuana filled the room. Everybody was moving to the music and some people were singing along with the band. They segued to "Wheel in the Sky." After playing for more than an hour, Journey stopped with a flourish and left the stage. The audience was on its feet, begging for an encore.

Journey came back on stage and played "La Do Da" to a standing ovation.

When it was over, J.J. led the merry group to the backstage entrance. People were already there trying to get in without passes. J.J.'s gang showed their passes and got right in. They headed for the hospitality suite.

They walked down a hall packed with people to the door that led to the suite. The band was already in there talking to fans and signing autographs. Flynn went to try to talk to Steve Perry. Stephanie and Don went to the table, where there was a ton of coke.

J.J. joined them and started talking up Stephanie. Don kept doing coke. Miles, Skye and the Playboy Bunny-type mingled among the throng.

Flynn and Steve Perry talked for a long time. The others eventually had to wait for him before going outside to find the limo.

"Flynn has got to be in heaven. Talking to Steve Perry so long. I loved Journey and especially his voice," said Stephanie.

"He's coming over to the station tomorrow if you want to meet him," said Skye.

"I'm in," said Stephanie.

Finally, Flynn joined the group and J.J. led them to the exit. When they got outside the limo was waiting for them. They jumped in and the car sped away.

"Titans of rock-and-roll!" Flynn took his half-smoked joint out of his pocket and Don lit it for him. "Steve Perry is a really cool guy. I had a blast. Thanks, J.J."

"Miles, you've been so quiet tonight," said J.J.

"Just taking it all in. Maybe I need some more coke. Perk me up a bit," said Miles.

Don was there on cue with the snorter. After Miles took two snorts he motioned for Flynn to hand him the joint. He passed it over and then around. Everybody seemed to want a hit.

"Something to mellow out the coke," said Skye.

They rode in silence to Flynn's apartment. When they got there, Flynn stepped out and leaned in to gently take Stephanie's hand.

"You coming?" he asked.

"Absolutely," she said.

Up in the apartment, Flynn and Stephanie sat outside on the balcony. It was a beautiful Chicago night and they were going to take advantage of it. On the glass-topped table, there was a glass of scotch and a white wine. Flynn went inside for a minute and came back with a joint. He lit it and took a toke. Offered it to Stephanie, who declined.

"J.J. sure is nice to take us to all these concerts," she said.

"He loves the music almost as much as I do. We've always been connected that way. It's always been all about the music. Even during my radical days, the music was everything."

"Sorry I missed that era when I went to San Diego State just a few years ago. I feel like I should have been there with you guys. Oh, well. I'm just a babe in the woods."

"You know, I've always been looking for one true friend. I think J.J. is it. We've lasted all this time. Since the late sixties. It was the best of times. Music was king. It'll probably never come again."

"One true friend...." Stephanie reached into her pocket and pulled out a snowseal full of coke. "Do you mind if we go inside so I can lay out some lines?"

"You go ahead. I'll finish this joint out here. It's too nice out to be inside."

Stephanie went into the living room and opened up the snowseal. She poured the white powder onto the coffee table. Made lines with a business card and snorted with a dollar bill already rolled up and ready.

"Want some coke?" Stephanie shouted out to the balcony.

"No thanks. I'm in such a good place now after being at the concert. No coke. No stimulant that makes me hyper," Flynn answered back.

"That's okay. More for me." Stephanie snorted another line.

★ ★ ★

Flynn was in his office the next day listening to Steve Dahl and Gary Meyer on WLUP. Madison knocked on the open door.

"Enter," said Flynn.

"You're at it again. I'm gonna tell J.J. you've been listening to those guys," said Madison.

"They're high-larious."

"Your best friend works at WQXA. He wouldn't be pleased." She changed the subject. "You got your notes on Herman Wouk?"

"I know him as *The Winds of War* guy. Great book. Haven't read *War and Remembrance* yet."

"Hope Brett has read something. He's not the most literary guy."

Flynn got up and grabbed his clipboard. "He knows the right questions to ask just about anybody. You know how good he is. Nobody in daytime talk-shows does it better."

"That's so true," said Madison.

They walked to the booth together. Inside, they donned their headsets and Flynn checked in with Jeremy and Isaac. Zeke was waving through the glass, signaling that he was ready.

"Cue the opening music," said Flynn. "Zeke, start the countdown."

"Five, four, three, two...." One was silent and he cued Brett.

"Welcome to *The Brett Adams Show*. We have a very special author here today. Herman Wouk."

Herman Wouk walked out from stage right and joined Brett on the stage. They shook hands and Brett pointed him to his chair. He held up a copy of *War and Remembrance*.

"*War and Remembrance*. It's a masterpiece. I just finished it."

In the booth, Madison sighed with relief.

"Tell us about it," said Brett.

JUNE

STEPHANIE WAS IN HER OFFICE at the Playboy building. She had a small cubbyhole outside the palatial office of the Editor, Bobby Marin. There were framed *Playboy* covers in every available space on the wall.

She was typing a letter on her IBM Selectric typewriter. She had a phone with five buttons on it. None of them were lighting up. Bobby Marin came out of his office. "You proofing next month's Editor's column?" he asked.

"No, I'm working on one of your letters. The column comes next. What do you think I'd be doing?" asked Stephanie.

"Talking on the phone," Bobby teased.

"Who, me? She who always does her work on time."

"Are you still holding out on going out with me?"

"Bobby, I told you. What happened in California after that seminar stays in California. We work together now. I couldn't go out with you. You're my boss."

"It didn't stop you from getting cozy out there. You might say you used me to get a job."

"Everybody uses everybody."

Bobby touched Stephanie's shoulder affectionately. "You certainly are the cynical one. But I don't care. Make an exception, go out with me."

"Bobby, last I heard you were married. Give it a rest."

"Well, how 'bout at least lunch?"

"I can do that."

Her phone rang and she started laughing. Bobby shrugged and headed back into his office. He couldn't hold back, "See what I mean. I'll leave you to your love life."

Stephanie waited a minute, then spoke into the phone. "Hi. I didn't think you'd call. What? I can't do that. Flynn wouldn't be a happy camper. Well, yeah. Okay. See you in a little while." She hung up the phone, grabbed her purse and stuck her head into Bobby's open office door. "Let's do lunch tomorrow. Something's come up."

Bobby wasn't happy, but he waved her off.

Stephanie walked out of her area, down the hall toward the elevators, passing closed doors with secretaries outside them. They were all trained in keeping people out of the way of their bosses. She waved to a couple of the women and pushed the button for the elevator.

Outside on Michigan Avenue, she hailed a cab and as luck would have it one pulled right up. She jumped in and told the driver where to take her. Traffic was heavy on the Avenue during the midday hour. They continued south and eventually landed in front of Grant Park. Stephanie paid the driver and got out of the cab.

Grant Park was an oasis in the middle of the city. It was a beautiful June day in the 70s without a cloud in the sky. A little breeze came off the lake to make it almost perfect.

A huge fountain dominated the park and Stephanie headed toward it. When she got closer she could see J.J. sitting on the edge of the stone structure. He had two bag lunches with him and he was enjoying the way the sun streaked through the water into the fountain. The park around them was full of people on this rare, almost perfect Chicago day.

"Turkey or tuna?" J.J. asked.

"That's how you greet me? What about 'How are you, my dear adorable creature'?" asked Stephanie.

"Sorry. Okay, how are you, my dear adorable creature?" said J.J.

"I'll take tuna, by the way," said Stephanie.

"Have you told Flynn about us?" J.J. asked.

Stephanie balked. "There is no us. We've just had lunch a few times."

"You should tell him, though."

"Why? He's good to me. And he pays for everything."

"Pays. The magic word. Promise me you'll tell him."

"No. I'm not going to ruin a good thing."

"You want me to tell him what happened with Don at Butch's?"

"What do you know about that?"

"Don tells me everything."

"Oh, God. What kind of a guy tells."

"Don is Don. He was pretty excited about the whole thing. Maybe you could go after him next."

"Up yours!" exclaimed Stephanie.

"Nice talk." said J.J. "Are you a 'prick tease' kind of a girl?"

"I haven't heard that expression since high school."

"Well, are you?"

"I've had my share of men."

"So, what's the big deal, then?"

"N.B.D."

"He's with us even when he's not with us."

J.J. bit into his sandwich and turned his face up to the sun. Stephanie took a pair of sunglasses out of her purse and put them on. Then she took a bite of her sandwich.

"WLUP is killing us in the ratings. That morning show with Steve Dahl and Gary Meyer is a smash hit. We've got nothing like that," said J.J.

"They're great," said Stephanie.

"Don't tell me that. I thought you at least would be loyal to my station."

"I like to laugh. Those guys are funny. You never know what they're going to say."

"I thought you liked Skye in the morning."

"I have to tell you I surf the dial at that time. Whatever wakes me up better I stick to."

"You're no fun. Do you want to go out with me officially tonight?"

"I'm seeing Flynn. This is just a fun lunch. But there is no us."

"We'll see."

★ ★ ★

The sun began its descent, landing its last rays on the sidewalk along the lakefront where Flynn and Stephanie were strolling. People on roller skates zoomed by and a number of men and women on bicycles were riding recklessly around them.

"Hey, watch it. We're walking here," said Flynn to a group of bike riders. He then protectively took Stephanie's hand.

"Chicagoans are so desperate for sun they'll do anything. I always get a change of heart about the city in the summer. It really comes alive," Stephanie said as she picked up the pace.

"No hurry. We've got until eight when the movie starts. Where do you want to eat?" Flynn asked.

"Let's go to The Waterfront. I love seafood."

"We'll walk as far as Belmont Harbor, then turn around and head for The Waterfront."

★ ★ ★

Night had fallen on Chicago as Stephanie and Flynn left The Waterfront restaurant. They walked over to Oak Street and down the block to the movie theater. It was a dry, mild evening and they savored every minute of being outside. The marquee was lit up with *The China Syndrome* and the names Michael Douglas and Jane Fonda beneath it. Flynn bought two tickets and they went in.

When the movie was over they left the theater surrounded by a mob of people. They stole away and started walking toward Flynn's apartment.

"I notice you are wearing low-heeled shoes. Way to go. I knew you could do it," said Flynn.

"When you told me we'd be walking the lakefront I chose wisely," said Stephanie.

"Good thing. We've been walking all night. I don't want it to end. When we get to my place we'll sit on the balcony."

They got to Elm Street and walked the short distance to Flynn's apartment. Billy was Johnny-on-the-spot and opened the front door immediately.

"Hey, man, Billy! What's doing?" asked Flynn.

"I be doing fine. I keep opening the door for everyone so I can sneak a little of a June night in Chicago," Billy said.

He beat them to the elevator and pushed the button. When Flynn and Stephanie got into the apartment, Stephanie went straight out the sliding glass door and sat down in one of the balcony's two chairs. Flynn went into the kitchen to make drinks. He joined her on the balcony and handed her a glass of wine. He had a scotch. They each took a sip and simultaneously sighed.

"So, what did you think of *The China Syndrome*?" asked Flynn.

"Jack Lemmon stole the show. He was fantastic. And Michael Douglas is pretty easy on the eyes."

"No, I mean the content."

"Pretty scary to think a nuclear plant could go offline like that."

"I think it was a pretty significant piece. Especially after what happened in Russia with Chernobyl. It could just as easily happen here."

"Where's your little mirror?" Stephanie got up and went out to the living room to find it. "I'm going to lay out some lines."

"I don't want any coke tonight."

"Flynn, come on, party with me."

Stephanie found the mirror on the coffee table and brought it back out to the balcony. She began the ritual of laying out lines. Instead of the rolled-up dollar bill, she had a new tool. A faux-gold snorter. She showed it to Flynn before snorting up a line. She looked for her purse, which she'd dropped on the living room couch, so she brought it out to the balcony. She pulled out a vial of pills.

"What's that?" asked Flynn.

"Quaaludes. It's the new thing. I got them from Don," said Stephanie.

"Who else?"

Stephanie took one of the pills and washed it down with wine.

"Aren't those downers?"

"Yeah, a perfect sidekick to cocaine."

"I wouldn't mix my drugs."

"Why, you do it all the time with pot and scotch."

"Pot's different than coke. You know that."

"Everyone to their own drug. Want one?"

"No thanks."

Stephanie used her new tool and snorted up another line.

A little later, they were making love in the usual place on the rug. Stephanie seemed lethargic and Flynn was not happy. He pushed her off of him. He was mad now and he called her on it.

"I don't like what those Quaaludes do to you."

"The best way to remedy that is to do another line." She had brought the little mirror with her from the balcony. She leaned over the coffee table and snorted a line.

"Enough coke. Jesus. And now the pills. I don't want you to have anymore."

"It's a free country," Stephanie said with an audible sniff. "I'll do what I want."

Flynn rolled over and got up. Stephanie snorted another line.

★ ★ ★

At the WQXA offices, J.J. entered the broadcast studio and found Skye listening to WLUP.

"Skye, what are you doing?" asked J.J.

"It's 'Won't Get Fooled Again' on the air. You know, The Who. It's a really long song so I thought I'd tune into the competition," said Skye.

J.J. was livid. "I can't believe it. At my own station. I'm sick of those guys Dahl and Meyer. You should be thinking up something new and unique for your morning show instead of sneaking a listen to them."

Skye turned down the speakers. "All right, man. All right."

J.J. stormed out of the studio and went down the hall to his office. He just sat down at his desk when Miles knocked on the open door.

"What's your beef? I can tell you're mad," said Miles as he entered the office.

"I'm sick of WLUP. I just caught Skye listening to Dahl and Meyer while a long song was playing. I couldn't believe it," said J.J.

"You'll feel even worse when I tell you they beat us in the ratings."

"Oh, man. This is turning out to be a terrible day."

"There's more."

J.J. slicked back his hair and prepared for more bad news. "What?"

Miles sat down in his visitor's chair. "WLUP is up for a live broadcast at ChicagoFest. We're still in the running, so we'll have to see."

"We did ChicagoFest last year. We should be cool. Don't even think about not getting that."

"Something will work out, J.J."

"I have a headache."

"Cheer up. We've got Eric Clapton on June 12th. This weekend. We're sponsoring it, remember? Limo, the whole song and dance."

J.J. smiled. Up in the corner his office monitor speaker played the last strains of "Won't Get Fooled Again."

★ ★ ★

Flynn and J.J. were at the Boul-Mich Bar on Michigan Avenue. It was the local hangout for the *Chicago Tribune* and *Chicago Sun-Times* reporters and all media-types. It was crowded, but the two friends had seats at the bar.

"Eric. Original Rock God. Even though I'm a Hendrix, Clapton is beyond fantastic. What time is the limo picking us up?" asked Flynn.

"In about a half an hour. They're picking up Stephanie at the Playboy building and Don, Miles and Skye are meeting us here any minute," said J.J.

As if on cue, the three of them walked into the bar. Flynn noticed them at the front entrance and waved them over.

"Well, if it isn't Mr. Cocaine, The General Manager and the DJ. There should be a song about it," quipped Flynn.

"There is a song about it. 'Cocaine' by Clapton. He'll probably play it tonight," said Skye.

"It's a cover for him. The song was written by J.J. Cale," said J.J.

The bartender, Teddy, came over to take their drink orders.

"Hey, man, Teddy! Get these guys some refreshments," said Flynn. "Don, why are you so dressed up?"

Don was wearing a sports jacket and slacks. "The mood just came over me. It's not every day you get to see a rock icon."

The room filled up behind them as the after five crowd made their way in. Don took a sip from his drink and then headed to the back to the restrooms.

Flynn laughed. "What would that guy do without a men's room?"

J.J. jumped in to defend him. "You know he's a dealer and likes to sample the product. We'll have some in the limo."

Thirty minutes later, the five of them left the bar and crossed Michigan Avenue to be ready for the limo that would be heading south. They stood there while rush hour passed them by on the Avenue. Then they saw it coming. A big, black, shiny stretch limo. The chauffeur saw J.J. waving and pulled over. They opened the back door and began piling in. Stephanie was already in there on the back seat. Flynn and J.J. slid in next to her. Skye, Miles and Don took the seat facing them.

"I got to ride in the limo all by myself down Michigan Avenue. How cool is that," said Stephanie.

The chauffeur pulled back into traffic and headed toward West Madison, where the Chicago Stadium was located. The stadium was the home of the Chicago Blackhawks and the Chicago Bulls. It had an 18,000-people capacity with standing room for rock concerts, when the site wasn't hosting sports.

"Did you guys know that the Chicago Stadium was the site of the first NFL Playoff game in 1932?" asked Flynn.

"Mr. Factoid," said Stephanie. "You're always showing off."

"It's a great stadium. I've seen the Blackhawks play there. A friend of mine had season tickets last year," said Miles.

"It's gonna be a full house tonight. The concert is sold out," said J.J.

Don had a new coke tool. A little gold spoon paired with the amber vial. He dug into the bottle and pulled out a spoonful, took a snort, then handed both spoon and bottle to Stephanie. She took a snort in both nostrils. J.J. was next, then Skye and Miles. Flynn was last and when he had a snort he returned the bottle and spoon to Don, who then pulled a joint out of his jacket pocket and handed it to Flynn.

"Just like the sixties, Don, you're getting it embellished in your bird dog. Way to go," said Flynn as he took the matches and lit up the joint.

Miles, Skye and J.J. also took a hit off the joint. Stephanie declined.

"Hippies going to a concert. I'm in heaven. And I get to see an ORG," said Flynn.

"That's right," said Stephanie. "Eric Clapton is an Original Rock God. Flynn, don't pee in your pants."

"No need for that kind of talk," said Flynn. "Everybody in this limo loves Clapton. It's just far-out."

"Don't forget far-out," said Stephanie sarcastically.

J.J. passed out the All-Access plastic necklaces and they all strung them around their necks. The limo arrived at the stadium and pulled up right at the front entrance. They only had to walk a few feet to get inside the stadium.

When they got inside, it was a mob scene. They found their section with J.J. leading and went down the aisle to the VIP seats. There was no standing room area, they had filled it up with folding seats. The group was seated in the very front, the best seats in the house.

Almost immediately, the lights on stage went on. The opening act for Clapton was Muddy Waters. The musicians came on to a huge standing ovation from the audience. They grabbed their instruments and broke into "Baby Please Don't Go" and the crowd roared again. Muddy went through his full repertoire of songs and really got everybody going. When he finally left the stage, the crowd bellowed for an encore. He came back out and played "Got My Mojo Working," to screaming thousands.

Flynn and company settled for a minute as Muddy and his group left the stage. The lights went dark on stage. They waited for their idol to appear.

When the lights came back on, Eric Clapton and his band were on stage. The audience went wild. Eric began with "Lay Down Sally," then segued to the well-known "Cocaine."

The audience jumped to its feet and sang along. The songs kept on coming. There was "Wonderful Tonight" and "After Midnight" and half a dozen others. The group left the stage as the crowd tried to coax them back.

Flynn and the gang were on their feet clapping and shouting for Eric to come back. His drummer, Jamie Oldaker, came out first and went behind the drums. Then guitarist Albert Lee sauntered onto the stage. They were coming back in pieces. Keyboardist Dick Sims went to his place and bassist Carl Radle plugged in. Finally, Eric Clapton came out. The band was pumped. After a cue from Eric they broke into the iconic "Layla" for their encore number. It brought the house down.

Eric and the band left the stage while receiving a standing ovation. Down on the floor J.J. was leading his little group out of their seats and toward the backstage area. Flynn, Stephanie, Don, Miles and Skye showed their All-Access Passes to a guard and they were let in followed by J.J. He headed them to the hospitality suite down the hall.

Inside the suite were Eric Clapton and Muddy Waters chatting in one corner. The other band members were mingling and drinking. There was the usual bar and in another corner people were snorting coke off a glass tabletop. Stephanie and J.J. headed straight toward it. Flynn got a joint stuck right in his face. He took a toke.

Flynn pushed his way over to where Eric was standing. He was determined to meet him. A path was finally cleared and he met up with the master. He introduced himself to Eric and they fell into a conversation about guitars and rock music. The party went on around them, but they were too engaged to notice.

Stephanie and J.J. were hanging near the coke table.

"Are you going home with Flynn tonight?" asked J.J.

"That's the plan right now," she answered.

"What about us?"

"There is no 'us' at this point. I'm not going to say anything about the couple of times we've been together. He would really freak out."

Miles and Don were suddenly beside them and they stopped talking.

"Flynn's talking to Eric. Skye with Albert Lee. We're left to our own devices," said Miles.

"This is the best afterparty yet," said Don as he got ready to take a snort. He sniffed and handed the coke tool to Miles.

The party stretched into forever. Then in the wee hours, people began to trickle out. Flynn had been talking to Eric and his band members and practically had to be dragged out of there.

Outside, the limo was waiting for them. They saw it from the exit doors and waved to the chauffeur. He pulled over to them. They all piled in. After the noise of the concert and afterparty the inside of the limo was blissfully quiet.

Flynn spoke first. "Eric Clapton is far-out. He knows everything about rock music and I was able to hold my own."

"I didn't think such a big star would give you so much time," J.J. chimed in.

"You should have brought him over to our circle," whined Stephanie. "You should have let us in on the fun."

"We were so engaged I lost track of time," said Flynn.

Miles reached into the champagne bottle holder and pulled out the bottle from earlier. It was warm but there was a half-bottle left. He took a long swig from it, held it up to the group. There were no takers. But when Don brought out his little gold spoon and amber vial everybody took a turn.

"Good coke. That's my thing," said Don.

The limo headed down the street. The chauffeur opened the glass partition and asked the group, "Are you all going to the same place? Or do you want multiple drop-offs?"

"We're going to the Street of Dreams," said Flynn.

"What's that?" said the confused chauffeur.

"Butch's on Division Street," said J.J.

"Oh, that I can do," said the driver.

When the limo pulled up, they all jumped out and went into Butch's. It was almost 2 A.M. but the place was still packed. There were no seats at the bar, so they went into the side room and were able to find a table. They pulled out chairs and sat down. Almost immediately, a waitress came over and took their drink orders.

Flynn continued his dialogue about Eric and the concert. Stephanie got up with Don and went to the restrooms. When she came back, she was feeling pretty frisky.

"Why didn't you introduce us to Eric Clapton?" she asked for the second time that night.

"We were engaged. You could have come over. You and J.J. were talking pretty heavy," answered Flynn.

"What's that supposed to mean?"

"Nothing. Just that you two were looking pretty cozy."

"Well, you left me alone."

"Alone among thousands. Pretty good trick."

J.J. broke in, "Enough. Enough already. We all had a good time. That's the main thing. Another VIP concert trip. I loved every minute of it."

The waitress brought their drinks. They clinked glasses.

★ ★ ★

The next day, Flynn and Brett sat in the Wrigley Bar after the taping of the show.

"I'm glad you had some time. I wanted to talk to you about an idea I have," said Flynn.

"Shoot," said Brett.

"I've been thinking about starting my own show with a focus on rock music."

"You mean directing that kind of show?"

"No, I mean hosting that kind of show. A weekly with one musician or the entire band per show. Want to call it *Rock the Town*. Chicago is a great rock band city. Bands are coming and going through here all the time. And I thought it would be cool to have a whole show devoted to music."

"Sounds like a good idea. But two things: Who's going to direct my show? And will the network go for it?"

"I'd be leaving the show. I'd help you find somebody else. And I thought you could help me with the network. Who would I talk to? Could you put in a good word for me?"

"The head of the network is Barry Sanders. I know him, of course. I might be able to help you get a meeting with him. But, Flynn, you're a great director. You're my director. I don't feel so great about you leaving."

"It can't be helped. I couldn't do both. But there are other directors working at the network. We'd find somebody good for you."

"Flynn, I'm not happy about this."

"Sometimes it's just time to move on. I've been thinking about this music show idea for a long time."

"Okay, let me think about it. See if I have any clout with the network boss. He leaves me alone pretty much because our ratings are so good. I might be able to get you in to see him at least."

"Thanks, Brett. We've always had a great working relationship. I appreciate anything you can do."

"Let's have another drink. I would miss you. You're part of the show."

"I'd miss you, too. But we'd still be at the same network."

"I'll see what I can do. For now, let's just drink."

"Hey, man, Hector! Can we have another round?"

★ ★ ★

At five o'clock straight up, Flynn sat at the bar of The Palm restaurant. Frank, the bartender, came over.

"Flynn, bet you want scotch," said Frank.

"You know me, man. Don't forget, one ice cube," said Flynn.

Just as Frank brought the drink, J.J. arrived and grabbed the barstool next to Flynn.

"I knew I'd find you here," said J.J.

"Yeah, it's definitely one of my hangouts."

"I had a terrible day. Miles was all over me about the ratings for Skye's morning show. Dahl and Meyer swept the morning show ratings across the board," said J.J.

"I have to admit they're pretty funny."

"Flynn, I found Skye listening to them last week during a long Who song. My own guy. He better watch out or he's going to be out of a job."

"J.J., he's the best deejay you've got. Hang on to him. Be cool, man. It'll all work out."

"We'll see. How's Brett and the show?"

"He's fine. It's fine. Shrinks and more shrinks. But I have to tell you about my idea. I've been waiting till we actually had some time with just the two of us."

"What idea?"

"I want to start my own TV show. Be the host of a music-oriented interview show with a different rock star each week. They may or may not come on with their band. A real music show, J.J. I want to call it *Rock the Town*."

"It's been tried before and never went anywhere," J.J. said.

"Not on my network. Brett is going to try to get me in to see Barry Sanders. Head of the network. I want it to run on Saturday night. Late. It'll be my dream coming to life," added Flynn.

J.J. seethed with jealousy. "You can't do it, Flynn. It'll never happen. What do you know about being a host, anyway?"

"I've been working on a talk-show for seven years. I know every position right down to the cameraman." Flynn sipped his drink.

"It'll never fly. You're better off staying a director," said J.J.

"I thought if anybody you'd be supportive," complained Flynn.

"I just don't think it would work. How would you get musicians to come on the show?" asked J.J.

"I'd ask them personally. Then later, after we've become popular I could work with somebody like a guest coordinator."

J.J. changed the subject. "The Neil Young *Rust Never Sleeps* album, recorded live during his '78 tour with Crazy Horse. It's coming out next week on July 2nd."

"Far-out! You know how much I love Neil Young. See, he would be the perfect guest for *Rock the Town*."

"Forget that show, Flynn. Take my advice. In the meantime, I'll get you a copy of the album."

"Thanks, man. By the way, speaking of all things music. WLUP is cooking up a promotion against disco music at Comiskey Park. Coming up in mid-July. You wanna go?"

J.J. pushed back his hair to emphasize his frat boy good looks. He was feeling pretty insecure. "I can't go. It would be disloyal to WQXA."

"You might change your mind. It's gonna be big."

"Let's have another drink." J.J. waved to the bartender.

★ ★ ★

Stephanie was in her office at the Playboy building. Her boss, Bobby, was leaning up against her desk flirting with her. She feigned innocence, but was getting a kick out of the attention.

"You better not let Hef see you practically on my desk," said Stephanie.

"He's in L.A. We always know when he's going to be around," said Bobby.

"Well, let me know next time so I can wear my best outfit."

"You thinking of changing jobs and becoming a Bunny?"

"Yeah, right."

"You've got the body for it. Hef only takes the best."

"How's your wife doing, by the way?"

"Why do you have to ruin my fun?"

"Too bad. I gotta go anyway. It's five o'clock. Closing time. I'm meeting Flynn at the Monroe Street Yacht Club."

"Fancy. Fancy."

Stephanie grabbed her purse and headed out.

The sun was beginning to melt into the horizon, spilling its rays eastward toward Lake Michigan. The terrace at the Yacht Club was crowded with people who were just digging the sunset to the west and the warm night in June. It was clear and dry, low humidity, in the mid-70s. A perfect Chicago summer evening.

Flynn and Stephanie came out onto the terrace carrying their drinks. They spotted a corner table right next to the railing and raced to get it before anybody else took it. The waves below them were crashing against the rocks. It was picturesque and very romantic.

"I can hear the waves crashing. Far-out. This night should go down in the record books," said Flynn.

"N.B.D.," quipped Stephanie.

"You're using my words. But you're wrong. It is a big deal. How many nights in Chicago are like this?" asked Flynn.

"Not many. You said you had something to talk to me about." Stephanie sipped her martini.

"Since when do you have a martini instead of wine?"

"It's a new thing. I'm tired of wine. Besides, it goes better with coke."

"I hope you didn't do any coke. We're here to eat."

"I only had one toot in the cab." She reached into her purse and pulled out a Bullet Snorter. "I got one of these from Don. It's portable. Goes anywhere."

"Well, wait at least until after we eat."

"I will. So what's the big news?" Stephanie asked.

"I'm going to try and start my own TV show. *Rock the Town*. It'd be a weekly show with rock musicians as guests. I would be the host and executive producer."

"You're kidding, of course. You wouldn't want to give up being a director on a talk-show for something like that."

"Thanks for your support. You sound like J.J. It would be the perfect job for me with all my musical background. Brett's going to try to get me a meeting with the head of the network so I can pitch the idea."

"What about the money? Would you make as much as you do as a director?"

"Haven't even thought about the money. It's not about the money. It's about the music."

"Well, I don't know. Sounds pretty risky."

"We'll see. Now for part two on the evening's agenda. I think it's about time we moved in together. You can bring your stuff over to my place. We can even start sleeping in the bed."

Stephanie was caught off guard. "Flynn, I…."

"You can think about it. But don't take too long. The mood might pass."

"I don't know what to say. I'm shocked, I guess."

"Well, here's another shock." He took a small, velvet Tiffany's box out of his pocket and handed it to her.

She opened it and inside was a gorgeous turquoise ring. She oohed and aahed and tried it on. "It's perfect. I love it. But what does it mean?"

"It means we're going steady."

Just then, the waiter appeared at their table to take their food order.

★ ★ ★

Flynn sat on his balcony smoking a joint. The sliding glass door was open to the living room where Stephanie was making lines with a one-sided razor blade.

She yelled to Flynn out the door. "You want a line?"

"No thanks. I'm smoking a joint. Come out here. We have to appreciate every minute of this beautiful Chicago weather. Hey, that's like an oxymoron."

Stephanie snorted a couple of lines with her shiny gold snorter.

Flynn watched from the balcony. "You've got all kinds of new tools."

"Don has everything. I got this small mirror, too." She kept snorting lines until she was satisfied. "I'm coming out now."

She left all her drug paraphernalia on the coffee table and joined Flynn on the balcony.

"I'm in a Rolling Stones kind of a mood." He got up and went into the apartment to his record collection and rifled through it until he found *Let It Bleed*. He pulled the album out of its cover and put it on the turntable. Then he returned to the balcony and handed the album to Stephanie. The Stones classic music poured out of the speakers in the living room and could be heard easily by them out on the balcony.

Stephanie checked out the album cover, turning it over to read the song titles.

"'Gimme Shelter' is my favorite cut on the album," said Flynn.

"I've never heard this album. It must be ancient."

"If 1969 is ancient. I just think of it as classic. Someday they're going to have a music format on the radio just for classic. J.J. and I have had this discussion."

"Well, he should know." She was still reading the titles on the back of the album. "Oh, this one I know. 'You Can't Always Get What You Want.' They should teach that in school."

"I'm going to get a beer. You want another drink?"

"A vodka martini."

"I just happen to have vodka and vermouth. I even think I have some real martini glasses. Somebody gave them to me sometime, whatever. I'll be right back." Flynn stepped back into the apartment and headed for the kitchen.

Stephanie stared at the ring now displayed on her finger. She sniffed a couple of times and looked longingly at the coffee table inside. She decided against any more coke.

Flynn was back with a beer and a fancy martini glass full of vodka. She took it and gulped the first pull.

"Easy, easy." Flynn put his beer on the table and looked out on the cityscape and patch of lake. "Too bad we can't make love out here. It would be really cool."

"I thought you said we could use the bed. It would be the first time."

"Yeah, I only do it if I'm serious about a girl. There's only been one other. So we have to make it special."

"Let's take our drinks in the bedroom," Stephanie suggested.

Flynn took her hand and led her off the balcony and toward the bedroom. By this time on the album, "Gimme Shelter" came on. He had to stop and listen to it loud on the living room speakers. Stephanie was annoyed. When the song was over they continued on to the bedroom.

They placed their glasses on the nightstand and started kissing. Flynn helped her to lay down on the down comforter. The room had a queen-size bed, two nightstands, a dresser and a hat rack. Very minimalist.

Flynn and Stephanie undressed each other and began making love. It was a long session and they were spent at the end. Flynn rolled over and cuddled Stephanie. She grabbed her drink off the nightstand and drank the rest of it down.

★ ★ ★

J.J. was sitting in his office with his feet up on the desk talking on the phone.

"Why don't you meet me at the Allerton Hotel?"

He paused as the person on the other end of the call answered.

"No, it's not a seedy place. It's just out of the way. Nobody we know will see us."

Another pause.

"Noon straight up. A true nooner."

He took his feet off of the desk and sat up straight.

"Okay, I'll see you there."

JULY

FLYNN AND STEPHANIE DESCENDED THE stairs from Wacker Drive down to the boat dock on the Chicago River. A big banner heralded the event: "Boat Cruise 4th of July Extravaganza." One of the boats in the Wendalla line of cruisers was boarding for the night out on Lake Michigan to watch the fireworks.

Flynn handed the two tickets to the deckhand at the top of the plank. At the top, you could go either to the bow or the stern. A good-sized crowd was headed for the bow and Flynn and Stephanie got caught up in it. When they reached the front of the boat they saw all the decorations for celebrating the nation's birthday: streamers, banners, lights all done in red, white and blue. They took it all in before heading inside to the bar. The bar area was also decorated in everything red, white and blue. They ordered drinks and sat down on the bench that wrapped around the room.

Four familiar faces entered from the door to the bow of the boat. It was J.J., Miles and his beautiful blonde date Maggie, Don, and Skye. They rushed over to where Flynn and Stephanie were sitting.

"Well, if it isn't the Four Musketeers plus blonde," said Flynn.

Miles introduced them to Maggie. She was spilling out of her low-cut blouse. They all said hello. Then J.J. went up to the bar for drinks.

When they had seated themselves on the bench, they could feel the boat moving forward. They were on their way down the Chicago River.

"Let's go outside and enjoy the view and the ride," said Stephanie.

They all went out the bow-side door. Outside, it was twilight on the river and they stood there while the boat went under the Michigan-Wacker Bridge. It was a mellow night. Temperatures in the 70s. Very humid. The boat tilted a little and Stephanie in her heels teetered a bit. J.J. was there to latch onto her. Flynn was at the railing taking in the full view.

More people came out on deck. There were about fifty people in the front now, everybody talking and gawking.

When they hit the open water of the lake, it became a little rougher and most people tried to find a place on the wraparound benches.

Stephanie and Maggie sat down. The guys were standing in front of them. Don snuck the Bullet Snorter out of his pocket and handed it to Stephanie. She discreetly took a hit in both sides of her nose. She handed the snorter to Maggie and she followed suit.

When they were a couple of miles out on the lake, the boat stopped and anchored among a small armada of all kinds of boats. Everything from cabin cruisers to small speed boats. In the distance were the barges, where all the fireworks were waiting for their grand display.

Right around nine o'clock when it was completely dark, the fireworks boomed from the barges. They lit up the night sky in an array of colors and styles. Everybody on the Wendella boat was at the railing, thrilled to see the extravaganza that was promised. The fireworks kept going and going. Nobody left the railing for a drink or any reason. They were mesmerized by the display of firepower.

When the finale came, it was spectacular. The boat people were cheering as the last of the fireworks came to an end. It had been thirty minutes of pure thrill and it was a letdown when the boat pulled up anchor and started back to the river and the dock.

Stephanie and J.J. offered to go into the bar and get everybody drinks. They walked carefully on the moving boat and went inside.

"We had fun at the Allerton, didn't we?" asked J.J.

"Yeah, it was great. But the guilt isn't worth it," said Stephanie. "I'm going to stop this thing, whatever it is, right now."

"You're not going to get out of it that easily. I want to see you. Plain and simple."

"It's just not going to work out. Flynn thinks we're exclusive. He even gave me this ring." She showed him the ring on her left hand.

"It's just a ring. It's not like you're married or anything."

Don was suddenly there. They hadn't even ordered the drinks yet.

"Where are the drinks? What have you been doing? Everybody is waiting," said Don.

As if on cue, Flynn, Miles, Maggie and Skye were coming in the door heading straight for the bar.

"We got tired of waiting. I'll order my own drink," said Flynn.

After they all got a drink, they went back outside to the front of the boat. The sky was midnight black and filled with stars. So clear they were able to pick out some of the constellations.

They were mesmerized and quiet all the way back to the dock.

★ ★ ★

July 12th brought a steaming-hot, stick-to-your-clothes kind of day. Flynn and J.J. arrived by cab at Comiskey Park on the near-southwest side of the city in the Bridgeport community. Comiskey, home of the Chicago White Sox, was a behemoth stadium. Chicagoans came out in droves to watch the baseball team and enjoy the sunshine all summer long.

They got out of the cab and headed to the entrance gates. There was a special promotion that day. If you brought a disco album you were admitted for 98 cents. There were signs all over with the WLUP logo. It was Steve Dahl's special disco promotion. He planned to blow up the records after the first game. Flynn and J.J. handed over the disco records they had brought and paid their beyond cheap entrance fee.

They climbed to their seats above first base and immediately grabbed two beers from the vendor who was walking by. The game was the White Sox versus the Detroit Tigers and it was the second inning of the first game.

After the game, Steve Dahl, WLUP's morning man, appeared on the field and headed to the pile of thousands of disco albums that had been placed there for him to blow up. He ceremoniously lit the fireworks under the albums and started to blow them up. Suddenly, fans were out of their seats and rushing the field. In minutes, thousands were tearing up sod, burning signs, knocking over a batting cage and flinging records. Flynn and J.J., up in their seats, watched with fascination.

"Let's go down there. This is too good to miss," said Flynn.

"Oh, why not. Just hope nobody sees me," replied J.J.

The pair climbed down the stairs and raced onto the field joining the thousands already down there wreaking havoc on the field. On the White Sox scoreboard a message was flashing: "Please return to your seats." Nobody cared and they kept raising hell. Then, the chanting began: "We hate disco. We hate disco." Steve Dahl was in the middle of it all egging people on and grinning madly.

Flynn and J.J. participated by throwing stray albums onto the exploding mess. They decided to leave the stadium while they could still get out of there. They found an exit near the dug out where the stunned White Sox team waited for the second game of the doubleheader to start.

Out on the street, it took Flynn and J.J. a long time to find a cab because there were thousands of people who couldn't get into the stadium rioting outside.

When they found a cab, they stared out the window at the mess that had taken place on the outside. The cab was stuck in a traffic jam that had started as a result of the blowing up of disco records.

Finally, back at Flynn's apartment they could breathe. They sat on the couch with beers watching the local news on TV. The TV anchorman was calling the fiasco "Disco Demolition."

"Today at Comiskey Park, where the White Sox lost to the Detroit Tigers in the first game, there were bigger doings going on on the field. WLUP's morning man, Steve Dahl, was staging a promotion where if you brought a disco album to the game you would get in for 98 cents. Thousands showed up and stormed the field as Dahl blew up the records with fireworks. The riotous group took over the infield burning signs and flinging records. An estimated 59,000 took part in the infield mayhem. Outside the park were 15,000 more who couldn't get in but made trouble anyway by stomping on their disco records. Howard Cosell blamed Harry Carey for contributing to the carnival atmosphere."

The screen cut to outside Comiskey Park, where Steve Dahl was being interviewed by the on-scene reporter.

"I never thought a stupid disc jockey like me could draw this kind of a crowd to a disco demolition. I mean, I've been promoting the burning of the records on the Loop for a while now, but I never knew this many people hated disco music as much as I do. I never dreamed all those people would tear up the field," said Dahl.

The screen cut back to the anchorman. "The second game of the double-header with the Tigers was cancelled. The field was in no condition for playing. The estimated 59,000 on the field, and 15,000 outside stopped the famous Chicago White Sox from playing. WLUP, the highest-rated Chicago rock station, had no comment."

Flynn was laughing his head off, "We were there watching a little piece of history unfold."

"Don't tell anyone at my station I was there. Miles would kill me. But I wouldn't have missed it for the world," said J.J.

"59,000 people. Can you believe it? That was so cool to see all those albums blown up. What a brilliant promotion. I'm surprised the White Sox management allowed it in the first place," said Flynn.

"They had no idea all those people would show up, let alone that they'd charge the field. It felt pretty cool to be among all those disco haters. Too bad WQXA didn't think of it." J.J. smoothed back his hair and sipped his beer.

Flynn got up from the couch and turned the TV off. "The radio promotion of the decade. Far-out!"

★ ★ ★

J.J. was sitting at his desk in his office at WQXA. Miles came in without knocking.

"WLUP has outdone us again. 'Disco Demolition' day and all those thousands of radio listeners. We better start doing some special promotions or we'll take another dive in the ratings."

"I'll come up with something," said J.J.

"Get with our promotion director, what's her name, Betsy?"

"She's the worst promotion director ever. It's just like a title to her. She never comes up with anything."

"Well, then, you come up with something, J.J. You're the programming guy."

"All right. All right. I'll think about it. Maybe something with Skye."

"Get on it."

Miles swiftly left J.J.'s office, leaving him to stare into space. He had no idea how to top "Disco Demolition."

★ ★ ★

Flynn was outside the booth on the stage of *The Brett Adams Show*. Brett was primping and acting nervous in anticipation of the taping. Behind them the studio audience streamed in noisily.

"They keep on coming. That's a good thing," murmured Brett.

"It's because you've got a celebrity on instead of a shrink," said Flynn.

"Who is this guy, anyway?" asked Brett.

"Didn't you see the movie. We had passes. It's *The Warriors*. Michael Beck. You at least read your notes, right?" said Flynn.

"The one about gangs?"

"Jesus, yes, that's the one. Is this going to be a terrible show?"

"I'll rally. I can almost always think of good questions."

Flynn took this opportunity to get Brett's full attention. "Did you talk to the head of the network about my show idea?"

"Not yet. But I will. I promise. I always keep my promises."

"Thanks."

Flynn walked off the stage, across the floor where the camera guys were. "Hey, Jeremy. Hey, Isaac." The floor director was there, too. "Hey, Zeke. Guys, get ready, we've got an actor on today. Let's do a great show."

When he arrived inside the booth, Madison handed him his clipboard.

"Michael Beck. I'm so excited."

"Did you see the movie?"

"Of course I did. I loved it."

"I'm glad somebody did. Brett hasn't seen the movie." Flynn donned his headset and resigned himself to knowing the show might not be great.

"Cue the opening music."

★ ★ ★

Flynn and J.J. were sitting on the balcony of his apartment. The last stream of sunlight beat down on them while they sat and sipped Old Styles. The temperature was cooling off and a beautiful summer night enveloped the city of Chicago.

Flynn went into the apartment and brought back the album Neil Young's *Rust Never Sleeps*. J.J. checked out the cover art and Flynn took the LP into the living room and put it on the stereo. Neil Young's unique voice filled the space and spread out the sliding door to the balcony.

"I saw this concert last year. It was one of the best shows I've ever seen. He had sand people in robes coming out on stage," said Flynn.

"I missed it, but I love Neil Young," said J.J.

"Most of the album was recorded live on the 1978 tour."

"Oh, here comes 'Hey, Hey, My My.'" The strains of the song reached the balcony and they listened intently.

"The song is called officially 'Hey, Hey, My My (Out of the Blue).' What's your favorite Neil Young overall?"

"'Cowgirl in the Sand.'"

"Mine is from the *After the Gold Rush* LP. 'Southern Man.' I don't think Lynyrd Skynyrd liked it too much."

"He was too busy with 'Free Bird.' He's the real voice of southern rock."

Flynn left the balcony to get a joint from his stash on the coffee table in the living room. He lit it and went back on the balcony.

"So, what's happening with Tiffany? Last I heard she had asked for a legal separation," said Flynn.

"We're divorced now. She sent me papers," said J.J.

"I'm really sorry. Bummer ad infinitum."

"I thought she loved me. We were together six years. Never knew she was unhappy."

"That's why I never married. Women are hard to read."

"So what's the deal with Stephanie?"

"I asked her to move in."

J.J. almost fell out of his chair. "You're kidding me? Flynn, the confirmed bachelor. A woman moving in."

"She hasn't said yes yet."

"Be careful. She's a handful."

Flynn handed him the joint and J.J. turned it down. He reached into his pocket and pulled out a Bullet Snorter. He did a hit in each nostril, then handed it to Flynn.

"Does everybody have one of those portable snorters? Don must be pretty busy. Sure, I'll have a hit." Flynn stuck the snorter into his nose and sniffed. "I didn't get any."

"You have to push that little gadget down and let the flake fall into the top part."

Flynn did as instructed and took a big sniff. He handed the tool back to J.J.

"Do you like that feeling in your throat after a hit? I love that."

Flynn took a toke off his joint. "I'd rather smoke and drink scotch."

When the album came to an end, darkness had fallen like a blanket around the city. Flynn lit a candle on the table. "Let's stay in the Neil Young mode. I'll put on *After the Gold Rush*."

J.J. took another hit off the Bullet. "Go for it. It's a great album. We'll do a Neil Young night."

"Far-out!"

★ ★ ★

Flynn sat at the Boul-Mich bar sipping his second scotch. The five o'clock crowd was pouring in. The music from the speakers on either side of the bar was Aerosmith's "Dream On." The bartender, Teddy, was frantically trying to make drinks. He came up to Flynn.

"You want another Johnnie Walker Black, one ice cube?" he asked Flynn.

"Hey, man, Teddy! Sure do. And make a vodka martini straight up for my girl, who should be here any minute."

As if on cue, Stephanie was behind Flynn. She touched his shoulder. He turned around and hugged her.

"What took you so long? I saved a stool for you. Sit down before somebody else steals your seat."

"Some of us have to work till five. Then I decided to walk down Michigan from the Playboy building. The weather is so nice, I didn't want to waste it sitting in a cab," said Stephanie.

She was dressed in tight, black jeans and a low-cut blouse. Black two-inch heels rounded out the ensemble.

"You look great," said Flynn. "Some of the guys in here noticed, too."

"Wow. You're jealous. I can't believe it."

"I'm not jealous. I'm just saying."

"I heard about the Disco Demolition. Wish I'd been there."

"It was perfect. All those disco records blowing up."

Teddy arrived with her martini. She took a sip. Then noticed there were no olives. She asked Teddy for three olives. He was back in a flash with a toothpick full of them.

"There's some disco I like. Donna Summer's 'Hot Stuff' is pretty good. And the Bee Gees. Aren't they disco?"

"They're sort of unique. Can't fit them into a category. But you can't really like disco. No true rocker does."

"Did J.J. end up going with you?"

"Yeah, he was there. Wishing it was his promotion. There were 59,000 people inside and more outside. It says a lot about Chicago radio. But it wasn't his station so I think it took the fun out of it. We actually stormed the field."

"In publishing, we don't have promotions like that. It's all about the editorial content. And of course, Hugh and the Bunnies."

"Yeah, people read *Playboy* for the editorial content. Sure. But what about the centerfold. Every adolescent boy's paradise."

"Don't be a male chauvinist pig."

"Don't kid yourself about *Playboy*."

They were quiet for a minute, sipping their drinks. Behind them, the bar had filled up considerably. It was hard to hear the music through the din, but the speakers spilled out Led Zeppelin's "Whole Lotta Love." Flynn could hear it and started to beat time with his drink straw. Stephanie waved to Teddy for another round.

"Drink up. The movie starts at eight. I'm seeing it for the second time. I think you're going to like it."

"About this movie, *The Warriors*, is it pretty violent?"

"It's about gangs, yes. But the violence is not gratuitous. It's going to be the next cult hit. It's got everything. A love story and great music. You'll see."

"I can't wait."

Stephanie noticed that some of the guys were looking at her. She sat up straighter and fluffed her hair. Flynn noticed.

★ ★ ★

After the movie, Flynn and Stephanie were back in his apartment sitting on the couch. The Doors "Don't You Love Her Madly" was playing on the stereo. They had Old Styles in bottles. Stephanie had her amber vial and little gold spoon and was snorting coke.

"What happened to the Bullet?" asked Flynn.

"I only use it when I'm mobile and need something portable," replied Stephanie. "Want some?"

"No thanks." Flynn lit a joint instead, then handed it toward Stephanie, who declined.

"I smoked a lot in high school in San Diego. I think I got tired of it. Coke is so much better." Stephanie snorted again.

Flynn got up and opened the sliding glass door to the balcony. "Got to cherish every moment of summer. I can feel a light breeze. It's wonderful. Let's go out here."

She came out and they sat in the chairs staring at the sky. A full moon was just edging across their viewpoint. There was a bit of a haze around it. Some passing clouds. They were mesmerized.

"So what did you think of the movie?" Flynn asked.

"'Warriors, come out to pla…yay. Warriors, come out to pla…yay.'"

"That says it all. And I love the part when they asked the psycho why he killed Cyrus. 'I just like doing things like that.' Perfect."

"I loved the Baseball Furries and The Lizzies. I didn't even mind the violence," said Stephanie.

"Loved the music. Joe Walsh at the end with 'In the City.' It all blended together for a great movie," said Flynn. He took a toke off his joint, then put it in the ashtray. "You thought any more about moving in with me?"

"Yeah. No. I don't know. It's sort of soon."

"Not for me. I want to be near you. I've never lived with anyone before. Believe me, girls have tried."

"We'll see, Flynn. We'll see."

Flynn embraced her and they began kissing heavily right away. After a while he led her inside and into the bedroom. They slid onto the bed and began making love frantically.

★ ★ ★

Flynn was in the booth at the television station. Through the glass he saw the studio audience making their way to their seats. He looked down at his notes and saw that Dr. Zorba from Yale Medical Center was the guest. He laughed to himself and then donned the headset adjusting the little microphone so the crew on the set could hear him. Brett came out on the stage and took his seat. The audience saw him and started clapping. He gave them a little wave, then looked down at his notes. Flynn, in the booth, asked for the opening music. The Floor Director did the countdown and they were on their way.

"It's *The Brett Adams Show*. Welcome, everyone. I'd like to introduce today's guest, Psychologist Dr. Wayne Zorba," said Brett.

Zorba entered from stage right and slowly made his way to the empty chair. He looked small and totally lost. In the booth, Flynn moved the microphone away from his mouth and said to the booth crew, "Oh, no. It's gonna be one of those shows. Embellish that in your collective bird dogs." The booth gang, including Madison, laughed heartily.

★ ★ ★

After the show, Flynn was in his office with Brett, sitting in one of the visitor chairs in front of his desk.

Brett moaned. "Zorba, shit. That's the worst interview I've ever done. I thought he was either going to fall out of the chair or fall asleep. The audience, in fact, looked like they'd fallen asleep."

"N.B.D., Brett. You usually hit it out of the park. One strike won't hurt you," said Flynn.

"It was really quite lame. I can't seem to let it go," said Brett.

Flynn put his feet up on the desk. "We should have had Eric Clapton on when he was in Chicago. That would have been a fantastic show."

"Maybe you should do the casting."

"On my show I want to do everything. *Rock the Town* will do just that. Have you talked to the network honcho yet? I'm all ready. Just need word from up top and a timeslot," said Flynn.

"I've been dragging my feet on this because selfishly I don't want you to go. You're the best talk-show director at the network."

"Thanks, Brett. I appreciate that. But it's time for me to move on."

"I promise I'll talk to him. His name is Barry Sanders, by the way."

"I know his name. I just want to know him."

"I'll do what I can."

★ ★ ★

The cab pulled up to the entrance of Wrigley Field, the famous home of the Chicago Cubs. The landmark stadium sat right in the middle of a residential area filled with townhouses and single-family dwellings. A man in a booth outside the ballpark was selling pennants and knick-knacks all bearing the Chicago Cubs logo. Flynn, J.J. and Don stepped out of the cab and went to the ticket window. They were able to get seats just up from first base in the tenth row. A favorite spot of Flynn's. They climbed up to their row and sat down. When a vendor came by, they immediately got beers in plastic cups.

The Cubs were at bat and the first batter struck out. The second batter hit a single and raced to first base. Then the third batter hit a double and the first guy moved to third base. Next up slammed the ball over the fence for a home run. The Cubs had three runs and the San Francisco Giants nothing, all in the first inning. The cheers in the crowd were wild and lengthy.

"If you see that beer guy, grab another one for me," said Flynn. "There's nothing like beer and baseball on a fantastic July day in Chicago."

"I think it's hot," said Don. He was fiddling with his Bullet Snorter very stealth like so no one could tell. You could hear him sniffing. He handed the tool to J.J.

"It's not the heat, it's the humidity," said J.J. "I've never gotten used to it even after all my years in Chicago and Michigan before that. When it's hot in California it's a dry heat."

"That's high-larious. Dry heat. Like it makes it better. It's still hot," Flynn chimed in.

J.J. took a hit off the Snorter and handed it back to Don.

"Hey, guys. There should be a new rule: 'There's no coke in baseball.' Do you two ever go anywhere without it?" asked Flynn.

Don spoke first. "Nowhere without it. It's my business. It's what I do."

"I'm just along for the ride," said J.J.

The beer vendor came by and Flynn bought three beers and passed them out. They were settled in and happy to be watching the Cubs play.

The next two guys struck out and the Cubs took the field. Willie Hernandez, the pitcher, took on the first batter for the Giants. He struck him out. The crowd went wild.

The game continued and the Cubs ended up beating the Giants. The guys were hot and sunburned when they left the stadium and went down the street to the Cubby Bar. It was a local joint strictly for the baseball crowd with a small TV above the bar where you could watch the game if you couldn't or wouldn't get into the stadium. The bar was loaded with baseball pennants and all kinds of baseball memorabilia. The three stooges sat at the bar and ordered more beers. The after-game stragglers were coming in and the bar was filling up.

Flynn said, "Cool ending. Hernandez is a good pitcher. Did you guys know that this is the 64th season for the Chicago Cubs at Wrigley Field? They don't play at night. Did you know that? The owner won't let there be any night games."

"I remember hearing that. They'll have to change it someday. It's all about the money, anyway," said J.J.

Don was sneaking a snort. Flynn sipped his beer and soaked up the atmosphere of the Cubby.

"Hey, Don, man, are you a White Sox fan or a Cubs fan? Everybody in Chicago has to be one or the other."

Don sniffed a couple of times, then answered, "It's just baseball. I don't care which team."

"Oh, that won't do. Did I tell you guys Brett is going to help me get in to see the head of the network about my show idea?"

J.J. spoke up. "I told Don. I said it was going to be called *Rock the Town* and you'd never get it off the ground."

"You'll see. Nobody believes in me. But I believe in me. I'm going to do it," said Flynn.

"Good luck," J.J. and Don said in unison.

★ ★ ★

Stephanie was at her desk outside Bobby Marin's office. He came out of the inner office and asked her to come in.

"Sit down, Stephanie," said Bobby.

"What's this all about? You never have me come in here," said Stephanie.

"I'm going to have to let you go."

"You're firing me? You're kidding me. On what grounds?"

"I don't need any grounds. It's just not working out with you. You're on the phone too much. Making mistakes in fact checking. You name it."

"I don't think that's it at all. You're firing me because I won't sleep with you."

"That has nothing to do with it."

"Yes, it does. I slept with you out in California once and that was it, but you could never accept it. You brought me here to Chicago so I could be your play thing."

"You're wrong. You slept with me to get the job. Now you think you can do anything and still keep your job."

"There should be a law against this. I could sue you."

"There is no law. I want you out. Clear out your stuff and leave."

He handed her an envelope.

"Here's a couple of weeks' severance pay."

"Bobby Marin, you are an asshole. Complete and total. This should not be able to happen. Who made you God?"

He dismissed her with a wave of his hand

Stephanie got out of a cab in front of Flynn's apartment building. Steve, the daytime doorman, opened the door and greeted her.

"Hi, Steph," he said. "How's it hanging?"

"Terrible. I just got fired from my job."

"Oh, sorry about that. Flynn just came in. I'll buzz him and tell him you're here."

Flynn stood outside his apartment door as the elevator opened and Stephanie stepped out. He noticed that she was dressed up in work clothes and silently groaned. Then he swept his arm inside the apartment as a gesture to enter.

"I thought we were going for a walk on the lakefront," said Flynn.

"I know. The shoes. Yes, they're high-heels. No, I didn't bring any tennis shoes. I'm just suddenly not in the mood for walking," whined Stephanie. She then proceeded to take the shoes off and throw them at the fireplace. "I don't care about my fucking shoes."

"You sound really irritated. What's up?" asked Flynn.

"I lost my job. I was fired."

"You're kidding. What happened? I thought your job was going great."

"I think it's because I wouldn't sleep with my boss, that asshole Bobby. He's been after me the whole time I've worked there. When he asked me recently to spend the night with him while his wife was out of town, I said no. He seemed okay with it, then this. There should be a law against this kind of firing. I didn't do anything wrong. And I always did my work on time without mistakes."

"Can't you talk to Heff or the Managing Editor? There must be something that can be done about it."

"Bobby Marin is one of the top Editors. The buck stops with him. I'm fucked."

Stephanie broke into tears and Flynn held her until she stopped crying. Then she flopped down on the couch and took a snowseal full of coke out of her purse. She grabbed the little hand mirror Flynn kept on the coffee table for her and started to make lines with her little razor. Then she took the gold-plated straw out of her purse. She kept it all in a little leather pouch. Everything you needed to snort coke.

"I'm fucked. I won't even be able to afford coke now. I don't have that much in savings. Oh, Flynn." She began crying again. In between the crying, she snorted. She was sniffling a lot.

"Now's the perfect time for you to move in. You can stay here and look for a new job."

She took another snort before answering. "I think you're right. I'll move in with you. Oh, Flynn. You're a lifesaver."

★ ★ ★

J.J. was in his office at WQXA. Betsy, the Promotion Director, was sitting in one of the visitor chairs.

"So, tell me again what we're doing for ChicagoFest," said J.J.

"We've got a booth and Skye's show will be broadcast live from there. We're also going to give away free tickets to the Fest on his show," said Betsy. She twirled her hair and looked very uncomfortable.

"We need something more happening in the booth," said J.J. "Come up with a few more ideas."

The phone rang and he answered it. "Hold on a minute. Betsy, work on those ideas and get back to me. I gotta take this call."

She nodded and got up and went out of the office. J.J. came around the desk and shut the door.

"Hello, Steph. What's up?" He put his feet up on the desk. There was a long stretch of silence on his end of the phone while he listened to her. Then:

"If you move in with Flynn, what's going to happen to us? I know there is no 'us,' but I don't get it after what we've done already. Why don't you just come clean with Flynn?"

Silence.

"Free rent? Nice Elm Street apartment. You're really quite the little witch. Since you're out of work, I'll pick up lunch. Corona Café. Noon. Gotta go."

Miles had opened his door and started to come in uninvited.

"You could knock, you know. It's not that hard," said J.J.

"I'm your boss. I don't knock. You're always on the phone. Done any programming brilliance lately? How are the promotions going?" asked Miles as he sat down in one on the chairs.

"ChicagoFest is in two weeks. You know all about the live broadcast already. Plus, Betsy's working on giving away free tickets to the fest on Skye's show."

"Anything else?"

"As a matter of fact, it's a real coup if we can pull it off. Tom Petty's new album *Damn the Torpedoes* will be released in October. I thought we'd get Tom and all The Heartbreakers and throw a release party at the Drake."

"Now you're thinking. That's a great idea. You've got your job for another day," said Miles. "And the Fest? You've got that covered, right?"

"We're all set."

"You've got your job at least till ChicagoFest."

"You're a real swell guy, Miles," J.J. said sarcastically.

★ ★ ★

Stephanie got out of a cab in front of Flynn's apartment building. She was carrying her entire wardrobe with the help of two friends. The night doorman, Billy, opened the door for them.

"You're either moving in or going to a rummage sale," quipped Billy.

"No jokes, Billy, this is hard enough as it is," said Stephanie.

Billy went behind the desk and rang Flynn's apartment.

"Go on up. He's expecting you."

After they got all the clothes in the elevator, there was barely room for the three girls. When they got to the 18th floor, Flynn was outside his apartment with the door wide open for them.

"Oh, my God. My closet isn't big enough. What is all this stuff?" Flynn asked.

The girls came in and threw everything on the couch. It took over the entire couch.

"Flynn, this is Nancy, my roommate that was. And this is Sarah, the new roommate for Nancy."

"Hey, ladies. I'm surprised you didn't bring furniture."

"All the furniture is Nancy's. All I really have are my clothes and a few odds and ends."

"You guys want a drink or something?" asked Flynn.

Nancy spoke for the two of them. "We're meeting some people at Butch's for a drink."

"You have good taste in watering holes," said Flynn.

"Thanks, Nance. You've been great. And Sarah, you too. I know you'll be great roommates together."

The girls hugged each other and said goodbye. Nancy and Sarah left the apartment.

Flynn led Stephanie into the bedroom and showed her the half-of-a-closet that he had cleared out.

"Flynn, you've got to be kidding. This space won't do. I've got to get one of those metal rack things and put it over there" She pointed to an empty space in the corner.

"Whatever you need to do."

"In the meantime, I'll hang up what I can."

Stephanie went out to the living room and grabbed an armful of hangers. Flynn tried to help, but she waved him away.

"I've got them separated by season. It's summer now, so I'll put in those outfits first. I'll save winter for later."

Flynn gestured over to his big, overstuffed chair. "The stuff that won't fit you can dump on that chair. Then when you get the metal rack you can hang it up. I cleared out three drawers for you in the dresser. We might have to get another one. We'll see. In the meantime, I haven't welcomed you properly." He took her in his arms and kissed her passionately.

"Oh, Flynn. I've got too much stuff," she said as she broke away from him.

"We'll figure it out. The main thing is, you're here. Let's put on some music and take a drink outside to the balcony."

Stephanie moved the summer clothes into the bedroom closet. And piled up the other stuff on the big chair. She had some things left and moved them over on the couch so she could do her coke.

She grabbed her purse and took out the little leather pouch she carried her coke tools in. She poured some coke out of the snowseal onto the little mirror and made some lines. Then she used her gold-plated spoon to take a hit. She handed the tool to Flynn, who was standing by the record collection looking for an album to put on the turntable.

"How about *Are You Experienced*? I'll put it right on 'Foxy Lady' in honor of you."

"I still think you're obsessed with Jimi Hendrix."

"There's that shrink word again. By the way, whatever happened to you going to a shrink?"

"I quit. You and your 'I hate shrinks' finally wore off on me. I'm cured."

"That's good timing, now that you're moving in. You can let go of your problems surrounding men. You're with me now."

"I may start up again with therapy, but for now I'm here."

Flynn got a beer and made a martini for Stephanie. He brought the drinks out to the balcony and placed them on the table. The night was as crystal clear as a summer lake. Stars stood out like diamonds in the sky. They paused for a minute to appreciate how beautiful and rare this night was.

Flynn made a toast. "To Stephanie, the first woman I've ever lived with. You're as beautiful as this delicate Chicago night."

"Thanks, Flynn. Here's to the first night of our new arrangement."

"'Arrangement' sounds like you're talking about furniture. It's more like a lover's tryst," Flynn added. He took a long pull on his beer.

Stephanie got up to go into the living room. "I'm gonna get another toot. You want one?"

"I'm in heaven, woman, let me be."

AUGUST

BELMONT HARBOR WAS SPREAD OUT with an array of small-craft motorboats and sailboats nestled in a little offshoot of Lake Michigan. The weather was typical of August, hot and humid. But already there was a breeze picking up on the lake. Standing on the pier, where boats picked up passengers, stood Flynn, Stephanie, J.J., Skye and Miles. A 40-foot cabin cruiser, helmed by Ernie Mendez, maneuvered its way to the pier. A two-man crew secured the bow and stern lines on the pier. Ernie stepped down from the captain's chair and greeted the gang of five.

"Climb aboard. We want to get out on the lake before it gets dark," shouted Ernie.

The group clambered onto the boat. Stephanie had to be helped by Flynn because of the high-heels she was wearing. When they got into the stern of the boat they were greeted by about ten people already on board. Stereo speakers were mounted high on the top of the wheelhouse. The Lynyrd Skynyrd song "Free Bird" blasted all over the boat. Ernie went back to the Captain's chair and yelled out to the two guys on the crew.

"Cast off, guys. We're on our way."

The two guys undid the ropes and the cruiser pulled away from Belmont Harbor. The breeze was pleasant and the humidity seemed lighter already as they bobbed through choppy water. Ernie had one of the crew take over at the helm and went down to the crowd in the back of the boat. He introduced everybody and a lot of shaking hands and smiles were exchanged.

Ernie spoke to J.J. "I've got the radio set to WQXA, just for you. It's also easier for me not to have to worry about the music."

"Good choice. We have a great nighttime show. We'll hear some good cuts off good albums," said J.J.

"Free Bird" ended and the music segued to The Doors "Light My Fire."

"Let me show you guys around the boat," said Ernie. The back of the boat had a cushioned wraparound couch and two swivel tall chairs near the Captain's perch. Down a couple of stairs was the galley. A full kitchen with refrigerator and stovetop. There was a bucket on the counter filled with ice and cold beer. A booth of sorts was another couple of steps down and was occupied by two couples around the built-in table. Beyond that was the stateroom sleeping quarters. Enough room for four to sleep comfortably against the side of the boat and a porthole leading to the bow. Ernie led them through it up to the bow of the boat. There were more people up their sitting on the cushioned benches facing each other. They then walked on the outer railing back to the stern of the boat.

"Well, Flynn. Happy Birthday! Is this the big three-oh?" asked Ernie.

"You weren't supposed to tell anybody, Ernie. I didn't want to broadcast it."

"August 8th. I knew that. It must have slipped my mind," said J.J. "So, happy birthday, dude," said J.J.

"This is news to me. Is that why we're on this boat cruise?" Stephanie asked.

"Ernie and I are new Monroe Street Yacht Club friends. He keeps his boat there, too and somehow must have found out it was my birthday," said Flynn.

"I'm good buddies with the management there. They know every member's birthday and they told me," Ernie said. "I was going to take you out this summer anyway. So, it just worked out."

Through the speakers came the voice of the night DJ Zorro. "You're listening to WQXA. Friday night rock till you drop. And what would a Friday night be without the Rolling Stones? Here's 'You Can't Always Get What You Want.'" The inimitable sound of The Stones poured down on the boat gang.

Flynn was talking to one of the guys as they stood looking out at the lake. The sun setting in the opposite direction sent slanted rays onto the water as they headed east. The effect was mellow and mesmerizing.

Stephanie and J.J. went down to the galley just in time for the coke to come out. One of the girls was chopping up lines from a rock of cocaine. She shaved enough off the rock for a half a dozen lines. Then a gold-plated straw was passed around. Everybody took their turn. Two people got up to go outside, so there were two places empty at the table. J.J. and Stephanie grabbed them so they could be close to where the coke was. Ernie burst into the galley.

"This is the best spot on the boat. I made sure I got a rock of cocaine. From Don, of course," said Ernie as he sniffed up two lines. "Where is Don, by the way?"

"He was sick," answered J.J.

"Coke dealers don't get sick."

"I know, but it's true. No Don tonight."

"Well, we've got plenty. And reefer, too," said Ernie. He reached into a cigarette holder and revealed a bunch of rolled joints. He picked one up. "I'll just take this outside to Flynn. I know he'll want to have some."

Ernie joined Flynn and one of the Art Directors from Leo Burnett. "I see you've met Harry. He's one of the best creatives we have. And he's as into music as you are, Flynn." He lit the joint and took a toke. Then handed it to Flynn.

"My birthday toke. Ernie, you rascal. You told everybody on this boat that it was my birthday," said Flynn.

"I couldn't help myself. It's your big three-oh."

"Don't keep saying it. I'm still 29 until midnight."

The sun had set and it was dark on the lake. Ernie had dropped anchor and the party went on and on. A crescent moon hung low in the sky surrounded by a ring of fog. The light gave off an ambient glow. Just enough so the partiers could see each other. Ernie had also turned on some low-level lights that added to the atmosphere.

Inside in the galley, Stephanie and J.J. were still sitting at the table doing lines. They were chatting up some other friends of Ernie's from Leo Burnett. Somebody had found a bottle of champagne and they were drinking it out of paper cups. The music was now Queen, "Another One Bites the Dust."

Flynn left the back of the boat and was looking for Stephanie. When he found her in the galley, she gestured for him to join them. She and J.J. had not moved from their spot. For Flynn, it was standing room only. Ernie came down and reached into the refrigerator and pulled out a small cake.

"Couldn't have a birthday without a cake," said Ernie. Then he led the group in a round of "Happy Birthday."

Flynn was embarrassed. J.J. handed him the snorter and shaved off some coke from the rock.

"My birthday snort," he said.

Stephanie moved over on the cushion, but there was still no room for Flynn to sit down. He gave her a dirty look and went back up the stairs to the main area in the stern of the boat.

A little after midnight, the cabin cruiser slipped into its mooring at the Monroe Street Yacht Club. Ernie and the two crew guys docked the boat up against a seawall. The group from the boat, laughing and talking, were in full-party mode as they disembarked.

"Flynn, where to now? It's your day. Your choice," said Ernie.

"Street of Dreams, where else?" said Flynn.

"Division Street? Butch's? Perfect. Let's go get a bunch of cabs to take us all over there," said Ernie.

Four cabs pulled up at Butch's. One right after the other. And the boat party got out and went inside. At one in the morning, Joco, the bartender was frantically busy behind the bar. The group had to squeeze their way up to the bar to order a drink. Suddenly, out of nowhere, Don appeared.

"I thought you were sick," said J.J.

"I had a miraculous recovery. Actually, I don't like boating so I didn't come with you guys. I knew where I could find some business, so here I am," said Don.

The minute Stephanie saw Don, they were on their way back to the bathrooms. Flynn watched them go with an angry expression on his face.

When they returned, Stephanie was worrying her jaw back and forth from all the coke she had snorted that night. She grabbed Flynn from the crowd.

"Let's dance," she said.

"Not now. I haven't even gotten my drink yet," Flynn said.

"I'll dance with you," said Ernie.

"Good. Come on," Stephanie said. She led him back into the side room, where people were dancing between the tables.

Stephanie danced with Ernie, then a couple of the guys from the boat party. She didn't stop for a minute except to change partners.

Butch's was still busy after 2 A.M. It was a 4 A.M. bar, so everybody kept drinking. Stephanie was now dancing with J.J. Flynn had finally gotten a barstool and was listening to the music blasting out of the speakers on the side of the bar. Joco had the FM dial turned to WLUP and Led Zeppelin's "Heartbreaker" was playing. When the song ended, the overnight DJ, Jed the Fish, spoke up:

"This is WLUP. I'm Jed the Fish and we're doing a Led Zeppelin marathon. Stay with us and you won't miss your favorite L.Z. song. Keep your dial on the Loop."

The music poured out into the bar as Flynn flagged down Joco for another drink. He was just drinking and watching the dancers. Only a handful of people were left at the bar.

Stephanie was now dancing with Don. When the song ended, she went back to Flynn at the bar.

"Dance with me, Flynn. Come on."

"You seem to have your choice of partners. Leave me alone, I'm drinking 12-year-old scotch."

"You're such a stuffed shirt. No fun at all. Get with Don. Join the party."

"A stuffed shirt?"

"At least you could get me a martini."

Flynn flagged down Joco. Stephanie took the stool next to him. When her drink came, she gulped down half of it, set it on the bar, and went back to the dance floor. J.J. was dancing with one of the girls from the boat party, so she grabbed a stranger and began dancing.

At ten minutes to four, Joco announced "last call." He turned off the music and started to clean up behind the bar. Nobody wanted a last drink.

A few minutes later, J.J., Don, Stephanie, Flynn, Ernie and the people from the boat party were out on the Street of Dreams. Division Street was lit up like it was daytime. People all on the street after the 4 A.M. bar closings.

"We can keep going at my place," said Ernie. "Let's get a couple of cabs." The boat partiers were game.

"Thanks, Ernie. For everything. The whole night. The boat ride was really special," said Flynn. "But Steph and I are going to call it a night."

"You bet." Ernie and the gang took the first cab.

"I want to go to Ernie's," said Stephanie.

"We're walking home," said Flynn.

"No cab?" asked Stephanie.

"Elm Street is too close to take a damn cab. Come on."

Flynn pulled Stephanie away from the people waiting for the second cab. When it pulled up, J.J., Don and the rest of the people got into it and were gone.

Flynn dragged Stephanie down the street. They were halfway to his apartment building when one of her heels broke. She stopped and picked up the bottom half of the shoe.

"How do you expect me to walk? I've only got one working shoe."

"The flat part's still good. Come on."

She hobbled the rest of the way to Flynn's. Billy saw them coming up the walk and opened the door.

"Flynn, Stephanie. You guys are out late. What's the occasion?"

"My birthday," said Flynn.

"Well, Happy Birthday, Flynn. You old man, you," said Billy. "What happened to your shoe, Stephanie?"

"It died. Because Flynn wouldn't take a cab."

Billy walked over to the elevators and pushed the button. "You can probably glue that heel back on."

"Yeah, right."

When they got into the apartment, Flynn went directly to the sliding glass door to the balcony and opened it. The night remained beautiful, stars lighting up the sky. He sat down at the outside table with a joint. Stephanie was in the living room putting out lines on the little mirror. Flynn took a couple of hits and then put the joint out. He went back inside.

"I'm going to bed. You going to join me?"

"No. I'm doing lines."

Flynn went into the bedroom and came back out with a quilt and a pillow and threw them at Stephanie.

"You can do the couch tonight. I'm done with the partying."

"N.B.D.," said Stephanie.

"Use my words, but I'm not buying it. You sleep on the couch."

Stephanie snorted up a line with defiance. Flynn shut the bedroom door.

★ ★ ★

Navy Pier was an abandoned maritime shipping facility. Fifty acres of concrete that extended into Lake Michigan. The site was the home of ChicagoFest, a ten-day music and food event. Booths were set up the whole length of the pier. There was a main stage for rock groups alternating with the headliners and sixteen smaller stages for other music groups. Right in the swing of things, was the WQXA live broadcast setup. Skye Matthews was sitting in a makeshift DJ booth doing his show from the Fest.

"You're listening to WQXA live from ChicagoFest. Tonight the headliner is Muddy Waters and there is a rumor going around that he may be joined by John Belushi and Dan Aykroyd. They're in town shooting a movie. We'll keep you posted. In the meantime, we've got Cheap Trick playing on one of the smaller stages. So, get on down here for a total music lover's dream…."

Stephanie and Flynn arrived at the booth. They were wearing shorts and hats to protect them from the blistering hot and humid August day. Flynn was carrying two cans of 16-ounce Old Styles. Stephanie had a plastic cup full of white wine. J.J. saw them and came over to greet them. Flynn handed him one of the beers.

"Thanks, dude. How long you guys been here?" asked J.J.

"We've been wandering around to the small stages to see what groups are playing. We listened to a group called Cheap Trick for a while. They were pretty good. And a group called Asleep at the Wheel. We've been eating and drinking all along the way," said Flynn.

"I'm so hot. And I'm wearing the wrong shoes," complained Stephanie.

"So, what else is new? Hey, J.J., man, how'd you get such a primo location? Just about every Chicago radio station is set up here. And you right up near the main stage. Pretty cool move. I saw the Loop logo way down the other way," said Flynn.

"I had to pull every trick in the book, but we got the locale. Miles is thrilled and Skye couldn't be happier," said J.J.

Stephanie squirmed and pretended to sit down. "You got any chairs back there? I need to get off my feet."

J.J. took Stephanie to the back of the booth, where there were some folding chairs. He opened one up for her and she sat down. She took off one of her shoes and rubbed her foot.

"How's it going living with Flynn?" asked J.J.

"Well, it's fine when I'm not sleeping on the couch."

"Whaddaya mean?"

"Whenever Flynn gets mad at me, which is all the time when I'm snorting coke, I sleep on the couch."

"You shouldn't be living with him. You should be with me."

"He's got a great place. A doorman building and everything."

"Well, I don't like it."

"You don't own me. I'm gonna do what I'm gonna do. You got any coke?"

"Don's coming down later. We'll have some for the big Muddy Waters show on the main stage tonight."

"Good. I can't wait."

"I'm going back to Flynn. You coming?"

She massaged her foot some more. "A little later."

J.J. walked back up to the front of the booth, where Flynn was drinking his beer and talking to some of the WQXA staff.

"I'm just taking in the entire ChicagoFest experience," said Flynn.

"This will make it even better," said J.J. as he handed Flynn two tickets.

"Great seats for Muddy Waters tonight."

Flynn took the tickets and put them in the pocket of his shorts. "Hey, man, cool. Thanks. Where's her majesty?"

"She's in the back sitting down. I'll show you."

★ ★ ★

The sun was setting to the west and streaks of sunlight were beaming on Lake Michigan. The humidity had dropped and it promised to be a beautiful night in Chicago.

The main stage was completely full. Thirty thousand Chicagoans waited anxiously for Muddy Waters. Flynn, Stephanie, J.J., Don, Skye and Miles were in the third row center. They had already seen Muddy open for Eric Clapton a few months before, but it didn't tamper their excitement.

The lights came up and Muddy Waters came on with his band. They broke into "Baby Please Don't Go" and the crowd went wild. The acoustics were great and the fabulous horn section was blowing backup. When their set was about over, they broke into "Hoochee Coochie

Man" and suddenly The Blues Brothers, Jake and Elwood (John Belushi and Dan Aykroyd) walked onto the stage. All hell broke loose in the audience. They jammed with Muddy, then as a finale they finished up with "Sweet Home Chicago."

The audience began to break up and the gang of Flynn & Company started walking down the pier. They passed the smaller stages all with music pouring out over the lake. They stopped at one stage to listen to the German band The Scorpions. Even from the outer edges of the stage the group sounded fantastic.

It was 2 A.M. and the Flynn party had moved to The Blues Bar off North Avenue. Even Jake and Ellwood (aka Belushi and Aykroyd), still wearing their dark glasses and black-and-white suit ensembles, were front and center on the dance floor.

Later, Flynn was talking to Belushi at the bar. Belushi brought out a snowseal of coke and dumped most of it on the top of his hand and snorted the whole mound off in one try. He poured what was left on Flynn's hand and he followed suit. There was so much coke in this bar it seemed like a convention of snorters. And they were snorting right out in the open. No bathroom visits. Joints were going around, too. ChicagoFest had become DrugFest.

Stephanie and J.J. were dancing in front of the jukebox to Pink Floyd's "Money." The place was packed with media types and friends of the Blues Brothers. Belushi was suddenly off his barstool and out on the dance floor. The dancers moved back and gave him the total space. He broke into a wild dance, all by himself on the dance floor, and turned the bar upside down. He was dancing like a wild man when Aykroyd stepped in to dance with him. They brought the house down with their pure adrenaline.

The party continued until 4 A.M., when the bar closed. Some of the dancers had to be dragged off the dance floor, including J.J. and Stephanie. Flynn joined them and they walked outside. It was warm, but not too hot. The sky was clear and stars twinkled out like jewels.

J.J. grabbed the first cab. Flynn and Stephanie stood on North Avenue a long time after that. There were no cabs in sight.

"You wanna just walk home?" asked Flynn.

"No, I don't. I don't have the right shoes," said Stephanie.

"You never have the right shoes. Chicago is a walking city. Can't you ever remember that?"

"Don't yell at me. I already don't feel so good from drinking all day and night."

"Don't forget how much coke you had."

"What, are you counting my lines now? You had some, too. And lots of beer."

"When it comes to coke, you win!"

"I didn't know it was a contest."

"It's more like a marathon race."

"I'm going home."

"We live in the same place, remember?"

"Then I'm taking my own cab. I don't want to be with someone who's always taking my inventory."

"Here's a cab now." Flynn waved it over and opened the door for Stephanie. She climbed in and shut the door on him.

"Hey!" shouted Flynn.

Stephanie rolled down the window as the cab pulled away. "Get your own cab."

Flynn fumed as he stood on the Avenue waiting for another cab.

Sometime later, he reached his apartment building and got out of the cab. The night doorman, Billy, was there to open the door.

"Your lady roommate already went up," said Billy.

"Thanks. I know she'll be thrilled to see me," Flynn said sarcastically.

"She seemed furious. Not that it's any of my business," said Billy.

"That's all right. I'm furious, too," said Flynn.

Billy went to the elevator and pushed the button. Flynn followed and stepped in the elevator as the doors opened.

Flynn stuck his key in the door and entered the apartment. Stephanie was sitting on the couch hunched over the coffee table. She was doing a bump of coke.

"Oh, coke. Something new. Thanks for leaving me on the street. It took me almost twenty minutes to find another cab at 4:30 in the morning."

"I don't want to fight with you."

Flynn raised his voice two octaves. "Well, I want to fight with you. Starting with you and J.J. getting pretty cozy on the dance floor. What's up with that?"

"Nothing, he's a good dancer, that's all."

"And this shoe thing with you. You've got to stop with that. Wear shoes you can walk in. We walk here. This is Chicago, not California."

She snorted another line just to spite him. "I'm going to the bedroom."

"Like you'll sleep with all that coke in you."

"I don't care. I just want to be away from you."

"So be it. I'll sleep on the couch. Bring me a pillow and a quilt."

"Get it yourself." Stephanie got up and headed to the bedroom. She slammed the door.

"Fuck you!" shouted Flynn.

★ ★ ★

The next day around noon, Flynn woke up on the couch, all stiff and cranky, glad that it was a Sunday and no work. He rolled off the couch, and stumbled into the kitchen to start the coffee maker. He turned around at a sound from the living room. When he went back in, Stephanie was there gathering up her things.

"What are you doing?" Flynn asked.

"I'm going to a friend's apartment."

"Who? Where?"

"None of your business."

"How do I reach you?"

"I'll call you."

Flynn stiffened, his temper edging to show up again. "Let's talk about it. I don't want you to leave."

Stephanie stuffed her coke paraphernalia into her purse. "I won't have anybody telling me about my cocaine. It's my choice. I won't hear of anybody, especially you, taking my inventory." She pushed some clothes down into a duffel bag, turned around and walked out the door.

Flynn was left standing there with a blank expression on his face.

★ ★ ★

The next day, after the taping of *The Brett Adams Show,* Flynn and Brett were crossing over the Chicago River Bridge from Wacker Drive to Michigan Avenue. The day was a scorcher. Chicago was having a heat wave. Temperatures in the mid-90s with matching humidity. They arrived in front of the Wrigley Building and went inside.

The Wrigley Bar was empty. They had their choice of seats and went for the barstools. The bartender, Hector, stepped over to take their order.

"Flynn, how you doing?" asked Hector. "You still drinking Johnnie Walker Black with one ice cube?"

"You've got that down, Hector." Flynn introduced Brett. "This is Brett Adams. From the show of the same name."

"Oh, yeah. The talk show with all the shrinks. You told me about that, Flynn."

Brett and Hector shook hands.

"I'll have a vodka martini. With Stoli," Brett said.

"Both drinks coming right up," said Hector.

The two men waited for their drinks before starting to talk. Then they clinked glasses and toasted each other.

"To another day of fame and glory," said Brett.

"You've got that right. So, any news on me seeing the network honcho? Did you talk to him?"

"Barry Sanders. He's a pretty decent guy. He's a happy camper as far as our show goes. The ratings are through the ceiling."

"Brett, don't keep me in suspense. What did he say about *Rock the Town*?"

"He said he liked the idea, but he of course wants to know all about it from you. Call his secretary, Mary Ann, and she will fit you into his schedule. It might be in September, because he's got some broadcasters' convention to go to end of August."

"That's fantastic, Brett. He didn't say no. That's the big thing. I'll get my shot."

"I wish you the best. But at the same time I would hate to find a new director," said Brett.

"It'll all work out." Flynn sipped his scotch. A slight smile began to spread across his face.

★ ★ ★

Stephanie pulled up in a cab outside the Elm Street apartment building. She got out, almost slipped in her high-heels, then steadied herself and headed for the door. It was after eight and Billy was on duty. He opened the front door for her.

"Hi, Stephanie. I guess I don't have to ring Flynn. You live here now. That's pretty cool."

"You better ring him. He doesn't know I'm coming."

Billy went behind the desk and rang Flynn's apartment. "Stephanie's down here. Yeah. Okay." He hung up the phone and turned to Stephanie. "He said to send you up."

"Thanks."

Flynn stood outside the apartment with the door open. He saw Stephanie coming out of the elevator. She quickened her pace and met him at the door. The minute she got close enough she began crying.

She hugged him and said, "Oh, Flynn, I'm so sorry. I should never have walked out. Never said those things to you. Please forgive me."

He took her arm, led her into the apartment, and shut the door. Inside there was a scotch on the coffee table and a joint in the ashtray.

"Want a drink?"

"Wine will do."

Flynn went into the kitchen to get it. Stephanie plopped down on the couch. When he came back out, he gestured to the balcony.

"Let's sit out here. Bring my drink."

They sat down outside. It was hot and humid, but the sky was crystal clear and the stars twinkling into infinity.

Stephanie sipped her glass of wine. "This is good. I could use something. I've been out pounding the pavement all day looking for a job. It is horrible and humiliating."

"Why don't you ask J.J. if he's got something at the radio station? They're always hiring people."

"I did. He doesn't." Stephanie reached over to Flynn and started kissing him. "Let's make up." He kissed her back. She led him into the living room all the time kissing and they were back on the couch.

They kept kissing until Flynn picked her up and put her on the floor.

"Our place," purred Stephanie.

Heavy petting turned into full-blown sex. Stephanie lay naked on the rug, Flynn was half-dressed. He went into the bedroom to get the quilt. He came back with it and they cuddled up under it.

"I've missed you, you know. I'm glad you're back. Don't go away again. I might not take you back a second time," said Flynn.

"I'll be good," said Stephanie.

"And get some new shoes."

★ ★ ★

The studio audience was streaming into *The Brett Adams Show*. Brett was on the stage with makeup and hair people doing their thing. Flynn was in the booth ready to go. Madison entered and handed him some notes.

"You should love today's guest. Shrink extraordinaire," she said.

"Don't tell me you read *How to Be Your Own Best Friend*," said Flynn.

"I read it in college. The author's got a new one out now."

"I can see that from the notes."

Outside the booth, the audience was settling down. Brett sat in his chair. Flynn cued the opening music and Zeke standing in between Jeremy and Isaac started the countdown. Brett went into his routine.

"Welcome, studio audience. Nice of you to join us today for Mildred Newman, psychoanalyst and author of several books. Among them, her famous early seventies classic, *How to Be Your Own Best Friend*. Come on out here, Mildred."

Mildred entered from stage right and Brett got up to shake hands. They took their seats.

"Mildred, you made such a hit with *How to Be Your Own Best Friend* you're practically a household name. Now tell us about the new one, *How to Take Charge of Your Life*." Brett held up the new book to the camera.

Back in the booth, Madison tried not to laugh. But Flynn did it for her. Then they both bent over with laughter.

"Don't shrink me, Madison. I've got to hold it together here."

Now the whole booth was laughing.

★ ★ ★

The next day, outside the Allerton Hotel, J.J. paced. When he saw Stephanie coming down the street, he waved to her frantically. She was hobbling along on her two-and-a-fourth-inch heels. When she got to him, he grabbed her and quickly went into the hotel.

He already had a key so they went straight to the elevator. They got off on the 8th floor and went directly to 802. J.J. opened the door for her.

Once inside, they looked around the unadorned room.

"Jes, J.J. You had to pick a rundown hotel. This is pretty depressing."

"It has a bed, doesn't it? I wanted something out of the way where nobody we know would see us."

"Well, you succeeded. No one would come to the Allerton. I hope the sheets are clean."

J.J. pulled down the bedspread. Checked out the sheets and began to take off his clothes. Stephanie kicked off her shoes.

A little later, after they had had sex, they were lying under the covers.

"It was everything I hoped it would be," said Stephanie. "All these months was like the longest foreplay ever."

"You gonna tell Flynn now?" asked J.J.

"Hell, no. Are you kidding? I just moved back in. I'm not giving that up. I've got no money and he's paying for everything. I've got it made." Stephanie reached for her purse on the nightstand. "I've got some coke. Flynn bought it for me from Don. Can you believe it? Let's have some."

They got out of bed and threw their clothes on. They sat at the tiny table in the room and set up the coke on Stephanie's small portable mirror. She had the gold-plated snorter with her and they snorted up a storm.

"Good coke. Don always has the best. I've got to go back to work. Can we do this again?"

"Maybe. But can't we go to the Ritz Carlton?" asked Stephanie.

"You're too much. Not only is it expensive, but we might see someone," said J.J.

"Why are you so paranoid? We're just having a good time. I've got to go, too. I've got a date with Saks Fifth Avenue."

"What are you using for money?"

"I've got a credit card, J.J., what do you think?" said Stephanie.

"I want to see you again." J.J. was putting on his shirt.

"Me too," said Stephanie.

★ ★ ★

It was a blistering hot day in Chicago and Flynn was drinking coffee out on the balcony. Stephanie was in the living room setting up lines on the coffee table. After snorting a couple, she joined Flynn outside.

"Don't get too high. We've got a big day ahead of us," said Flynn.

"What's the big deal?" asked Stephanie.

"WLUP is having 'The Loop's Day in the Park' at Comiskey. It's an all-day event with Journey, Santana, Thin Lizzy, Eddie Money and Molly Hatchet." He showed her the ad in the newspaper sitting on the table.

"But it's so hot. And there will be a zillion people there," said Stephanie.

"This isn't a limo event. And don't tell J.J. We're just going to buy tickets at the door just like everybody else. It'll be fun. We can drink beer in the stadium and listen to music all day. Put on some shorts. Come on. We're going," Flynn said as he downed what was left of his coffee.

A cab pulled up to Comiskey Park and dropped Flynn and Stephanie at the front entrance. About twenty to thirty people were in line for tickets. They joined the throng.

When they were inside, it was a free-for-all. A crowd was on the infield right up close to where the bands were playing. The stands were packed and it was a pick-your-own seat setup.

Flynn and Stephanie climbed way up to some empty seats above the madhouse. They sat down and looked at how far away the stage was. It didn't matter, though, because they could hear the music of Eddie Money. He was performing "Two Tickets to Paradise." A walking vendor came by with beers in large plastic cups. Flynn grabbed two and paid the guy. They drank thirstily.

"How's the job hunt going?" Flynn asked.

"Not great. I've had about five interviews and nothing came of them. I'd be out on the street if it wasn't for you," answered Stephanie.

"Don't worry. You're safe with me," said Flynn.

Down on the stage, Eddie Money was leaving.

"Who's next?" asked Stephanie.

Flynn looked at the program. "It looks like Santana. They were great at Woodstock."

"You didn't tell me you were at Woodstock."

"I thought I did. It was one of the few times I dropped acid."

"I know you never told me that. How was it?"

"It was fantastic. So much so that I didn't do it again. I was afraid I liked it too much."

"And you're always talking to me about coke. Acid! See, you are a druggie."

"Sex, drugs and rock-and-roll. It was all part of the sixties. The drugs go with the territory."

"Speaking of drugs. I've got my Bullet Snorter with me. You want a bump?"

Stephanie took the snorter out of her purse and stuck it into a nostril. She sniffed. Then did the other nostril. She handed the tool to Flynn.

"Okay, I'll do one. Just for you." He took the snorter and sniffed coke into his nose.

"Yay, Flynn. Now we're cooking. Makes the music sound so much better."

"I always thought grass did that. In fact, I know grass does that. It really is my drug of choice."

"Well, coke's mine. And I think I'll snort to that!" She took the Bullet and did a second round.

"Santana's coming on. Let's have another beer."

SEPTEMBER

SOLDIER FIELD WAS A BEHEMOTH of a stadium adjacent to Lake Michigan in the near South Side of Chicago. Home field of the Chicago Bears, who moved there in 1971. The historic structure was dedicated to the men and women of the armed services. The American football stadium had a capacity of 61,500.

J.J. and Flynn were sitting at the 50-yard line about 12 rows up. Perfect seats on a perfect day in September. Crystal clear, not a cloud in the sky, temperature in the low 70s. A pre-fall day that only Chicago could provide.

On the field, the Chicago Bears entered from the tunnel. Out came Walter Peyton and Willie McClendon, the famous running backs. On the other side of the field, the Green Bay Packers entered from their tunnel.

"Great seats, Flynn," said J.J.

"These are my season tickets. I go to every home game. I love this matchup. Green Bay and Chicago. Classic football every time. If I wasn't a Bears fan, I'd be a Packers fan," said Flynn.

They stood for the national anthem. When it was over the Bears got ready to kick off to the Packers. The kick went into the end zone and the ball was brought up to the twenty-yard line for the Packers' first crack at scoring points. They got off their first play, a run up the center. The game was on.

A walking vendor came by with beer in large plastic cups. Flynn bought two and handed one to J.J.

"Thanks. So, what's going on with you? What's happening with your idea for the rock show?" asked J.J.

"I have an appointment in two weeks with the head of the network. I get a chance to pitch my idea," said Flynn.

"What's it called again?"

"*Rock the Town.*"

"I like it. Hope it works out for you. I'm thinking about moving back to California. There might be a Program Director job opening at KROC. I'm going out there in November. They're talking about a new format called 'classic rock.' It would basically be the same as album-oriented rock, but with a twist. Can you imagine the possibilities?"

"It sounds cool. But I would hate to see you go. All those limos to the concerts. Just kidding. I would miss you."

"Speaking of limos. There's a concert coming up with the group Rush. Here's the catch, though. It's at Alpine Valley Music Theatre in East Troy, Wisconsin. It's about an hour and fifteen minutes up there. I'm trying to arrange a limo that would do the drive, then wait for us, then drive us back. Miles is balking because of the expense, but I think I can talk him into it."

"I've heard about that venue. Seating on the lawn. And some seats under a dome."

"We'd have dome seats. Up front like always. But I haven't put the whole thing together yet."

"Rush is a good rock group. I'm not that familiar with every song, but it would be cool to go to Wisconsin for a rock show."

"It would just be for that one day. Limo both ways. Lots of champagne and coke in the car."

"Are the usual gang of rockers invited?"

"Yeah, it would be you, me, Stephanie, Miles, Don and Skye. Miles may or may not have a date. We could all fit into one of the stretch limos."

"Far-out! An outdoor concert in September. Perfect!"

Down on the field, Walter Peyton was running for the end zone. The offensive line was clearing a path for him. He was running by all Packer defenders. He pushed his way past them. He was in the end zone for a touchdown. The thousands in the stands cheered him on.

There was celebration by the Bears in the end zone. Then the kicking team came out and they missed the extra point. A collective sigh went out from the fans.

Flynn and J.J. enjoyed every minute of the game and being outside. The Bears pulled in a win at 6 to 3. But it was a low-scoring game and not that thrilling.

"They just pulled it off," said Flynn. "You busy later? I'm meeting Stephanie at the Twin Anchors for some ribs."

"Okay, I'm in."

Flynn and J.J. walked down out of the stadium and made their way through the mass of people leaving. In front of the entrance, there were a couple of cabs waiting. They grabbed one of them and were off.

The cab pulled up to the near-north rib hangout. J.J. and Flynn slid out of the cab and headed to the entrance of the Twin Anchors. Inside, it was dark and cool. The bar was crowded and all the drinkers were watching a small TV atop the bar. It was the sports report about the Bears game. It was all guys and all sports fans sitting on the cushioned barstools. J.J. and Flynn took stools at the end, near the front door.

"I want to be able to see Stephanie when she gets here. I can do that from here. Pretty soon this place will be standing room only. It gets busy around dinnertime," said Flynn.

"I can't wait for those ribs. My mouth is watering just thinking about it."

The front door opened and Stephanie stepped into the Twin Anchors. She was wearing a low-cut dress and the usual heels. Her long, straight hair looked like she'd just stepped out of the salon. She saw the guys and glanced quickly at J.J. Flynn patted the seat he had saved for her.

"You look like you're going to a party," he said. "I'm not complaining. You look great. But this is just a rib joint."

"I'd never been here. I wasn't sure what the attire should be," said Stephanie.

"Hi, Steph," said J.J.

"Hi." They took a quick, furtive look at each other.

Flynn got up to talk to the host about a table. Stephanie took this opportunity to talk to J.J.

"What are you doing here? This is very uncomfortable. You should probably go."

"Are you kidding? I wouldn't miss this for the world. You're here with your boyfriend and your boyfriend. Pretty cozy, if you ask me," said J.J.

Flynn came back and said, "We've got a table. Come on. We don't want to lose out on those ribs."

Stephanie and J.J. got up and followed Flynn to a nice table in the corner of the main room. As they sat down, people started coming in the front door.

They took seats at a round table with a red-and-white checkered tablecloth. The waitress was there in seconds and they ordered a round of drinks. They were silent while they perused their menus.

When the waitress returned Flynn ordered for them. "Three rib dinners with fries and coleslaw."

Somehow, they made it through the mostly silent dinner and dug into their ribs.

★ ★ ★

Flynn walked down the plushy carpeted hallway on the 25th floor, where the executive offices of the network were located. He was not wearing a suit. Just a button-down blue shirt and a black summer weight blazer. He was also wearing black jeans and a fancy pair of cowboy boots. At the end of the hall, a secretary sat like a police officer ready to keep people away from the boss, Barry Sanders. She eyed Flynn suspiciously.

"I'm here to see Barry Sanders," said Flynn.

"Do you have an appointment?" the secretary asked.

"Yes, Flynn. 2 P.M."

"And your first name?"

"It's just Flynn. No first name."

She sighed a bit, then picked up her phone and announced to Barry that his 2 o'clock was here.

"The door is open. Go right in."

Flynn opened the door to more plush carpeting. Barry Sanders was sitting behind a huge antique desk. Floor-to-ceiling windows offered a view of the Chicago River and the Wrigley Building. When he saw Flynn, he got up and stuck his hand out. They shook hands and then Barry gestured him to one of the visitors' chairs in front of his desk.

"Sit down, Flynn," said Barry.

"Thanks. Nice view," said Flynn.

"Just one of the perks of the job. So, Brett tells me you have something to talk to me about."

"Yes."

"By the way, the ratings are in on *The Brett Adams Show*. You guys are doing a great job. I have nothing to complain about."

"Well, here's the thing. I want to start my own show. Host my own show. It would be all about the Chicago music scene. *Rock the Town* is my working title. The show would feature rock stars, bands touring through Chicago. The content would be interviews, performances and memories. Every week there would be a featured artist like Mick Jagger, Tom Petty, Eric Clapton, the Midwest giants Styx. Whoever was in town doing a concert would drop by the show and talk about their music. It would be a rock talk-show for all those millions of fans out there who love rock music."

"Sounds interesting. But you're a Director on a talk-show. What makes you think you could be a host?"

"I'm a musicologist, of sorts. I've been following rock music since the mid-60s. I know the groups, the trends, the old stuff and the new stuff. It would be a natural for me to interview these musicians. I've been working on a talk-show for a long time, now I want to do my own show. It seems like the natural next step in my career."

"We'd have to sell it, though. You'd need a sponsor. You'd have to come up with one. The timeslot I've got. Ten o'clock, Saturday night. An hour. Before the news and before *Saturday Night Live*. Then again, maybe late night. I'll have to think about it."

"I'll come up with a sponsor. I can do that. No problem."

"You'd also need a killer first guest. A big introduction to the show."

"That I can definitely do. I've got a whole lineup in my mind."

"Do you have a start date in mind?"

"Yeah. January 1st. Or at least that first week in January. The first Saturday."

"You get a sponsor and a killer guest. We'll talk about it. I'll think about it. Thanks for coming in. Go get a sponsor." Barry was dismissing him from the meeting.

Flynn got up. "Thanks, Barry. I'll find a sponsor. You can count on it."

THE YEAR THAT ROCKED

★ ★ ★

The late-afternoon sun was streaming in through the front door of The Palm. At the bar, Stephanie, Flynn, Don, Miles and Skye were having drinks. J.J. came from the payphone at the back of the restaurant near the restrooms.

"The limo is on its way. Drink up. It'll be a little over an hour in the car," said J.J. He pushed his baseball cap up so he could see better.

"So glad you're here, Don," squeaked Stephanie. "Let me talk to Flynn for a minute."

She whispered into Flynn's ear. Then he reached into his pocket for his wallet and pulled out five twenties and gave them to Stephanie. She took it greedily, then gestured to Don and they went back to the restrooms. They reappeared a little later, both visibly high.

"You must really like Stephanie if you're giving her money for coke," said J.J.

"She's out of a job. You know that. And she's back living with me," said Flynn.

"When did that happen? I thought she was staying with a girlfriend."

"She begged me to take her back. Sort of."

"Be careful, Flynn. She's a handful." J.J. took a long pull on his bottle of beer.

A little later, a limousine chauffeur came through the door and announced, "The J.J. Watts party of six, your driver is here."

Flynn paid the bar tab as the others rushed out the door. In a minute, he joined them outside where the long, shiny black limo was double parked. The gang was getting into the limo. Inside, there were seats facing each other. Three people to a side. Flynn slid in next to Stephanie. J.J. had two grocery bags with him and he started to dig things out of them as the car took off. He brought out a bottle of champagne, cheese and crackers and some plastic cups. He opened the champagne with a flourish and began passing out the cups.

The limo reached the expressway and headed north to the tollway to Wisconsin. Inside, Don and Stephanie were passing around their Bullet Snorters. Flynn passed around a joint, but only he and Skye were smoking.

"You guys will be the first to know. I met with Barry Sanders, the head of the network, and he was open and positive about my rock-show, talk-show idea. I just need to find a sponsor and a killer first guest. He's got a Saturday night timeslot open and I'm just like far-fucking-out. I really want to do a music show," said Flynn.

"God, if you can pull it off. We could do some cross-promotions with the radio station," said Miles.

"Any ideas for sponsors?" asked Skye. "This town needs a good rock-show. What's the name, Flynn?"

"*Rock the Town*. The format would be interviews, performances, memories. All the stuff you always want to know. But never do," said Flynn

"Good luck, Flynn. I'll believe it when it's on the air. These things have a way of sometimes not working out," said J.J.

"Don't be negative. Positive energy only," added Flynn.

The group kept snorting and talking as the limo sped along the tollway. The landscape changed to farmland and they saw cows grazing in the fields.

"How cool it is to be out of the city," said Stephanie. "Real grass. Not the smoking kind."

"Skye, you're the DJ guy. What do you think of Geddy Lee of Rush?" asked Flynn.

"He's pretty cool. Bass guitar and lead vocals. Rush is a Canadian rock band. One of the few popular ones from Canada to really make it."

"Aren't they only a three-person band, just like the Police?"

"Yeah, there's Geddy and Alex Lifeson on guitar and the drummer Neil Peart. Wait till you hear the sound that comes out of only three. It's fantastic!"

J.J. broke into the conversation, "I've had Rush on our playlist forever. I can't remember a time when QXA wasn't playing them. I'm psyched to see them," said J.J.

The limo pulled up to the picturesque outside arena called the Alpine Valley Music Theatre. It was the main attraction in the sleepy town of East Troy, Wisconsin. There was seating on the lawn where people had already started to show up. The main stage and ticketed seating area had a concrete dome covering the area that looked like a symphony would play nicely in that spot. The acoustics would spread out from the dome and onto the lawn.

The chauffeur slid open the glass partition to the back seats. "I'll be right here when the concert ends. This zone is set up for limos and VIP cars, so don't worry. Come fast when the show is over."

"Thanks," a collection of voices rang out as they stepped out of the limo.

J.J. led them up to the entrance and handed the ticket-taker six VIP tickets. Then he led them out to the massive lawn area. "We'll sit out here for a while and then move to our seats when the sun goes down."

"Far-out," said Flynn. "I'll go hunt us up some beers. Steph, why don't you come with me and help carry them."

Stephanie and Flynn walked toward the concession stands. They got the beers and also saw a stand with lawn blankets for sale. They picked up one and headed back to their space on the lawn, handing the beers to everyone. Stephanie made everybody get up so she could spread the blanket down.

There were at least a couple of hundred people on the lawn. They drank and did the Bullet Snorter and laughed and talked. The sun began to set in a beautiful array of orange and yellow streaks. From the lawn, it felt like it was setting just for the people sitting out there. The sky was crystal clear and the temperature dropped just enough to be comfortable. When it was dark, J.J. rounded everybody up and took them over to their seats under the dome. They walked to the third row and sat six across. The stage was dark. Very quickly, bright lights flooded the stage and Rush came out. It was just the three of them, but they were a powerhouse of rock musicianship.

They played "Xanadu," "The Trees," "Working Man," "Finding My Way," and "Bastille Day."

Then there was a drum solo by Neil Peart. J.J. and company were really digging it. It went on and on and the thousand or so under the dome were on their feet cheering. Alex and Geddy came back to life and they finished the set. They bowed and went off stage. But the crowd wouldn't let it go. They wanted an encore.

Rush came back on stage and broke into the song "In the Mood." More craziness from the crowd. They were finished and left the stage. The J.J. group left their seats and started to move through the crowd. Everybody was pushing and shoving. He was finally able to make a path through the throng. He led them out to the limo pickup and there was the car just waiting for them. They all piled in and the chauffeur took off before the thousands came out to the parking lot.

"I'm jazzed," said Flynn. "Tell the driver to take us to The Street of Dreams."

"He won't know what that means. It's a Flynnism," said J.J.

Miles was closest to the sliding glass partition and he opened it and said to the chauffeur, "We're all going to the same drop-off place. Butch McGuire's on Division Street."

"You got it," the driver said. "On my way."

When they arrived at Butch's, they got out of the limo to a beautiful night with a hint of fall in the air. The full moon was hanging low in the sky and stars were visible and sparkling with no fog to block the view.

"I almost hate to go inside. We only get a few nights like this in Chicago," said Flynn. He lingered a while and took in the night. The others were already in the bar.

When he came in, there were no seats at the bar. It was two deep with people and everybody was shouting their drink orders. Flynn rounded up the group and headed into the side room.

The music was loud and pouring out of the wall speakers. It was AC/DC's "You Shook Me All Night Long."

There was one table left. It was big enough for the group and had six chairs. Sheer luck. They all sat down. Stephanie was whispering to Don. They both got up and headed toward the back. When J.J. saw them leave, he got up and followed them.

Flynn said to Skye, "I think I've got an idea for the sponsor for my show."

"Cool. Who is it?" asked Skye.

"The *Chicago Tribune*."

"Wow. If you could get them you'd be set."

"I'm gonna do my best."

Stephanie, Don and J.J. came back to the table. Flynn wrapped his arm around Stephanie's shoulder.

"Did you have fun back there in the bathroom? You spend a lot of time in bathrooms."

"Yes, I did have fun. What's it to ya?"

"Nothing, I was just asking."

J.J. weighed in, "It's always fun back there. You should do it sometime."

"No way. You wouldn't catch me going to the bathrooms. That Bullet Snorter thing is okay. But no bathrooms," said Flynn.

J.J. reached into his wallet and brought out a couple of passes to a private screening of *The Last Waltz*. He handed two over to Flynn. Then gave out the rest to Miles, Skye and Don.

"Far-out. I saw it last year when it came out. The best rock-and-roll film ever made."

"The movie distributor is doing a special promotion to show it again on a big screen, so they're doing it at the private screening room on top of the Chicago Theatre," said J.J.

Everybody pocketed their tickets and murmured thanks.

"I've never seen it," said Stephanie.

"You're in for a thrill," said Flynn.

"I like thrills."

Don, who had said nothing in his coked-up-state, mumbled, "Cool." Then he looked down into his drink like the meaning of life was in there.

Skye and Miles were talking shop in their corner of the table.

J.J. got up. "I've gotta go. Big day tomorrow with Martin Scorsese in town for the screening. See you guys tomorrow night."

"Why is everybody making such a big deal about a movie?" Stephanie asked.

"It's not just a movie. It's rock-and-roll history. The filming of The Band's last gig with Neil Young, Van Morrison, Joni Mitchell, even Bob Dylan joining them on stage. It's just fantastic. I can't believe I get to see it twice," said Flynn.

Miles said, "I've never seen it either, Steph, so don't feel bad. And I'm in rock-and-roll radio."

"I'm like Flynn. I saw it last year. But I could never get enough. And a private screening is like riding in a limo," Skye added.

The music pouring out of the wall speakers segued to The Who's "My Generation."

The group kept on drinking into the wee hours.

★ ★ ★

The next night Flynn and Stephanie arrived by cab in front of the Chicago Theatre on State Street. When they got out, they headed to the side of the building and found the entrance door. Inside was a small hallway and an elevator. They pushed the button and the elevator doors opened into the smallest space they'd ever seen. There was a sign over the up button that read: "4 passengers max. Do not exceed limit." Since they were the only ones in it, they pushed the button and the doors slid shut. When they got to the top floor, they exited to find J.J. there to greet them.

"Glad you could make it. There were only fifty passes so consider yourselves members of the elite," J.J. said.

"Thanks, J.J.," said Flynn.

J.J. led them into the screening room. It was small. Only about fifteen rows with a dozen seats across. The screen, however, was big. Dominating the room. Flynn quickly picked out the middle row and took Stephanie down to the center. They had a perfect view of the screen. About twenty-five people were scattered about the other seats. J.J. checked his watch and went down the aisle to the back row. There was a phone next to one of the seats. He called the control room behind him and told them to start the movie in ten minutes. While he waited, another twenty people or so came in and found seats.

J.J. picked up the phone again. "We're ready to rock-and-roll. Show the film."

Up on the screen, The Band was featured at a soon to become historical farewell concert at the Winterland Ballroom in San Francisco. Flynn was enthralled as they performed "The Weight" with Levon Helm singing the lead and Robbie Robertson playing the guitar. As the film progressed, they saw Van Morrison, Bob Dylan, Neil Young doing "Helpless" with Joni Mitchell in the wings accompanying him with a soprano solo. Even Neil Diamond came out and did a number. It was just one fantastic performance after another. A stylistic concert film that captured the essence of The Band.

When the film was over, Flynn couldn't move. He was too jazzed to get up. People started leaving the screening room and he just sat there. Finally, Stephanie nudged him. And when J.J. stood at the end of the row waiting for them, he got up.

"Let's go over to the Wrigley Bar. It's close," he said.

There was a mob scene in front of the elevator. At four people at a time allowed in, it was taking a long time to get downstairs. Flynn, Stephanie and J.J. were the last ones in the elevator. When they finally got outside the theatre, they walked to the corner of Michigan and Wacker and crossed the bridge over to the magnificent architectural achievement: The Wrigley Building. It was all lit up in the dark, beautiful September night. The temperature was mild, still summerish and Stephanie was limping along in her sandals. They reached the building and went in and headed for the bar. It was pretty crowded, but they found three stools at the bar.

Hector, the bartender, was there instantly. "Flynn, J.J. How's it going? What do you want to drink?"

Stephanie said, "I'll have a vodka martini."

"Hector, man, you know me. Line up the 12-year-old scotch," said Flynn.

"I'll have a bottle of Heineken," said J.J.

Hector went down the bar to get the drinks. When he came back with the drinks, they toasted each other.

"I've never seen anything like that film. I still think it's the best concert film ever made. Even better than *Woodstock*. I even liked Neil Diamond's performance and I'm not a huge fan. Neil Young blew me away with 'Helpless' and with Joni in the wings. Unreal. It's sad that The Band broke up, but what a sendoff," said Flynn.

"I liked Joni's number 'Coyote.' I liked the whole thing. A lot of people I've never seen play," Stephanie said. She grabbed her purse and jumped off the barstool. "I'll be right back. J.J., you gonna join me?"

They left Flynn there by himself. A long time later they returned. They were sniffing and laughing at the same thing.

"What took you guys so long? How much time does it take to take a couple of hits? Nobody asked me," said Flynn.

"You know you don't do bathrooms, Flynn. You usually don't want any," said Stephanie.

Well, tonight's a special night. You could have at least asked," said Flynn.

"Sorry." She and J.J. shared a laugh and a sniff. All of a sudden, they couldn't stop laughing.

"What's so funny?" asked Flynn.

J.J. answered first. "The elevator at the screening. The tiniest thing I've ever seen."

"Yeah, it was pretty small," said Stephanie.

"Small," J.J. was cracking up.

Stephanie giggled. "Small."

★ ★ ★

Flynn and Stephanie were lying down on a blanket in the middle of Oak Street Beach. It was a beautiful September day, very summer-like, in the mid-80s with not too much humidity. The beach was crowded, Chicagoans taking advantage of a rare perfect day.

Stephanie adjusted the top of her bikini. "It's not the ocean. But it'll do."

"What, are you kidding? That's the mighty Lake Michigan out there. One of the great lakes. Emphasis on 'great.' I can't believe I'm actually wearing a bathing suit," said Flynn. He had the Sunday *Chicago Tribune* with him and he looked down on the Arts Section.

"Oh, my God. We're really missing something at Madison Square Garden in New York City."

"What is it?"

"It's called 'No Nukes: The MUSE Concerts for a Non-Nuclear Future.'"

"What's MUSE?"

"Musicians United for Safe Energy, it says here. It's an activist group that includes Jackson Browne, Graham Nash, Bonnie Raitt and John Hall. They started it and it has become this big concert. Also playing are James Taylor, The Doobie Brothers, Tom Petty and the Heartbreakers, Poco, Bruce Springsteen and the E Street Band, Crosby, Stills and Nash. Man, what a lineup. I wish I'd known about it we could have flown to New York to be part of it."

"You'd take me to New York? Flynn, you're so good to me."

"Too late for No Nukes. Maybe we'll just take a weekend there sometime." He referred to his newspaper again. "Looks like they're making a live album of the concerts. Oh, cool. We can hear everything on a record. Not the same as being there, but it'll have to do."

Somebody came by their blanket and kicked sand onto Flynn. He brushed it off and stood up. "I hate sand on me."

Stephanie continued lying on the blanket, sand-free. "You'd be terrible in California. The big, old Pacific Ocean would be out to get you."

"It's not the water. I just don't like sand."

"Why don't we call it a day. We've been out here for a couple of hours. I'm probably getting a sunburn."

"I know I've got one. Yeah, let's get out of here. We'll go back to my place and order takeout for dinner."

They got up. A couple of guys on the beach whistled at Stephanie, looking great in her bikini. She smiled and pulled back her hair.

"Don't encourage them. I'm the only one who can look at you in that bathing suit."

"I think it's nice."

"C'mon, let's go."

★ ★ ★

Flynn was in his office. Feet up on the desk reading *Rolling Stone*. Brett Adams knocked on his open door.

"Hey, Flynn. Good show today. How did it go with the head of the network?"

"Pretty good. The thing is, I have to find my own sponsor. Not such an easy task."

"Got anybody in mind?"

"The *Chicago Tribune*."

"Nothing like starting at the top. The crème de la crème."

"It would be perfect. What could be more Chicago than the *Chicago Tribune* to promote a Chicago based show? Not to mention the rock music coming out of Chicago."

"Good luck. Let me know if there's anything I can do."

"Thanks, Brett. I'll keep that in mind."

Brett left the office. Flynn went back to reading *Rolling Stone*.

★ ★ ★

Flynn and Stephanie were walking down Elm Street toward Division and beyond. She was wearing inappropriate footwear. He was actually pushing her along.

"Can't we take a cab? Walking is killing me," said Stephanie.

"This is Chicago. It's a walking city. When are you going to get it?"

"Never." She came to a stop and adjusted a strap on her sandal.

After about a twenty-minute walk, they arrived at Morton's Steakhouse. Stephanie was practically limping by this time. They went into the restaurant and Flynn gave his reservation to the maître d', who sat them at a quiet table in the corner. As they sat down, they looked around and took in the old-world, comfy wood and leather ambience.

"How's the job search going?" asked Flynn.

"I'm hitting the ad agencies now. Nothing so far," answered Stephanie.

"Keep at it. You'll find something. In the meantime, you've got a great place to live. With me. I wanted it all along."

Stephanie looked down at her menu, avoiding the subject. Flynn perused his.

"I'm gonna have a filet mignon, medium rare." He put down his menu.

Stephanie looked up. "I don't feel like a big meat thing. I might just have a salad."

"We're at a steakhouse and you're not going to have a steak?"

"I'm not that hungry."

"Then why did we come here?"

"'Cause you wanted to."

"And you agreed right away."

"I didn't think it would take so long walking here. You tortured me."

"Now I tortured you. If you'd get some decent shoes. Oh, I'm not going to have this conversation again."

"Good. I wear the shoes I like and that's it. Comfortable shoes are for old ladies. I'm not going there."

"Comfortable shoes are for smart women."

"Then I guess I'm not very smart." She started crying.

"Not the waterworks. Not here. What is your problem?"

"I'm not happy living in Chicago."

"You've got a great place to live and a guy who's crazy about you. You'll find a job. It just takes time."

Stephanie kept crying.

The waiter approached their table. "Can I take your order?"

"Yes, I'll have a filet mignon. Medium rare," said Flynn.

Stephanie sniffled. "I'll have a cobb salad."

Flynn sighed and shook his head. Then he turned the menus over to the waiter.

★ ★ ★

Flynn was wrapping up *The Brett Adams Show* when Madison joined him in the booth. She handed him a bunch of papers and he looked them over. Then he took off his headset and prepared to leave the booth. He turned to her and handed back the papers.

"Come to my office. I want to talk with you."

They headed out of the booth, down the hall to Flynn's office. He went in and went straight to his chair behind the desk. Madison sat in one of the visitors' chairs.

Flynn wasted no time in getting right to the heart of the matter.

"Madison, are you happy working here?" She thought about it for a minute. "Yeah, I like it. But I have ambitions beyond being your Assistant Director."

"Good. Because I want you to help me with the new show I plan to produce and host."

"Really. What is it?"

"*Rock the Town*. A music-oriented talk-show featuring all the popular rock bands that are touring Chicago. I've already talked to the head of the network here and he said if I can find a sponsor I can do the show. They already found me a timeslot. I would also need a killer first guest. It could be a solo or a group that would come on the show. I need a co-producer/director and that's where you come in. Would you want to do it?"

"Oh, Flynn. A music show? You know how much I love rock music. It would be great. What do I do?"

"Well, for now you can help me with the sponsor part. I'm going after the *Chicago Tribune* and I need a lot of research on them and our network so I can put together a presentation for the newspaper."

"I can do that. I'm already on it. This is so cool. You've got to do it."

"Okay, we'll talk again soon. Go on and get on it. Don't let it interfere with Brett's show. We're still on it for now."

Madison got up and left the office very excited. Flynn smiled and put his feet up on the desk.

★ ★ ★

Stephanie got out of a cab in front of the entrance to Grant Park. The day was a magnificent early fall day in late September. Temperatures in the 70s with just a hint of humidity. The sun filtered through a grouping of clouds just enough to keep it warm, but not hot.

She walked over to the fountain, where J.J. was sitting on the edge with bags of food next to him.

"What a day to be in Grant Park," said J.J. He motioned for her to sit down next to him on the edge of the fountain.

"Yes, it's gorgeous. But we shouldn't be meeting out in the open like this. Flynn may hear about it," said Stephanie.

"Who's going to tell him. The birds in the sky?"

"Don't be cute."

"So, when are you going to tell him about us?"

"There is no us. How many times do I have to say it?"

"Then, what would you call what we are?"

"Friends."

"Friends who sleep together. Okay. Whatever. But if I get the job in Los Angeles and go back to California, I want you to go with me."

"What job is that?"

"Program Director of KROC. A new rock station starting from the ground up. They're experimenting with a new format: Classic Rock. And I'd be back in California. No more Chicago winters. And L.A. has a bigger music scene than Chicago. It's all happening out there. That's always been where the real action is."

"Wow. That would be great for you. Where do I fit in?"

"We'd live together and you could find a job. Maybe at KROC. Maybe in the promotion department. With your newfound knowledge of music, thanks to Flynn, you'd fit in."

Stephanie got a faraway look on her face. "California. No more Chicago winters. It sounds too good to believe."

J.J. handed Stephanie one of the bags of food. "Well, believe it. I'm flying out there sometime before Thanksgiving. If I can get the job, we'd be set."

Stephanie sighed. "California…."

"Yeah, California, here we come!"

"I'm not going to say anything to Flynn until you've got the job. No sense rocking the boat."

"You're going to have to tell him sometime."

Stephanie dug in her bag and pulled out a burger. "Yeah, sometime, but not yet."

J.J. bit into his burger. "Let's eat."

★ ★ ★

Flynn was in his apartment listening to music. He got up from the couch and walked over to the turntable. The shelves in front of him on both sides of the stereo setup were filled with at least a hundred albums starting back in the mid-60s. He picked up REO Speedwagon. "Ridin' the Storm Out" boomed through his giant speakers. He was playing air-guitar when the key turned in the lock in his front door. Stephanie entered with a load of Saks Fifth Avenue shopping bags. He turned the music down a little.

"Don't tell me you've been shopping. You don't have any money," said Flynn.

"I have a credit card for Saks. I needed some things." Stephanie started pulling pants and tops and lingerie out of the bags.

"Okay, give me a fashion show. Or better yet, just give me a show." Flynn went to her and put his arms around her.

"Flynn, you've always got just one thing on your mind."

"What's the second thing?"

"Music."

"Music and sex. What could be a better duo?"

"Whatever." Stephanie sat on the couch with her new things around her and took her little cocaine pouch out of her purse. She took out a snowseal, razor blade and the gold-plated coke snorter. She began to make lines on the little mirror that was permanently placed on the coffee table.

"Want a hit?" Stephanie snorted a line in each nostril. She handed Flynn the snorting tool.

"Okay. Just one," Flynn said. He snorted a line.

"You gotta do one in the other side of your nose or you'll be unbalanced."

"That's a new one. Oh, my God. To be unbalanced. Wouldn't think of it." He did a second line. "Want a drink?"

"Oh, Flynn. Would you make me a martini? I've been hard at work all day shopping."

Flynn went into the kitchen and came back in a few minutes with a martini and a scotch with one ice cube. "Let's sit on the balcony while we still can. October is almost here. My favorite month in Chicago, but sometimes toward the end it can start getting a little cold."

Flynn went onto the balcony and set the drinks down on the table. It was near sunset and the rays of the sun were shooting through the clouds.

"Hey, Steph, bring me my sunglasses. They're right on the sideboard in the dining room."

She came out onto the balcony with the sunglasses. Flynn put them on. "Embellish this in your bird dog: Enjoy every minute of this mild weather. Because you know what's coming."

"I know. Unfortunately. Let's do some more coke. I'll bring the mirror and stuff out here."

"You do that. But I'm not having anymore. Bring me a joint out of the box on the table. And some matches, too."

Stephanie went back inside to get all the drugs. She came back, handed Flynn a joint and matches. Then put her little mirror on the outside table and went through the ritual of making lines. She snorted two, then sipped her martini.

"You seem really distracted. Anything wrong?" asked Flynn.

"No. I'm fine," answered Stephanie.

"I'm going after the *Chicago Tribune* for my sponsor for *Rock the Town*."

"That's reaching pretty high. You might have to get somebody not as big as them."

"You've got to reach high. That's the whole point. My assistant, Madison, is helping me do research. I'm going to put together a dynamite presentation to the newspaper. Can you imagine. A Chicago institution backing a Chicago-based rock talk-show."

"Nice, Flynn. Nice." She lined up two more hits of cocaine and snorted them right up.

"You and J.J. are pretty negative about my new show idea. But it's gonna be great. I will literally rock the town. You'll see. Everybody will see. It's gonna happen."

Stephanie laid out yet another line and snorted it up. Flynn lit his joint and took a toke. They were in their own worlds.

OCTOBER

THE COOL BREEZE FLOATED DOWN Michigan Avenue, spreading golden leaves in its path. The sun was warm but not hot. This true fall weather made Chicago the ideal place to be. You could call it a real Indian Summer day that seemed brimming with possibilities.

Flynn walked down the Avenue catching the mood of the weather. When he passed the Wrigley Building, he looked up and breathed in its beauty. Then he walked across the bridge over the Chicago River, stopping to look down into the water. He finished crossing and waited for the light at Wacker Drive.

When he arrived at his office, Madison was right on his heels.

"I did that research on the *Chicago Tribune* and found out everything you ever wanted to know about the newspaper," said Madison as she handed Flynn a wad of papers.

He looked them over. "Fantastic. Is there information about the demographics? We want to be sure they know the show would reach the 18-34 age group. The group listening to rock music."

"It's all in there. Lots and lots about demographics," said Madison.

"You've outdone yourself. I'm taking you to lunch after the taping," said Flynn.

Madison laughed and clapped her hands. "You're gonna love today's show. It's Dr. Richard Osborne. Another psychiatrist that's written a book."

"N.B.D. It's such a beautiful day out, I don't even mind shrinks. Even though I hate them." Flynn gathered up his clipboard and the day's notes. "Let's go torture ourselves for another day."

★ ★ ★

While Flynn and Madison were having lunch at the Wrigley Restaurant, across town at the Allerton Hotel, J.J. and Stephanie were just finishing up a nooner in one of the hotel's rooms.

J.J. started putting on his pants. "Hey, babe. That was everything I thought it would be."

Stephanie buttoned her blouse. "Me, too. It was great."

"So, are you going to tell Flynn about us? And don't say 'there is no us.' There is an us and now you can say it."

Stephanie put on her open-toed sandals. "I'm not going to wreck a good thing. I have a place to live and he's giving me money for coke and essentials."

"You're brutal," J.J. barked.

"You're in this, too. He's supposed to be your best friend from college. Buddies for ten years, right?"

"Yeah, I've known Flynn a long time. But sometimes women come in between friends. It's an old story in dime-store novels."

Stephanie was ready to leave. "You heard any more about that job in L.A.?"

"I'm flying out there in November," said J.J.

"If that works out, I'll tell him then." Stephanie opened the door to the hall.

J.J. and Stephanie went down in the elevator and walked out of the Allerton Hotel down to Michigan Avenue.

"I'll call you, babe. Tom Petty and the Heartbreakers are doing a release party at The Drake Hotel next week. You and Flynn are officially invited."

"Who's Tom Petty?"

"Steph, get a grip. He's like the hottest rocker around. You need to know these things."

"I never know the names. I just know the music."

"If you want a job in L.A. radio, you better brush up." J.J. started to go south on the Avenue to pick up a cab to take him to the Merchandise Mart.

She went with him until he crossed the street to get a cab going in the right direction. "I'm going to Saks. I'm walking. See you later."

★ ★ ★

Flynn was sitting on his couch smoking a joint and listening to his stereo that was blasting Creedence Clearwater Revival's "Fortunate Son." He didn't hear Stephanie come into the apartment because he was so engrossed in the music. She was carrying a couple of shopping bags from Saks. She walked in front of him, so he could see her. Flynn jumped out of his skin. He had no idea she was there.

"Can you turn that down a little?"

Flynn got up and went to the stereo and turned down the music just as it segued to "Down on the Corner."

"We're listening to CCR. I saw them years ago. Wait for 'Have You Ever Seen the Rain.'"

"I'm going into the bedroom and hang up some of this new stuff," said Stephanie.

Flynn followed her in there as she placed the bags on the bed. She opened the closet door to try to find some space. Lined up on the floor were a dozen pairs of cowboy boots, different leathers, styles and colors.

"I've never noticed this before, why do you have all these cowboy boots?" she asked.

"I trade off in the winter. The salt on the street is hell on leather, so when one pair starts to get bad, I switch to another and wear that pair until it starts to get bad, and on and on," said Flynn.

"You are weirder than weird. You're wearing a pair now. It's not even winter."

"It's October. Perfect leather boot weather. They don't get wrecked in the fall. It's just that winter mess," said Flynn.

She moved some of Flynn's clothes to one side and started unpacking her new outfits. There was barely any room at all, but she managed to get everything in.

"All done. My new stuff won't get wrinkled. Can't you move some of your stuff to the other closet?" Stephanie said as she opened the other closet. "It's stuffed. No room at all. Oh, well, I'll just have to deal with it."

Flynn was just sitting on the bed staring at her. "Want a glass of wine? I got your favorite white French Bordeaux."

"Oh, Flynn. You sweetheart." Stephanie said as she walked back into the living room with Flynn on her heels.

He went into the kitchen and came back out with the wine and a corkscrew. He ceremoniously opened the bottle. He went back to the kitchen to get the wine glasses. He came back and handed Stephanie hers.

"I'm having some, too." Flynn sipped the dry white wine.

"Here's to ya," said Stephanie. They clinked glasses. She took a big gulp. "Oh, that is delicious. My favorite."

CCR's album was still playing on the turntable. Stephanie took her coke paraphernalia out of her purse and began the ritual of making lines on the little mirror. She snorted up two lines.

"So, any luck with the job hunting today?" asked Flynn.

"I blew it off and went shopping."

"How are you going to pay for all those clothes you keep buying?"

"Credit card. What do you think?"

"You're going to get into debt."

"No, I won't. I have you to bail me out."

"What are you getting me into?" Flynn sat on the couch next to her and sipped his wine. There was a half-joint in the ashtray, and he lit it and took a toke.

"You're the best, Flynn." She laid out two more lines and snorted them up.

Flynn didn't say anything.

★ ★ ★

The Drake Hotel was a Chicago landmark. Old-world charm with modern amenities. Flynn and Stephanie arrived by cab and got out right at the front door. Uniformed doormen were there to greet them and open the double-doors. Right behind them, in another cab, J.J. got out of the backseat, followed by Miles and Don. Ernie Mendez got out of the front seat. They went to the door and let the doorman open it. Stephanie and Flynn were waiting just inside the door.

"Oh, good. Hey, you two. We're all here," said J.J.

Inside the lobby, there were Persian rugs, Victorian-style couches, mahogany tables and tall, dark green, tree-sized plants. The group headed past the check-in counter and the concierge to a private room off the hall. J.J. opened a door to a huge conference room that looked like a rock concert was going on inside. A banner stretched across the back wall said: *Damn the Torpedoes*. Through the wall speakers "Refugee" played into the room. There was a bar set up in one corner. Near the bar, Tom Petty and his band, The Heartbreakers, were signing autographs. Flynn went right to Petty and started talking to him. The others went to the bar. They brought a beer back to J.J. and a wine to Stephanie.

J.J. broke in. "*Damn the Torpedoes* is going to be at least a platinum album. We got an advanced copy at the station and it's fantastic. Going to be their breakout album. Not that they weren't great before, but now everybody is going to know it."

"Refugee" segued into "Here Comes My Girl" and some of the people were dancing now in the middle of the room.

Suddenly, Don materialized out of nowhere. He didn't seem to be standing there before. He tapped Stephanie's arm. "You wanna go to the bathroom?"

"All right. Yes, I do," answered Stephanie.

J.J. walked over to the band and struck up a conversation with guitarist Mike Campbell. The keyboardist Benmont Tench joined them.

Miles and Ernie hung at the bar. Stephanie and Don returned from the bathroom. Don tapped Miles on the arm and they were off to the inevitable bathrooms.

The music had now segued again to "Don't Do Me Like That." The room full of people were swaying to the music. Everybody wanted to talk to Tom, but Flynn kept his attention and they kept on talking.

Stephanie walked up to J.J. and he introduced her to Mike and Benmont. They started talking all at once. They seemed to hit it off and the talking and the music continued.

Most of the record executives and producer-types were in one corner almost snubbing the Chicago radio people and media who were invited. They only left their corner to get drinks and return to their corner.

A waiter, carrying a tray of hors d'oeuvres, slipped in and around the crowd, offering up the array of hot goodies.

Later, when the party was clearing out, Flynn and Tom Petty were still talking. Stephanie had to practically drag him away as the rest of the gang was ready to go. They all said their goodbyes to the band and left them to their executives and managers. They walked back through the lobby and found themselves outside. Miles suggested The Palm.

They all agreed and headed a short block to Michigan Avenue. Then walked north about a block before heading east to The Palm.

The restaurant was busy with the late-dinner crowd, but the bar had only a few solitary drinkers and there were plenty of barstools. Stephanie, J.J., Flynn, Don, Miles and Ernie bellied up to place their orders.

"Hey, man, Frank! How's it going?" said Flynn.

"I'm good. Busy night," said Frank. "You want your usual 12-year-old scotch. With one ice cube?"

"Right on the money," said Flynn.

"I can't remember all the rest of you. What you drink. So, you'll have to tell me again." They did and Frank served everybody what they wanted.

J.J. sipped his drink and addressed Flynn who was sitting right next to him. "What were you and Tom Petty talking about? You didn't give anybody else a chance to talk to him."

"We just really hit if off musically. Then I told him about *Rock the Town* and the whole concept of the show. He was really keen on it. Thinks it's a great idea."

J.J. sipped his drink again. "What else did you guys talk about?"

"His beginnings in garage bands in Gainesville, Florida. And how he and the band Mudcrutch started out there. Then they all migrated to Los Angeles and became Tom Petty and the Heartbreakers. It's a fascinating story," said Flynn.

"Very cool. Very cool. Next time, share the stage. Others would have liked to talk to him," J.J. said with an angry note in his voice.

Stephanie jumped up and went to the back with Don. When she came back, she stood at the bar behind the barstools. She said to J.J., "That was a pretty nice party. I liked the music a lot. When does the album come out?"

J.J. answered, "Pretty soon. If I remember correctly it's October 19th. We'll be adding the songs you heard to our playlist. It was pretty cool listening to them with the band right there."

Flynn weighed in, "They're a real rock-and-roll band. None of this disco or jazzy stuff. Just good ole rock-and-roll. I love it."

"For once, I get it," said Stephanie.

Don, Miles and Ernie were talking up a storm down the bar and J.J. joined in with them. Stephanie moved in to talk to Flynn alone.

"Flynn, my sweet. Do you think you could buy me some cocaine? Don's holding and it's really primo stuff. Whaddaya say? Please."

Flynn reached for his wallet inside his coat and counted out five twenties. He handed Stephanie the one hundred dollars and she took it greedily. Then she went to the back of Don and tapped him on the shoulder. He was up in a flash and they were headed back to the bathrooms.

★ ★ ★

Flynn and Stephanie stepped out of a cab in front of his Elm Street apartment. The night doorman, Billy, opened the door and let them in. When they got up to Flynn's apartment, they took off their coats and sat down on the couch. Stephanie took off her ridiculous shoes and rubbed her feet. Flynn went to the kitchen and got a beer and a glass of wine. When he came back, Stephanie was setting up lines of coke on the table.

"Didn't you have enough of that at the bar?"

"I've never had enough," she said as she snorted up a line.

"How do you even sleep? That stuff keeps me awake at this time of night."

"That's the whole point. You're buzzed, so who needs to sleep?"

"Some of us have jobs in the morning. Speaking of that, how's the job search going?"

"Pretty slow. They're just doesn't seem to be any openings."

"Did you call that headhunter to help you get interviews?"

"Not yet."

"You should do that. They can be really helpful. You've got to start bringing in some money. Your coke bill alone is going to break me."

Stephanie cuddled up to Flynn. "But you're so sweet about it and you make a lot of money. I'll make it up to you. I promise." She leaned in and kissed him full on the mouth. They went down on the couch and kissed for a while, then Flynn took her by the hand and led her into the bedroom.

★ ★ ★

In the morning, Flynn was just about to leave for work when he saw Stephanie making up some lines of coke.

"You're doing that in the morning? What about interviewing?"

"I have nothing going today. I might as well be buzzed."

She put the gold snorter up to her nose and did a line. Then she sniffed deeply and did the other nostril.

"Call that headhunter. I left his card on the dining room table." He grabbed his jean jacket and headed out the front door.

Stephanie did two more lines. One in each nostril.

★ ★ ★

Flynn was in the booth on the set of *The Brett Adams Show*. Madison entered with a bunch of notes. Flynn took off his headset so he could talk to her for a minute. Outside on the stage, Brett took his seat and waved to the audience as they were taking their seats.

"Who have we got today?" asked Flynn.

"Doctor Flannigan. He's written a book called *Tell Someone Your Secrets*." Madison handed Flynn his clipboard.

"Oh, spare me. I better take some wakeup pills for this interview."

"I met him. He seems legit. He's a practicing psychotherapist in Elgin."

Flynn laughed. "Big city, that Elgin."

"Oh, come on, Flynn. Give him a chance."

"I always give every shrink a chance." He turned to the techs at the control panel. "Cue the music. Let's get this show on the road."

The music came up. On set, Brett fussed with his hair. "Camera one, Floor Director, you guys ready? On with the shrink show to beat all shrink shows."

After the show, Flynn stopped by Madison's little cubicle on the way to his office. "You busy for lunch?"

"Oh, I don't know. Maybe I can fit you in. Where would you be taking me?"

"Giovanetti's. Italian."

"Let me get one call out of the way. I'll meet you downstairs in the lobby."

★ ★ ★

Across town, Stephanie stepped out of a cab in front of the Allerton Hotel. Upstairs in a high-floor room J.J. was waiting. When the knock came, he opened the door with a big smile.

"Hey, babe. How's it going?"

"It's going. I feel sort of sordid meeting you like this."

"Well, it's a clandestine affair. What do you expect?"

Stephanie began to undress with no fanfare. "Any news about your job in L.A.?"

"I told you. I'm going out there before Thanksgiving. I won't know anything until I've talked to them. It'll be a big interview for me."

"I hope you get it. I can't get out of Chicago fast enough. Winter's coming. I can't bare another one."

J.J. took off his shoes and pants. He left his shirt on. Stephanie was already naked. They jumped on the bed laughing. They had sex in a sort of furtive way, but very intense. When they finished they laid back against the pillows, panting. Stephanie grabbed her purse and pulled out her little coke stash kit. When the lines were prepared, they snorted in bed. Then they stayed there and made love again. This time a little rougher.

★ ★ ★

Flynn and Madison sat at a corner table in the very traditional Italian restaurant. The waiters all had accents and the food was presented beautifully on large platter-size plates. Madison spoke up first after they were served.

"I'm ready to give you all the research on the *Chicago Tribune*. I think I know everything there is to know about that paper."

"Good. I'm ready to hear it," said Flynn as his sipped a glass of wine.

"The head of Promotion, who handles all media, is Gavin Larson."

"He's the guy to see?"

"The one and only. I've got his bio and all the other information back at the office. You can take a look at it when we get back. After reading everything there won't be anything you won't know about Chicago's number-one newspaper."

"Good work, Mad. I'll be writing a proposal for them to sponsor *Rock the Town*. The more I think about it, the more I think it's a perfect fit. I'm still working on getting a first guest, too. I want to knock their socks off."

"How's it going otherwise? With Stephanie and everything?"

"She still doesn't have a job. I'm paying for everything. She shouldn't be on the street too long after working at *Playboy*."

"Be careful, Flynn. You know your track record with women. You're way too nice. She might be taking advantage of you."

"Forget about it. Hey, do you want to go to the Eagles concert on the 22nd? They're playing at the Chicago Stadium. A great, big, wonderful rock concert. I've got tickets and All-Access Passes this time and we're going in a limo, of course."

"Will Stephanie and J.J. be there, too?"

"Of course. She's my girlfriend and he's my closest friend. Whaddaya think?"

"Good seats?"

"You know they are. I wouldn't be Flynn if I didn't have good seats to a rock concert."

"Okay, I'm in. Bring some joints. Nobody seems to smoke joints anymore. It's all coke. I still like pot."

"You're talking to the right guy. I want to hear The Eagles play 'Life in the Fast Lane'; so I can dream about that old way of life we used to have."

"Used to? I think you're still in the fast lane now."

"Maybe the middle veering toward fast."

"I'm sort of in the slow lane," added Madison.

"If you come to work as my Director you'll switch lanes fast."

"I'm game. You know I love the music as much as you do."

Flynn got reflective for a minute. "It's all about the music. Always was." He held up his thumb and index finger to make a circle. "And now I'm so very close to being right up there with music again."

"You'll make it, Flynn. I know you will." Madison made the same signal with her thumb and index finger.

★ ★ ★

A black stretch limo glided along on Michigan Avenue. It was a late October evening with the sun setting brilliantly over the buildings of downtown Chicago to the west. Inside the limo was the usual gang—Flynn, Stephanie, Don, Miles and J.J. Madison and Ernie were on the jump seats. The Bullet Snorter was being passed around. Don brought out another gram of coke in a snowseal and put it into a second Bullet. Flynn lit a joint and that went around, too. J.J. opened a bottle of champagne and handed out paper cups.

"I've never been in a limo this big with this many drugs," said Madison.

"Oh, this is old hat for us," bragged Stephanie.

"The Eagles are so hot right now. Just about every song is a hit or has been a hit," said Flynn.

Sipping champagne, J.J. spilled a little bit on his pants. He wiped it off and licked his fingers. While the fingers were wet, he took an extra snort out of the Bullet on one finger, then put that finger in his mouth and coated his teeth and gums with the coke. "Cocaine and champagne. Fit for kings."

"Save some of it for my Halloween party," said Ernie. "It's gonna be another blowout this year with a prize of a gram of coke for the best costume."

"I don't know what I'll go as this year, but I'll think of something special. But we're having fun right now. I'm totally in the moment. What could be better than a rock concert?" asked Flynn.

"Maybe sex. Maybe shopping," answered Stephanie.

"Shopping? Are you kidding? Compared to The Eagles. That's just not in the same ballpark." Flynn took the joint that was going around.

The limo pulled up to the Chicago Stadium. The limo chauffeur got out and came around to the back door to let them out. They practically ran and entered the VIP line. The stadium was a close-quartered, triple-tiered boxy white building with seating for 18,000. When they got inside, people were everywhere trying to find their seats and getting drinks and food. The gang moved down the aisle to just in front of the stage. There was a roped-off area for the VIP seating. The floor had been cleared and set up with chairs. They were sitting right where the Blackhawks and Bulls played their games on other nights.

The energy in the room was contagious. The stage was dark awaiting the entrance of The Eagles. The hypnotic smell of marijuana filled the air.

All at once, the lights came up and The Eagles came on stage. The crowd went wild. There they were in living color. Don Henley, Glen Frey, Joe Walsh, Don Felder and Timothy B. Schmit. Behind them was a display of lights that spelled out "The Long Run Tour." They strapped on their guitars and blasted into "Hotel California." The audience was with them all the way. The physicality of all that rock amplification was palpable. The whole stadium seemed to be pulsing. Flynn and company stood up and started rocking, blown away by the sheer magnitude of such a huge audience.

The band segued into "I Can't Tell You Why" followed by "One of These Nights," "Desperado," "Lyin' Eyes." Songs that covered the period from 1971-1979. They ended with "Life in the Fast Lane." Now the whole stadium was on their feet. Some people were dancing in the aisles. The band left the stage with a flourish. But the crowd wouldn't let them go. Moments later, they came back for the encore, "Take It Easy."

When The Eagles finally left the stage the celebrating continued and nobody headed for the exit. Flynn and J.J. led their little group to the backstage area. They all had their laminated All-Access Passes and showed them to the security guard at the door to the hallowed grounds.

When they got inside, they were surrounded by a mob scene. They followed the crowd to the overflowing hospitality suite. The Eagles were mingling with their management and fans. People were lining up for autographs. There was a bar setup in one corner. Flynn ended up there with Madison. J.J. and Stephanie had found the coke in a more private part of the room. Don, Miles and Ernie had lost their way and were missing somewhere backstage.

Flynn sipped his scotch. Madison had a beer. They clinked glasses.

"Let's try to meet Joe Walsh and Glen Frey. They're right over there. Come on," shouted Flynn.

Joe Walsh turned and Flynn was there. He stuck out his hand and they started talking. Madison did the same thing with Glen Frey. They were very friendly and accessible.

★ ★ ★

Hours later the gang left the stadium and went outside to the waiting limo. They had to find the right one because there were so many black stretch limos in the waiting zone. They finally saw their chauffeur waving to them and they rushed over and jumped in.

It was after 2 A.M. and Butch McGuire's was jammed. The bartender, Joco, was hustling drinks to the people sitting at the bar and the ones standing for lack of available barstools.

Flynn and Madison had managed to find two places near the door. J.J. and Stephanie were in the other room with Don doing the bathroom thing. Miles and Ernie were sitting at a table with a group of drunk and friendly Chicagoans.

Miles spoke up. "You can sit here. I'm wiped. I'm gonna go get a cab. The Eagles flattened me. I'm done."

A chorus of "goodbyes" came from the table. Ernie quickly chatted up a good-looking blonde.

Back at the bar, Madison asked Flynn, "What did Joe Walsh say?"

"We just talked about music. Theirs and every other rock group."

"Same with Frey. We just talked about music. It was so cool. Thanks for inviting me. We haven't been to a concert together since college."

"I remember those days well. It was all about the music. It still is."

"You've got to get your show on the air. I want it to be all about the music again."

"We're gonna do it, Mad. Together we can make it happen."

"I'm with you all the way. I'll even forgive you for rejecting me in college."

"We were friends. The best of friends."

"I know," Madison whispered.

★ ★ ★

Back in Flynn's apartment, Stephanie was vibrating on the couch. Flynn went to the stereo setup and turned the amplifier to FM radio. He dialed in WLUP. Queen's "Bohemian Rhapsody" poured through the speakers. He settled down on the couch while Stephanie snorted and he smoked a joint.

"Are you smoking another joint?"

"Look who's talking. Miss Snort Queen. You must have had a whole gram on your own."

"It's better than pot. I'm gonna have another snort right now." Stephanie laid out some coke on the table and used her gold snorter to sniff it up. "I'm letting you know now that I don't want to have sex tonight."

"Oh, that's cute. What's your problem?"

"I just don't feel like it."

"Well, maybe I do."

"Too bad. Why don't you just sleep out here." She went into the bedroom and came back with a blanket and a pillow.

"This is my house. You sleep out here."

"I don't want to listen to any of your sixties music. I've had enough music for one night."

"It's never enough. Besides, Queen is a 70s band."

"I know you, you'll sneak something in later."

"I'm listening to FM radio. They'll play what they play."

"You live in the past. I'm sick of it."

"I'm sick of you. Go ahead, take the bedroom. Be my guest. I'll listen to music all night if I want to."

Stephanie turned around and stormed into the bedroom. Flynn just stared after her.

★ ★ ★

Halloween had arrived in Chicago. The temperature had dropped into the thirties and the sky was clear with a crescent moon hanging to the north over Lake Michigan. Flynn and Stephanie sat in the back of a cab in their Halloween costumes. Flynn was Darth Vader and Stephanie was Princess Leia. The cab driver was laughing at them in their ridiculous getups.

"You must be going to some party dressed like that," he quipped.

Flynn lifted his Vader mask up on his head so he could talk. "Our friend Ernie has a big shindig every year," said Flynn.

"Any prize for the best costume?"

"If you're not a narc, I'll tell you."

"I'm not."

"A gram of cocaine."

The cab driver whistled. "Wow, that's worth getting dressed up for."

Stephanie spoke for the first time. "I hope it's me."

The cab turned off at Montrose on the upper North Side. The row of townhouses and apartment buildings were very upscale. Ernie's place was a white stucco four-story building with gargoyles at the front entrance.

Flynn paid the cabbie and they got out of the cab and entered the walkway to the building. The front door was propped open. They went in and headed straight for the elevator. When they reached the fourth floor the door opened and you could already hear the party spilling out. Few people were recognizable because of the masks they were all wearing. There was a priest and a nun couple. The priest was wearing a strap-on-dildo. There was a box that looked like a dice. Ladies in black tights and black tops with cat ears on their head. Flynn saw another Darth Vader and winced. Then he recognized Don Bennett in drag.

Flynn pulled up his mask to talk. "Hey, man, Don! Who are you supposed to be?"

"I'm Klinger from M*A*S*H. Turn on your radar, Flynn. You shoulda guessed who I was. I know who you guys are. Not very original."

Flynn pushed the mask farther up and just left it on his head. "Thanks, I needed that. I feel stupid enough."

Don gestured into the apartment. "Come on in and check out the bar."

Flynn and Stephanie left the hallway and followed Don into the apartment. It was huge, very modern with a built-in bar that wrapped around the living room. In front of each barstool on the bar top were little piles of cocaine shaped like mini-Mt. Everests. Next to each pile was an array of coke tools. Everything from a gold snorter, rolled-up bills and a little vacuum cleaner snorter called The Hoover. People were snorting lines right off the bar. Stephanie took one of the razor blades and shaved off a line from the mountain. She snorted using The Hoover.

"Look at this, Flynn. It's a little vacuum cleaner snorter. Isn't it cute?"

"Adorable."

Ernie was behind the bar dressed in jeans and a leather jacket.

"Hi, Flynn. Steph. *Star Wars* standouts, huh?"

"You're not even wearing a costume. What gives?" asked Flynn.

"I'm a gang member from the movie *The Warriors*."

"But you're only wearing jeans and a leather jacket."

"You saw the movie. I'm one of them. Help yourself to some coke. Try The Hoover. Your assistant Madison is doing the drinks. She's coming down the bar now."

Madison was wearing fishnet stockings, small jazz dance pants and a leopard-print vest. On her head were two floating bee things attached to a headband.

Flynn had never seen Madison looking so sexy. He couldn't take his eyes off the fishnet stockings and the long legs.

"You look fantastic, Mad. Great costume."

"Thanks. What do you guys want to drink?"

"The usual. Scotch. And wine for…"

Stephanie had taken over a barstool and was making lines and snorting them from the mountain in front of her.

"…Miss Coke Head 1979."

Madison turned to get the drinks and Flynn's eyes followed her all the way.

The party went on and on. On one side of the room sitting at a baby grand piano, a woman dressed as a rabbit was playing by ear. It was a sort of jazzy, blues sound and the whole room was digging it. Madison and Flynn sat nearby on a couch sharing a joint. Stephanie was still up at the bar with Don and Ernie. Miles and J.J. were just coming into the party, both without costumes.

Ernie clinked a knife on a champagne flute to quiet the room and make an announcement. "I've tallied the poll for the best costume and we have a winner. It's Klinger from M*A*S*H, aka Don Bennett. He needs this prize like he needs a hole in the head, but thus he has won." The room broke out in equal parts applause and laughter.

Don jumped off his barstool and took a bow. Ernie handed him the gram of coke in a snowseal. He held it out in his hands for everyone to see, then he opened it up and added the entire gram to one of the Mt. Everest piles. People started high-fiving each other and clapped joyously at Don's generosity.

Flynn was laughing hysterically on the other side of the room. "Don wins the gram. That's high-larious! Of all the costumes in this room. That's too much."

"It's perfect. It couldn't have gone to a better costume. Maybe Don should dress in drag more often. He can really pull it off," said Madison. She took a sip out of a bottle of Old Style.

Flynn took a pull on his bottle of beer and said, "Did I tell you how fantastic you look? I never knew you had such great legs."

"I've known you for how long?" she asked.

"Well, you don't exactly show up in fishnets at work. Maybe you should."

"A compliment coming from you is high praise."

"Any word yet about the *Tribune* meeting?"

"I'm working on getting you in to see the Promotion Director, Gavin Larson. I think I told you. He's the man. I'm gonna set you up to see him."

"I've got to have everything set by the end of the year. That gives me two months."

"Have you told Stephanie and J.J. about your show idea?"

"Yeah, they didn't seem to care." He looked over to the bar. "They seem pretty cozy at the bar."

"Flynn, they're always cozy. Haven't you noticed?"

"I don't want to think about it."

"Okay."

J.J. and Stephanie were next to each other on barstools in front of a pile of the cocaine Mt. Everest. He slipped his hand up her leg. She pressed his hand down. They were both very high and very cozy.

★ ★ ★

A second party at Flynn's pad was still going at 3 A.M. Don, J.J., Miles, Madison and Stephanie were half in and half out of the deck. It was the last gasp of tolerable weather before November came in and they all wanted to take advantage of it. It was about 32 degrees, pretty balmy for an end-of-October night. Flynn was passing a joint around and they all had bottles of Old Style. In the apartment, the sounds of The Band from the album *Music from Big Pink* poured from the big speakers. They all started to come in from the deck at the same time. The coke was on the coffee table and all the tools were set up. Everybody took their turn having a snort.

J.J. was with Flynn over by the record collection. He pulled out The Band's second album just titled *The Band*. They changed albums and got into a conversation about the group.

"Do you have Bob Dylan and the Band *The Basement Tapes*?" asked J.J.

"Are you kidding? Of course I do." He went through his alphabetized collection and found it. He handed it to J.J.

"Very cool, Flynn. Hardly anybody has this one." Just then the song "The Night They Drove Old Dixie Down" came on.

"Levon Helm is the only drummer who can really sing. This is the best song on the album," said Flynn. Then he reached into the collection and found another oldie, Bob Dylan and The Band *Before the Flood*. He handed it to J.J.

"Looks like we're going to be here all night listening to Bob Dylan and The Band." He turned over the album to read the songs. "This one has that great rendition of 'All Along the Watchtower.'"

Flynn kept looking through his albums. He brought out *Nashville Skyline*. "Besides all the great music Dylan did with The Band. I think this album was Dylan's best. So far."

"Keep those records coming. I'm gonna have myself a bump of coke," said J.J. He walked over to the couch and sat down by the gang doing lines.

Stephanie snorted, then asked J.J., "You and Flynn talking music again? Don't you ever tire of it?"

Flynn approached and heard her. "Never. It's always all about the music. Embellish that in your bird dog."

NOVEMBER

J.J. WAS SITTING IN HIS office at WQXA. The music from the built-in-the-wall speakers was coming straight from the control room. It was Neil Young's "Hey, Hey, My My (into the black)." Flynn came into the room just in time to hear the song before it segued to "Sugar Mountain."

"Hi. I had Skye play tunes from the new Neil Young album *Live Rust* just at the time I knew you were coming." He handed the album to Flynn.

"Hey, far-out. This was recorded at the Cow Palace in San Francisco last October. It's got songs from the *Rust Never Sleeps* tour. I saw that tour last year when it hit Chicago. End of '78. Neil Young's one of the Original Rock Gods."

"It won't be released until next month, but of course I got an advanced copy," said J.J.

"I read that they won't be doing another tour on that material, so having this album for my collection will be great. Can I borrow this?"

"Yeah, sure. Maybe I can get another one so you can keep it. The first couple of songs are just Neil, his guitar and harmonica. 'Hey, Hey' is on there, 'Sugar Mountain,;' 'The Needle and the Damage Done,' 'Cinnamon Girl.' It's fantastic. You're going to love it."

"Far-out! Hey, man, do you want to have lunch at The Palm?"

J.J. jokingly looked down at his desk calendar. "I think I can pencil you in."

"Very funny. Bring a coat. It's November in Chicago. You might freeze your ass off or you might blow away."

They left the office, went down in the elevator and walked outside. The wind picked up off the lake, making 35 degrees feel like 25. The day was also gray and cloudy. Not even a little sun peeking through. Flynn and J.J. pulled their coats tighter around them as they made their way north on Michigan Avenue. When they got to the corner where you turned east to The Palm, a blast of Lake Michigan air almost knocked them down. They trudged forward.

People were coming out of The Palm and politely held the door open for them. Inside, the nearly empty restaurant was warm and cozy. They had their pick of barstools and they chose ones farthest from the door. The Palm bartender, Frank, was ready for them already pouring the scotch and getting a bottle of Old Style.

He placed the drinks in front of them. "Well, if it isn't the Bobbsey Twins."

"Hey, man, Frank! What's the skinny?" asked Flynn.

"Can I have a glass of water, too? I must be dehydrated from that walk down Michigan," complained J.J.

They clinked glasses and sipped their drinks. J.J. blurted out, "I'm up for a job in Los Angeles. Program Director of KROC. It would be a big step up for me and I'd be back in California."

Flynn took off his jacket and put it on the stool next to him. "Oh, man, I guess I should be happy for you, but that would mean you'd leave Chicago. How could you? L.A.? Oh, my God. The 405 and the smog. You haven't lived there since San Diego after college. It's been a long time. It's going to be different from Chicago. Really different. Does this have anything to do with Tiffany?"

"God, no. We're divorced. You know that. She's back in San Diego."

"But California. I thought you had become a real Chicagoan. The music scene, everything."

"L.A. has a bigger music scene than here. It's where it's all happening."

"Every major group plays Chicago, J.J."

"Okay, okay. I know. But at least I won't be freezing my ass off for five months of the year."

"California...."

"Here I come...."

★ ★ ★

Flynn opened the door to his apartment. Stephanie was sitting on the couch, lines of coke on the coffee table and new clothes spread out around her with empty bags from Saks Fifth Avenue on the floor.

"I can't even say hello without a disaster in my living room," said Flynn.

Stephanie held up a cashmere sweater. "You like it? Perfect for November weather."

"Since when did you ever dress for the weather?"

She held up a pair of open-toed sandals. Flynn shrugged. Then she held up a pair of Frye boots.

Flynn clapped and found the words, "Far-out. Now we're talking."

"I went to the special Frye boot place on State. Knee-high leather boots. I love these. Aren't they cool?"

"Yeah, and I especially like the heel."

"It's low and comfortable. Only an inch. Good for walking. Whaddaya think?"

"I think I want a beer and some music." He took off his coat and headed for the kitchen. He yelled back over his shoulder, "You want a fire? The wind was picking up when I walked home. Take a look at that album I just put down on the chair. It's an unreleased Neil Young album I got from J.J."

She picked it up. "*Live Rust*. Oh, here's 'Cinnamon Girl,' one of my favorites. When did you see J.J.?"

"Just now. At The Palm."

"What did he say? What's going on?"

"Nothing much. Why the sudden interest?"

"Didn't he tell you about the L.A. job?"

"How'd you know about that?"

"Oh, I hear things."

"Well, I hope he doesn't get it 'cause that would mean he'd be leaving Chicago."

Stephanie leaned over the table and snorted up a couple of lines. "No fire. Let's go out."

"Okay. Let me think of a great place."

"Would you ever move to California, Flynn?"

"Who, me? Are you kidding? I get acute anxiety just thinking about it. Driving on the freeway is pure hell. And the crowds. Pure hell!"

"When did you ever go out there?"

"Once in college to visit J.J.'s family. And another time on a business trip. Actually, two other times on business for the show."

"I'd do anything to get back there."

"Steph, you're here. And you're looking for a job, right?"

"Haven't done much about it lately. Been getting those unemployment checks. They keep me in maximum wardrobe mode."

"Get a grip. You've got to go back to work. It doesn't work for me that I'm paying for everything. I don't mind the short-term, but long-term you gotta work."

"Flynn, have another line. Cool out. Let's party. We've got coke, grass and Neil Young. What could be better?"

"Yes, let's go out to dinner. Don't do any more coke. You won't be hungry. I'm gonna take you to an old-school Chicago steakhouse. Gene & Georgetti."

"Okay. But we have to take a cab. I'm going to wear my new boots and it might rain or snow. Don't want to ruin them."

"Sure. Sure. Couldn't have wet boots."

"And that coming from the guy who changes his cowboy boots every time they start to get wet."

"N.B.D."

★ ★ ★

Outside it had turned really cold for a November night. A miserable mixture of rain and snow was falling. The cab was slipping and sliding a bit as the streets absorbed the mess. They reached north Franklin and pulled up right in front of Gene & Georgetti. As they walked in, the maître d' greeted Flynn like he was an old friend.

"Hey, man, Stefan! Do you have a nice, quiet table for us?"

"Certainly, Mr. Flynn. Right over here."

Flynn and Stephanie were led through the linen-covered tables with candles as centerpieces. It was all very romantic and charming. Stefan pulled out the chair for Stephanie at a table by a roaring fire. "Thank you," she said as she took off her coat. Flynn slipped Stefan a bill and he went off.

"What a great table. I'm actually warm. I can't believe it. I'm always freezing. How do you know Stefan?" asked Stephanie.

"Oh, we go way back. This restaurant has been a Chicago classic for years. I've always brought my friends here," answered Flynn.

Stephanie held up a leg with her boots toward the fire. "It's these new boots. Flynn, you were right. You've got to dress for the weather."

"Yeah, all you need now is a sweater."

"They're not sexy."

"Whatever you say. Let's look at the menus."

Stephanie took in the appetizers and shouted, "Let's have oysters-on-the-half shell."

"What's that thing? No oysters in a month that has an 'R' in it."

"Then I'm going to have a petite filet mignon and au gratin potatoes."

"Same here. Only a regular filet. Medium rare. I'm so glad you want to eat. You're making my night."

A waiter came over and took their drink orders and they gave him their food order at the same time. Flynn handed Stephanie a huge wine list. She perused it and decided on a Cabernet Sauvignon.

"Good choice. Red wine with meat. I'll even have some."

After they devoured their sumptuous meal, Flynn led Stephanie to the bar for an after-dinner drink. The bar was packed but there was a little table for two in a corner. They grabbed it.

A cocktail waitress asked them what they wanted.

"I'll have a Courvoisier and coffee," said Flynn.

"Grand Marnier," chimed in Stephanie.

"What are we doing for Thanksgiving? My parents out in Wilmette are having a thing. It's sort of a tradition."

"Flynn, I'm going to California. Didn't I tell you? Going to see my parents."

"Bummer. No, you didn't tell me. Guess I'll have to be alone with my family."

"You'll get through it."

"You don't know my family."

When they left the restaurant, icy rain was coming at them sideways. There wasn't a cab in sight.

Stephanie started complaining, "How can the temperature drop so fast? It's ridiculous. I'm freezing."

"That's Chicago. N.B.D. One minute one thing, the next another. Keeps it interesting. Come on, it's not that bad. Why don't you wear a hat?"

"It ruins my hair."

"Oh, God forbid. A hair out of place versus warmth."

A cab finally appeared. Flynn flagged it down with a lift of his arm.

★ ★ ★

Flynn sat at his desk with his feet up after the taping of *The Brett Adams Show*. Madison knocked on his open door and he waved her in.

"Flynn, I've got the demographics for the *Tribune*. Their arts section skews 25-34. Just our audience for a rock show." She slapped down a thick packet of papers on his desk.

He started to glance through them. This is great. And you got that appointment for me with this Gavin Larson guy, right? We've got the main bird dog?"

"The day before Thanksgiving. 2 P.M."

"Far-out. I'm going to knock his socks off with my *Rock the Town* idea. They're going to jump to sponsor it."

Through his wall speakers, WLUP was broadcasting an hour of Warren Zevon. "Werewolves of London" caught Madison's attention.

"Warren Zevon. I love this song."

"Stick around. They're doing an hour of only him." The song ended and "Lawyers, Guns and Money" took its place.

Madison took a visitors' chair and sat there digging the music. She stayed through "Excitable Boy" until the disc jockey broke the momentum.

"I better get back to work," said Madison.

"One more thing. Do you want to go with me to my family Thanksgiving? Steph will be out of town. We can turn the radio up loud and drive up Lake Shore Drive and Sheridan Road. They live in Wilmette."

"Me? You're asking me?"

"Yeah, well, why not?"

Madison mulled it over. "Well, all right then. Thanks."

★ ★ ★

Stephanie and J.J. stood at the check-in desk at the Tremont Hotel. The lobby was plush with lots of overstuffed couches and comfy pillows. All the wood made it very upscale. The clerk looked at them strangely when he saw that they didn't have any luggage. J.J. took the key and they headed for the elevator.

They got off on the fourth floor and went to their room. When J.J. opened the door, they entered a huge suite. It was beautifully appointed with marble floors, glass-topped coffee table and end tables and a Victorian velvet couch atop an Oriental rug.

Stephanie gasped. "Wow, this is fantastic. When you say you're going to upgrade, you're not kidding. Let's look at the bedroom." She led the way to open double-doors. A king-sized canopy bed took up most of the space. She threw her coat on the bed and kicked off her shoes.

"Let's order some champagne from room service," said J.J. He went to the phone in the living room and ordered up champagne and added some caviar to the order.

Stephanie started laying out lines of cocaine on the coffee table. "This is so convenient that the table is glass. A built-in coke mirror." She brought out her little pouch of tools and took out the gold snorter and did her hit. One in each nostril. "You better have some before the champagne gets here. We don't want the waiter to see all this."

"He'd probably want some. But we'll be careful. Let me have a couple of toots before you put it away." J.J. took his turn at the table. Stephanie put everything back in the pouch and then into her purse.

"So, have you decided if you're going with me to California for Thanksgiving?"

"I'm coming. I told Flynn I was going home. I hope you get this job. I've got to tell him about us. Then if we move, it'll be easier."

"You've got to tell him after Thanksgiving, no matter what. The sooner, the better. He's my best friend, remember?"

"Oh, right. That's why you're two-timing him. Let's face it. It's not very cool. But it just sort of happened."

"I feel bad. But you're mine now, babe. For good or bad."

"I hope it's bad!"

"You would."

Room service knocked on the door.

★ ★ ★

Flynn stood outside in front of Tribune Tower on Michigan Avenue. The wind was whipping off the lake and he pulled his scarf tighter around his neck as he stared up at the historic, tall building. As he went through the front door, the wind followed him into an overheated lobby. A security guard manned a front desk check-in. Flynn gave him Gavin Larson's name and the guard followed up with a phone call. He handed him a pass and Flynn headed for the elevators.

He got off on the 11th floor and found a secretary sitting outside the newsroom of the *Chicago Tribune*. She told him where Gavin's office was located. And pointed through the double-doors. When he entered, he saw a huge, buzzing newsroom with desks scattered all around and taking up every available space. There were office spaces enclosed in glass in a semi-circle on one end of the room. He headed toward the one in the corner. On the door was stenciled "– Gavin Larson – Promotion Director." Flynn opened the door and went in.

"You must be Flynn," said Gavin. He was very young, with a mustache, full beard and longish brown hair.

Flynn extended a hand and they shook. "That's me."

"I'm Gavin Larson. Barry Sanders at the network called me about you. And not to mention your persistent assistant. Between the two of them I got hooked."

"That's a good start." He looked out at the bustling newsroom. "You've got quite a lively newsroom out there," Flynn said to break the ice.

"Yeah, the glass saves me from total chaos. So, you have an idea for the *Tribune*. What's it all about? Have a seat and tell me about it."

Flynn sat down in the only visitor chair. He brought out a handful of papers from his canvas briefcase and began. "I'm the director of *The Brett Adams Show* at the network and I've had a lot of experience behind the scenes of interviewing writers, psychotherapists, doctors, lawyers and Indian Chiefs."

Gavin laughed and it set the tone for the rest of the meeting.

"*Rock the Town* is a unique, never been done before in Chicago idea. The set would be like a recording studio with speakers and microphones the only adornment. Two chairs facing each other with accompanying microphones. It would be a one-on-one, face-to-face interview with a rock musician. He would have an acoustic guitar to play bits of rock from his latest tour or album. Other band members could stop by and jam a bit. If they're touring they could plug their show a bit. But it's not about that. It's an intimate conversation with a rock star."

Gavin asked, "Who are you thinking about as guests?"

"Any rock-and-roll group that happens to be in town at the time. For instance, I talked with Glen Frey of the Eagles and Tom Petty of Heartbreakers fame. They like the idea. They get a chance at a whole new audience of Chicago rockers."

"What's the timeslot, Flynn?"

"Barry at the network mentioned an hour on Saturday, ten to eleven. But I think it should be a half-hour show. Intense and exciting for thirty minutes. Your part would be complete sponsorship. Opening title credits—presented by the *Chicago Tribune*, two commercials and closing credits. And of course, there would be newspaper ads in your paper about the show and your sponsorship."

"What's this shindig going to cost?"

"That's for you and network boss Barry Sanders to decide. He's just waiting for your call and you can figure that out. I'm not a money guy. I just need a commitment that you'll do it."

"I like the idea. I like it a lot. It would be perfect for the *Tribune*. And it would reach that elusive 18-34 audience that everybody's after," said Gavin.

"Are you in?" asked Flynn.

"I don't make the final decision. I'll talk to Barry then talk to my higher-ups and we'll decide. I like it, though, Flynn, as you said, 'Chicago has nothing like this.' And I think it would be a great fit with the paper."

Flynn left the proposal on Gavin's desk and took off.

★ ★ ★

Flynn, high as a kite on pure adrenaline, walked back to his office. As he crossed the bridge over the Chicago River, he skipped a little bit as the wind pushed him forward.

Madison pounced on him in the hallway outside his office. "Well, how'd it go?"

"Fantastic. Gavin Larson was cool. He really liked the idea for the show and he's going to talk to Barry and his people to get the final okay."

"Far-fucking-out!"

"You're quoting me. I love it. I am totally psyched."

They went into his office and he began taking off the layers. Madison sat in his visitors' chair. "Am I still invited to your family Thanksgiving tomorrow? I can't wait to see where you come from. This is going to be a real trip."

"I didn't uninvite you, Mad. I'm renting a car. I'll pick you up at Union Station."

"Trains run all day at Union Station."

★ ★ ★

Flynn and Stephanie were arguing in his apartment. She was packing a suitcase and talking to him at the same time.

"I told you I was going to California for Thanksgiving."

"It's not that. It's what you're going to do when you get back. You have got to find a job. I'm draining my bank account here."

"I know what I'm going to do when I get back," barked Stephanie.

"Anything. Waitress, hostess. As long as you're bringing in money," Flynn shrieked back.

The buzzer rang from downstairs. Flynn picked up the house phone and listened. "Your car to the airport is here."

Stephanie zipped up her suitcase and gave Flynn a peck on the cheek. "See you next week."

"Yeah, right."

She was out the door in a flash. Went down in the elevator to the waiting doorman opening the front door. Outside, a black town car was waiting. She got in and there was J.J. sitting in the back seat.

★ ★ ★

Madison and Flynn moved north on Lake Shore Drive in a rental car. It was a rare day with sun streaming through the windshield. The lake to their right was reflecting the sun in shimmering waves. They made their way down the drive to Sheridan Road. Destination, the suburb Wilmette.

"I've got some exciting news of my own," said Madison.

"Well, out with it," laughed Flynn.

"I'm moving downtown. I found a studio apartment in a brownstone at 20 Lake Shore Drive. It's on the third floor of a converted brownstone. When you walk in there are two huge windows facing the lake. It's small but cozy. Hardwood floors, a small kitchenette, bathroom of course. It's basically one big room, but there's all kinds of little nooks."

"Far-out!"

"I think so, too. Can't wait for you to see it. I'm moving in December 1st."

"Need any help?"

"I've got movers. I'm doing everything first class for my first Chicago apartment."

Flynn pulled off the road and stopped in front of a house right on the lake. It was a rambling colonial set on two acres.

Madison gasped when she saw the place. "Oh, my God. Palatial, exquisite. No wonder you have such good taste."

They got out of the car and before they reached the front door, Flynn's mother, Terri, came out holding a martini in her hand.

"Welcome to the party. So glad you could make it. Come in. Come in. Have a drink," said Terri.

Before they even took their coats off, Terri was taking them to the bar in the living room. Tom, Flynn's father, was playing bartender. Flynn asked for a scotch. Madison saw a bottle of red wine and went with that. On the couch were Flynn's twin sisters, Dee and Dawn. Flynn introduced everyone to Madison. Terri finally took their coats.

"Flynn's never brought a girl home before," said Dee. "Not that I can remember."

"You're kidding me," said Madison. She suddenly felt very special.

"How do you fit in?" asked Dawn.

"N. B. D., guys. This is my assistant director on *The Brett Adams Show*. She's my right-arm person extraordinaire. Former college friend, too." Flynn sipped his father's Johnnie Walker Black Label scotch.

"I never watch the show. I'm in my office during the day. Lawyers keep regular daytime hours, you know," chimed in Tom as he sipped his drink of the same scotch Flynn was drinking.

Flynn's mother was on her second martini. "I watch it every day. I love all those doctors who come on. You always learn something."

"I hate shrinks," Flynn complained. "That's the thing I'm trying to get away from. I told you I have a surprise and it's a new show that I'm going to host called *Rock the Town*. I'm not going to direct anymore if the show gets picked up. Madison will produce and direct. I'll probably end up with an Executive Producer credit."

Tom jumped in, "You can't leave a steady job for something so risky. That's crazy. What if it fails?"

"Well, I've almost got the *Chicago Tribune* for a sponsor."

"That changes the whole picture. The *Tribune*. Did you know they own WGN? 'World's Greatest Newspaper' is what it stands for. They're a dynasty. They've got Jack Brickhouse. Oh, Flynn. Sorry I doubted you for a minute. You must be on to something if the *Tribune* is involved," Tom said as he took a gulp of scotch.

"Nobody's doing anything like this show in Chicago. Dad, it's going to be a winner. I can feel it."

Madison placed her wine glass down on the table and spoke up in support of Flynn. "You guys don't get it. *Rock the Town* is all about the Chicago music scene with a one-on-one interview of a rock musician every week. The guest will share memories, performances, playing a little music. It'll be so perfect. And Flynn will be in heaven."

Flynn's mom put down her martini and lit a cigarette. "I can see why you'd want to do it. Ever since college you've been obsessed with all that music."

"Obsessed. Shrink word. But thanks, Mom, at least you sort of get it," said Flynn.

Tom turned his attention to the TV set that was on in the background. The NFL Thanksgiving Day game was on. Chicago Bears vs. Detroit Lions. The Lions just scored a touchdown. "The Bears are losing. This is terrible. Turn up the sound, Flynn."

The whole room watched the game and no one spoke for a while. Terri went into the kitchen to check on the turkey.

"Wait," burst out Madison. "I want to ask the question of the ages: What is Flynn's real name? The whole staff told me to find out. Especially Brett, who's known him the longest."

Terri came back in and answered, "We're sworn to secrecy. He changed his name legally so we just sort of forgot what the old ones were."

Dee said, "Some people think it's 'cause of the movie star Errol Flynn, but it's nothing like that. Too typical."

"Come on," pleaded Madison. "Somebody tell me."

"Embellish this in your bird dog, Mad. They're not going to tell. Maybe I'll tell you if the new show's a go and we'll have something to celebrate."

"I'm going to hold you to that."

Detroit scored another touchdown as Terri announced, "The buffet is ready. We can bring our plates in here so we won't miss the game."

Madison and Flynn followed the sisters into the kitchen to get their plates. There was an array of turkey, stuffing, mashed potatoes, gravy, green bean casserole, rolls and cranberry sauce. They all started loading their plates.

Madison plopped a big mound of mashed potatoes on her plate. "I didn't get the story on your name. The gang at the studio will be really disappointed."

"My family can be loyal when they need to be. Someday, someday. Let's eat and watch football."

"One wouldn't be the same without the other," added Madison.

★ ★ ★

It was the Saturday night of the long Thanksgiving weekend. Flynn walked from his apartment building over to Division Street in a snow flurry with a temperature in the low 30s. Amazingly there was no wind and it wasn't that cold. He passed Butch's on his way to Mother's.

He went in the front door and entered a long room with bar on one side, tables on the other. The back room was like a cavern and housed the bands that played live music on Friday and Saturday nights. Flynn took a quick peek in there, but nobody was setting up yet. So, he grabbed a stool at the bar. The bartender was right on it.

"Hey, Flynn. How's it going?"

"Hey, man, Zack! You still work here. That's cool. I haven't been here in a while. I don't know why. Mother's is on the Street of Dreams. You're included in Chicago's famous street. At least it's famous to me."

"You want scotch, right? The best. Straight up or one ice cube? I remember the important stuff," said Zack.

"Let's do straight up. The best tastes great that way."

Zack turned around to get his drink. A couple of girls came in and took stools next to Flynn.

One gorgeous blonde introduced herself to Flynn. "I'm Daphne. I'm here with my friends to see The BZZZZ. They're playing here tonight."

"I'm here for the same reason. I've never heard The BZZZZ."

"They're fantastic. We follow them around. This is Jan and Barbara, by the way. I guess some people would call us groupies, but we don't care. We love The BZZZZ. The guitar player, Michael Tofoya, is just the coolest."

"You ladies want a drink? Zack? Get these ladies what they want and put it on my tab," said Flynn.

"Thanks," a chorus of voices came from the girls.

They were drinking and talking when Flynn felt somebody right up behind him. He looked and it was Don. Then he saw Miles and Skye coming up to the bar.

"Unreal. You guys chose Mother's on the same night I did," ventured Flynn.

"Flynn, my man, you must have gotten the memo about The BZZZZ," said Miles. "We can't seem to get away from you even when J.J. is out of town."

Don jumped in, "I'm going to the bathroom. Anybody coming?"

"Don, you know I don't do bathrooms. You should know that by now," Flynn lifted up his drink and took it down in one slug. "I'm drinking here."

The bar music system had WLUP on and when Pat Benatar ended "Heartbreaker." The music segued to Foreigner's "Juke Box Hero." When the music stopped and the station went to commercial, the nighttime disc jockey, Jed The Fish, identified the song and the station.

Miles freaked out at the mention of the call letters and flagged down Zack. "Why aren't you playing WQXA? I can never get away from the Loop. Who decides what station you play?"

Zack shrugged. "The manager of Mother's. He always sets the dial to the Loop. Not much I can do about it."

"But our radio playlist is better. We play more hits," said Miles. "Can't you just turn the dial a little?"

"No can do. I'm not supposed to touch it. Sorry, bud." Zack went off down the bar to new customers.

By ten o'clock, Flynn, the girls, Miles, Don and Skye were happily buzzed. They heard a guitar tuning up from the other room and realized it was time for the entertainment to begin. Flynn settled with Zack and then followed the gang into the cavern.

The room was illuminated by soft track lighting. There were tables placed around in no particular order. Just far away enough from the stage to have a separation from the crowd to the musicians. The drummer was warming up. The BZZZZ also had a bass player, lead and rhythm guitars and frontman, who was testing the microphone.

Flynn and company took the table closest to the stage. The BZZZZ started playing one of their original tunes. They were a Chicago-based band who played more originals than covers and they were hot.

Daphne got up to go to the bathroom with Don. Miles went to get more drinks. Flynn was just mesmerized by the music of The BZZZZ. When all were seated again, they totally absorbed the first set of the heavy rock music. It was a good two hours before they took a break.

The guitarist and singer Michael Tofoya noticed Daphne, Jan and Barbara at the front table and came over. He was introduced to everybody and then he sat down next to Flynn and they started talking. Before long, the rest of the band trotted over and they had a table of BZZZZ. Flynn bought them all a round of drinks. They spent their entire break talking at the main table. Then it was time for a second set and they left the table to go play their brand of rock-and-roll.

Mother's was a five A.M. bar on Saturday nights. So, Flynn was still there at 4 A.M. with the girls and Miles. Skye and Don had left around two. The diehards were still there. By this time, the band was finished for the night and Michael and the drummer were still hanging out.

"You know you're on the Street of Dreams, don't you?" asked Flynn.

"I've heard that now and then. We play Mother's a lot. Why do you call it that?" asked Michael.

"Because Chicago is a city where you can go after your dreams. And this street with all its bars and night life symbolizes that. It's really just about the dreaming, honestly. What would we do without our dreams?" Flynn was verging on pontificating.

"No, I get it. Any aspiring band would. You make it in the clubs first. Then hopefully go on to greater heights," said Michael. "So, Flynn, you were talking about a show called *Rock the Town*. Chicago needs that. Tell me more about it." Flynn and Michael talked until the bar closed. Outside the bar, it was just starting to show a little bit of light from the sun coming up. They said goodbye. And the girls were going somewhere else with what was left of The BZZZZ.

Flynn walked down Division Street and headed for his apartment.

★ ★ ★

On Monday, the set of *The Brett Adams Show* was jumping. Everyone had had a long holiday weekend and felt refreshed and ready to start the busy season. They were also excited because Francis Ford Coppola was there with Robert Duvall to promote the official opening of his movie *Apocalypse Now*. Flynn was out on the floor talking to the two cameramen, Jeremy and Isaac. They were cracking jokes and talking about their Thanksgivings.

"Get over it, you guys. We've got a show to do," said Flynn.

"Flynn, you're no fun. You're just a slave driver," Jeremy bellowed.

On the stage, Brett was talking to Francis and Robert. He got them seated on either side of him in the three big chairs set up there for that purpose. Flynn went back into the booth and donned his headset. Madison came in seconds later.

"Cue the opening music," instructed Flynn. "Zeke, you ready with the countdown?"

"Ready and able." He started doing his thing.

Flynn barked directions to camera one. "Jeremy, get a closeup of Brett. Camera two, Isaac, zoom in on all three of them."

Brett introduced the director and actor. Footage from *Apocalypse Now* was spooling up in the booth. Flynn told the tape guy to roll and scenes from the movie came up on the monitor screens. Robert Duvall's character was standing on the edge of the water after bombs had been dropped in a horrible attack. He delivered the line: "I love the smell of napalm in the morning."

★ ★ ★

Flynn left the building as a freezing mix of sleet and snow rained down on the city. He bundled the coat and scarf around him as he crossed over the bridge to the Wrigley Building. The wind whipped around his legs as he struggled with the entrance door. Inside the comforting sight of wood and leather made it seem like a strange sort of oasis. J.J. was waiting for him at the bar already with an Old Style. Flynn slapped him on the back in a friendly greeting.

"Hey, man, J.J! How was California?"

J.J. was in a weird mood and Flynn noticed.

"You okay?"

"Flynn, I have things to tell you. First of all, I got a job as Program Director of the famous KROC in Los Angeles. I'm giving my notice and moving back to L.A."

"Wow. Fantastic. It's good and bad. You'll have a great job, but you won't be here anymore. Chicago won't be the same without you. But the music scene is great out there. Good for you!"

"Stephanie is moving out there with me."

You could have heard a pin drop the silence was so all pervasive. Finally, Flynn found his voice. "What are you talking about? She's my girlfriend."

"We've been hooking up. For a while now. I was going to tell you, but…."

"But what? When were you going to tell me? When was she going to tell me?"

"I'm sorry, Flynn. It just happened."

"We've been friends since college. You've always been my one true friend. Through all the thick and thin. How could you?"

"I said I'm sorry."

"I have one thing to say to you and then I never want to see you again. Fuck you, J.J. Fuck you!" He grabbed his jacket and raced out of the bar.

★ ★ ★

The cab pulled up in front of Flynn's apartment building. He raced for the front door, where Steve was already opening it for him. He barely greeted him as he headed for the elevator. When he got to his apartment door, he had trouble getting his keys out.

He flung himself into the apartment and came upon Stephanie doing lines on the coffee table. He approached the table and messed up the lines.

"Hey, what are you doing?" asked Stephanie.

"When were you going to tell me about you and J.J.? I just left him at the Wrigley Bar after telling him to fuck off," yelled Flynn.

"Tonight. I was going to tell you tonight."

"You're a whore. The worst kind. A coke-whore. How long has this been going on?"

"Not too long. And I'm not a coke whore. I just happen to like coke."

"You slept with my best friend. How could you do this? Of all the people it had to be him. Not that it would be okay with anybody, but J.J.? He's been my best friend since college. We've been super tight in Chicago. What kind of a person are you?"

"I'm sorry. I was going to tell you myself."

"Get out. Pack up your stuff and go to your lover. You're out of here. And have a nice time in your beloved California. I'll leave you with the same words I left J.J. Fuck you!"

"Flynn, I…."

"Get out! Get out!"

Stephanie finished the coke before she started packing.

★ ★ ★

Later, alone in the apartment, Flynn smoked a joint and drank a beer. He got up from the couch, went to the stereo system and rifled through his albums. He pulled out an old Byrds album with the song "Feel A Whole Lot Better" on it. He listened for a while and when the lyrics got to this part he sang along with it:

"…after what you did you can't stay on. And I'll probably feel a whole lot better when you're gone…."

He sat back down and let the song play out. It was cold enough for a fire. And he set about starting one. It was going to be a long night.

DECEMBER

FLYNN WAS IN HIS OFFICE after the taping of Brett's show. He had his feet up on the desk and was reading the *Chicago Tribune*. Madison came in and sat down in one of his visitor's chairs.

"You okay? You seemed sort of off during the taping. Even if it was another shrink. You usually get over it."

"Let's have a late lunch at Gio's." He grabbed his coat, scarf and hat and started to put them on.

"Flynn, hang in. Give me some time to get together. I'll get my coat and meet you at the elevator."

★ ★ ★

When they opened the front door of the office building the wind smacked them right in the face. There was a sleety mix of snow and ice and the temperature with the wind chill was in the teens. They bowed their heads and walked toward the restaurant.

The maître d' greeted Flynn and took them to a table near the fireplace. The fire was roaring and they unbundled and rubbed their hands in front of it. Madison opened her menu.

"So, what gives?" she asked.

"Stephanie and J.J. have been sneaking around behind my back. An affair right in front of my face. Stephanie hurts enough. But J.J.? I always called him my one true friend. What a joke. And to make matters worse they're moving to California together. J.J. got a job out there with KROC."

"Wow. I didn't see that one coming. Although I did see them cozying up at some of the concerts and bars. This is terrible. I'm really sorry. What a bunch of jerks."

"That's a nice word for what they are. You know, I think I saw it, too. But I didn't think it could be true. I thought I was really in love this time. That's how into it I was."

"She was always high-maintenance, Flynn. The trophy-wife type you always pick. At least the ones I've met."

"So, who should I pick? Someone like you who I have everything in common with and who shares my passion for music?"

Madison blushed. "Yeah, maybe. How bad could that be?"

"Okay, I'll be depressed until December 8th, when The Who are coming to town on their *Who Are You Tour*. You want to go? No more J.J. and his limos, but I've already talked to Miles and he's got a bunch of tickets and All-Access Passes. I'm picking up the limo. We don't have to change just because that asshole J.J. and Miss Coke Head stabbed me in the back."

The waiter came over to take their drink orders. Scotch for Flynn, red wine for Madison. She looked out the window and saw that the snow was picking up. She shivered a bit and moved her chair closer to the fire.

"You cold? It's only in the teens. Balmy for Chicago."

Madison changed the subject quickly. "So, what happened with the *Chicago Tribune*? Tell me again."

"I met with the promotion guy Gavin Larson. He was really cool and seemed to dig the idea. But he's got all these layers of decision makers to approve it before he commits. I don't expect to hear for a while. But I do have our network boss, his highness Barry Sanders, working in my favor behind the scenes."

"I do so hope it flies. I'm getting like you. Tired of the shrinks and the same old guests. And a chance to be the director. I'm crossing my fingers."

Their drinks arrived. Flynn held up his glass for a toast. "Let's drink to *Rock the Town*. May it be born and have a long life."

"I'll drink to that and to you finding that certain someone." Madison blushed again. This time Flynn noticed.

★ ★ ★

A long black limo moved south on Michigan Avenue toward the International Amphitheater on the city's south side. Inside a party was taking place. There was Flynn, Madison, Miles, Don, Ernie and Skye drinking champagne from paper cups. Don had his Bullet Snorter and was passing it around. When it came to Madison, she was a bit confused.

"How do you do this?" she asked Don.

"Turn that little plastic knob on the side and turn it upside down. The coke will go into the top. Then you just stick it up to your nose and snort."

Madison took a big snort. "It worked. Wow. Instant buzz. No wonder coke is so popular." She handed the tool to Flynn.

"It's great. As long as you don't do too much of it."

Don jumped in. "It's never too much."

"This is the first Who tour without Keith Moon. Kenney Jones will be on drums," said Flynn.

Miles jumped in. "As long as Pete Townshend is doing his jumping around that's good for me. There's nothing like the way he plays the guitar."

"I've been seeing The Who for years. I'll really miss Keith. Some say he was the best rock drummer of them all," continued Flynn. He lit up a joint and passed it around. Only Madison and Miles took hits. Don's Bullet Snorter came around again, but this time Madison and Flynn declined.

"I'm a one-hit snorter," said Madison. "Really not my drug. But I'm an old hippie when it comes to pot."

Miles started passing the laminated All-Access Passes around the back seat. Everyone took one and placed it around their neck.

A little later, the limo pulled up right in front of the Amphitheater. They got out and rushed into the lobby to get out of the cold. Their seats were in the VIP section right in front. They made their way down the aisle. On either side of them chairs were set up to fill up the entire floor space. They'd timed it out so they got there when the opening act was finished and the stage was dark.

Madison grabbed Flynn's hand. "I'm so excited. I've never seen The Who."

Flynn, surprised by the hand, squeezed back. "Get ready to rock, Mad."

The audience vibe was filling the stadium. Some people were chanting, "Who. Who." Others were clapping. Suddenly the lights came on and started sweeping through the Amphitheater.

From stage right, out came The Who: Roger Daltry, Pete Townshend, John Entwistle and the new drummer, Kenney Jones. They plugged in their instruments and moved directly into the song "My Generation." Flynn and company were almost blown out of their seats from the energy and sound. They played all their hits including "Behind Blue Eyes," "Pinball Wizard," "I Can See for Miles." They played for ninety minutes and covered several other songs from their rock opera *Tommy*.

When they quickly left the stage, the audience was on its feet clapping, shouting and stomping their feet for more. Things calmed down for a minute and then The Who raced back out on stage. For an encore they played "Won't Get Fooled Again" to the audience's enthusiastic approval.

Everybody crowded the aisle. Flynn and Madison headed toward the entrance to the backstage area. Behind them were Miles, Don and Skye. They all displayed their badge necklaces and were let into the inner sanctum. They walked down the mobbed hallway to the hospitality suite. They push their way into the room. The Who were signing autographs and shaking hands. Flynn eyed Pete Townshend and tried to get close enough to talk to him. He was surrounded by fans and groupies and wasn't digging it. Flynn reached him and introduced himself. They started to have a conversation. Madison and Miles went to the bar. Don went to the snorting crowd. And Skye tried to chat up Roger Daltry.

Later, on their way back in the limo Flynn was high on adrenaline. "I got to talk to Pete Townshend. He was really cool. And he said he would be on my show if the band was in town at the same time."

Miles inquired, "What's this new show? You haven't told me the whole thing."

"It's called *Rock the Town*. I would be hosting it. A different rock star every week. A one-on-one interview. The set's a recording studio. We'd share memories, performances. They'd have an acoustic guitar or electric guitar, sometimes other band members would show up. Just a show about rock-and-roll. The *Chicago Tribune* is my target sponsor. I've already met with them. The first guest is key. I need someone by the end of the year."

"Flynn, that is terrific. I hope it works out. Then you wouldn't be doing Brett's show anymore?" asked Miles.

"No. This would be my bird dog. And Madison here is going to produce and direct. I'd also have an Executive Producer and Creator credit."

Madison shared Flynn's excitement. "I'm ready to move up from Assistant Director. The music is part of me. I'm psyched."

Skye said, "Boy, would J.J. be jealous."

"Let's not bring him into it, okay?" said Flynn.

"Cool," said Don. "Very cool." He passed the coke tool around the limo and the whole gang took a hit each.

Flynn and Madison were the last two left in the limo. The chauffeur asked them for the address. Flynn looked at Madison, "You want to come up to my place?"

"Isn't it a little soon after you-know-who?" Madison answered.

"It's just a platonic thing. We'll listen to Crosby, Stills & Nash. Have a joint. Kick back."

"Okay."

They entered Flynn's apartment and the first thing Madison noticed was his record collection. She started looking through it and making wow noises. Flynn sorted through his kindling basket, pulling out the wood. He placed it on the grate with rolled-up newspaper underneath. He struck a match to the paper and it lit instantly. He waited for a while till the kindling took before putting a big log on the grate.

Madison continued looking through the album collection. She held one up. "Oh, here's the Crosby, Stills & Nash album."

"Yeah, the one with them on the couch. I've told you that story."

"That's the kind of story that would be great on *Rock the Town*."

By now they had a roaring fire going. Flynn got Madison a glass of red wine and a beer for himself. They sat down together on the couch and stared at the mesmerizing flames. Flynn lit a joint and passed it to Madison.

"It's nice to have company. I haven't really had anyone up here since I kicked Stephanie out," said Flynn.

Madison sipped her wine and toked on the joint. "Good move, by the way. She was trouble."

"With a capital 'T.'"

"You sure you're all right with it?"

"As the song says, 'I'll probably feel a whole lot better when you're gone.'"

"The Byrds?"

"Gene Clark wrote it."

"Nobody but you would know that."

"You know your music. That's why I want you on the show."

"Flynn, maybe this isn't the right time to bring it up, but I've had a crush on you since college."

"And you waited this long to tell me."

"You always had a girlfriend. Always with someone. I didn't think I had a chance."

"Wow. I'll have to think this over a bit."

"I know, it's too soon for another relationship, but I thought I'd finally tell you."

"All these years working together. I guess I'm pretty dense."

"I never let on. It was my little secret."

Flynn got up and placed the "Couch Album" on the turntable. The harmonies of CSN blared through his huge speakers.

Madison covered herself with a couch throw blanket. "Any news from the *Tribune*?"

"Not lately."

"You have a first guest yet?"

"I've talked to a lot of musicians about the show and left it up to them. If they want to do it, they know where to find me."

"I know you'll get a call. Who wouldn't want the exposure?"

"Some do. Some don't. Neil Young, for instance, would never do it. But Tom Petty was stoked and he's gonna be in Chicago in January. If everything goes, the first show is January 8th, 1980. Can you believe it. The 70s will be over. A whole new decade. Wonder what it will be like?"

"Brett's going to be pretty mad if we leave the show at the same time."

"I've already talked to him about it. He knows. He wishes us well because he knows how passionate I am about the new show."

"I'll be in the booth. You on the set. So very, very cool."

Flynn got up and put another log on the fire. "Far-out. *Rock the Town* is heading down the highway."

They smoked their joint and sipped their drinks. And they talked and talked until four in the morning. When Madison said she had to go home, Flynn rang down to the doorman, Billy, and asked him to get her a cab. Then he got her coat, helped her into it and walked her out the door to the elevator.

★ ★ ★

Flynn got out of a cab in front of Madison's brownstone at 20 Lake Shore Drive. He asked the driver to wait and he headed to the front door. He started the long ascent up to her third-floor walk-up. The stairs were deeply carpeted and everything was immaculate as he passed the first couple of apartments. He was out of breath when he reached her door and knocked. She opened the door with a flourish.

"Far-out!" Flynn had walked across the room to look at the view of The lake from her huge windows.

"It's cool, isn't it. As long as you like walking uphill to get here."

"It's worth it for this view. You look ready for a football game."

Madison was wearing huge boots that looked like an astronaut's, a big sweater and jeans. The jeans were tucked into the boots.

"What are those boots?" he asked.

"They're Moon Boots. Completely waterproof and lined with some super-warm material that can withstand temperatures in the teens and lower. You can walk through the slush puddles on the corners without getting wet. And wait till you see the coat." Madison opened the closet door and pulled out a down, full-length coat. Flynn helped her into it.

"It looks like a sleeping bag."

"It has the warmth of a sleeping bag." Madison looked at Flynn carefully. "I've never seen you in any coat but your ski jacket." His coat was knee-length, heavy duty mountain-climber quilted and had a hood with fur around it.

"This is my Soldier Field jacket. They sell them at L.L. Bean. I even have cowboy boots on that are a half-size too big so I can wear thermal socks."

"We are ready." Madison topped off the outfit with a warm wool hat.

Flynn got a kick out of her super-prepared outfit. "Today is December 16, 1979, and we're going to Soldier Field, kick-off temperature estimated at 28 degrees, by the way, and we're gonna see the Bears play the St. Louis Cardinals. And I've got a woman who is actually dressed for it. Madison, you've made my day even before football."

The last thing Madison picked up were her super-duper mittens. Flynn laughed as he looked around her studio apartment with approval. Then he opened the door and they went down to get the cab.

Soldier Field was crowded despite the cold temperature. Chicago Bears fans were fanatics no matter what the weather. Flynn and Madison made their way up the aisle to the tenth row just above mid-field. Flynn had brought a stadium blanket with him and he opened it across two seats.

"Let's get some beers. Or would you rather have coffee or something warm?" Flynn asked.

"No, beers, please. I'm warm as toast in this outfit."

Flynn flagged down a walking vendor who was selling Bud in plastic cups. He got two and they were all set for the kick-off.

By the third quarter, they'd had several beers. The Bears were winning and Walter Payton had just scored one of several touchdowns for the day.

"Don't they call him 'Sweetness'? Walter Payton? He looks pretty tough down there," said Madison.

"They do. He's one of the best Running Backs in the league."

Madison and Flynn toughed it out and stayed for the whole game along with the 42,000 and some loyal Chicago Bears fans. The Bears won the game 42 to 6 over the St. Louis Cardinals.

★ ★ ★

It was Monday morning on *The Brett Adams Show*. The audience was seated and everything was ready for the show to start. Flynn and Madison were in the booth with headsets on.

Flynn spoke to the board tech, "Cue the opening music."

On the monitor, Brett was in a close up as he introduced the doctor of the day. In the booth, Madison and Flynn shared a moment, trying not to laugh.

After the taping, Flynn was in his office when Brett walked in. "Hey, Flynn, good news. The head of the network wants to see you. I already met with him because he wanted to know all about you and how good you've been for my show."

"Far-out! Thanks for all your help. I'll never forget how you've tried to help me even though it will affect your show."

"Not to worry. We'll find another director, no problem. Of course, it won't be you. But I think you've had enough of shrinks to last a lifetime."

Flynn gave him a thumbs-up. Brett shook his hand and he left.

★ ★ ★

Flynn got off the elevator on the 20th floor. The executive office floor for the network. He wound his way down the deeply carpeted hall to the end corner office. Outside his office, protecting his fortress, was his smartly dressed secretary.

"Flynn, to see his highness," he announced.

The secretary giggled as she picked up an inner office phone. "Mr. Sanders, Flynn is here to see you. Okay." She hung up the phone. "You can go in."

Flynn entered the now familiar office with the fantastic view of Wacker Drive and the Chicago River.

They shook hands. Flynn spoke first, "How are you, Barry?"

"I'm terrific. And I have fantastic news for you. The *Chicago Tribune* is in. They've decided to sponsor *Rock the Town*. We've got a half-hour timeslot for you on Saturday nights at 10 P.M. You get six months to make it work. And I need to approve your first guest or guests. What rock guy and his band members, to be more specific."

"Far-out! That's the best news I could ever hear. I should know who the guest will be very soon now."

"You can use Studio C. Set up your recording studio set, hire a crew. This is all up to you now, Flynn."

"Thanks so much."

"No thanks necessary. This is business. It's all about the ratings and this show has winner written all over it."

"I can bring my own producer and director, too?"

"The whole nine yards."

★ ★ ★

Flynn was in his apartment sitting on the couch. Outside the mighty Chicago wind was roaring and rattling the balcony doors. He looked out and saw some snow flurries coming down. He lit a fire with the waiting paper and kindling. Then he thumbed through his huge record collection and pulled out the Van Morrison album *Moondance*. He got a beer from the refrigerator and sat back down and lit up a joint. On the coffee table, he noticed a rolled-up dollar bill. The last vestige of Stephanie's living there. He picked it up and reflected on it as Van broke through the speakers. He took a moment to reflect and grieve.

★ ★ ★

Flynn, Madison, Miles and Don were sharing a booth at the Park West music venue. They were waiting for Warren Zevon to come on. The small club was packed to the hilt. Up on the stage, the roadies and the crew were setting up. Don touched Miles on the hand and they got up to go to the bathroom.

"Why is blow always done in bathrooms?" asked Madison.

"'Cause you can't exactly lay out lines at the table," answered Flynn.

"What about that Bullet thing?"

"I guess that's only for the limos. Coke's a private drug. It's not like lighting up a joint and passing it around. Now that Stephanie is gone I haven't had much access to it. Except, as I said, in the limos."

"How are you doing with that whole mess with her and J.J.?"

"The betrayal hurts. But mostly because of J.J. That's the worst part of it. I'll listen to some sad music for a while and then let it go. Little by little."

Don and Miles came back from the bathroom already talking up a storm and pretty high. Don's jaw was moving back and forth and he was biting his lip. They sat down and took up their drinks.

Flynn jumped in, "I've been waiting to tell you all my big news. I wanted to pick the right time and this seems to be it. My television show idea for *Rock the Town* has been picked up by the network. I've got a timeslot. Saturday nights at 10 P.M. I'm going to be doing a weekly show with rock musicians and the Chicago rock music scene. The *Chicago Tribune* will be our sponsor."

Madison practically screamed. "Far-fucking-out!"

"That's my line," quipped Flynn.

Miles said, "Flynn, congratulations. This is big. Big for Chicago television. And it won't hurt radio either. Maybe you can run some ads with us promoting the show."

"We'll see, Miles. The sky is the limit. It's going to be great."

"Let's get another round of drinks," Miles said. "On me." He tried to flag down a waiter.

Madison lost control for a minute and kissed Flynn. She was beyond excited. The kiss took him by surprise, but he liked it.

"I've never seen Warren Zevon live. He's all over our playlist at the station. Oh, by the way, I hired a new Program Director to replace J.J. His name is Bud Stanton. He's coming over from WXRT. He knows a lot about album-oriented rock, so I'm glad to have him on the team," said Miles.

"Ever hear from J.J.?" Flynn asked.

"Out of sight. Out of mind. Hardly miss him. I think our DJs miss him, but you can always find a Program Director for a major market radio station. They're practically beating down the door," Miles added.

Madison turned to Don. "What is it exactly that you do?"

"I'm a professional concert goer and party animal. I do this and that," answered Don.

"Oh, I see. Aren't you a coke dealer, though?"

"Shhhh. We don't talk about that."

Everybody laughed as the darkened stage lit up with a wild flurry of lights. Warren Zevon came out on the stage with his band behind him. The crowd erupted with roaring and clapping. He broke into his hit "Werewolves of London" and the audience was hooked right away.

Flynn jumped in after the song. "I hope he's going to play every song from the *Excitable Boy* LP."

Just then Zevon started singing "Lawyers, Guns and Money."

"Love it," said Don.

"Sorry, guys. No All-Access Passes for this one. J.J. was better at that than I am. So, we'll just have to enjoy it from our private booth," said Miles.

"Guys, I'm trying to listen to the show," complained Madison.

"We'll shut up now," whispered Miles.

Flynn was already lost in the music.

★ ★ ★

When the concert was over, the group headed outside, where a near blizzard was starting to blanket the street. It was frigid. The temperature in the teens with a below zero wind chill. They desperately looked for a cab. At the corner of North Avenue they finally found one and jumped in.

"Where's the limo when we need it," quipped Flynn.

"Where to?" asked the cab driver.

"You guys going to the Street of Dreams?" asked Flynn.

"Yeah, Butch's or Mother's, Don?" asked Miles.

"Let's do Mother's."

The cab driver was listening. "Division Street, right?"

Through the limited visibility, the cab went slowly, slipping a little on the icy streets. After they dropped Miles and Don at Mother's, Flynn and Madison sat alone in the backseat.

"You wanna come up to my place?"

"I was thinking about it."

Flynn gave the cab driver the address.

Up in the apartment, Flynn lit a fire. Madison sat down in front of the fireplace anticipating the warmth that was just minutes away. Flynn headed for the kitchen and brought back a bottle of Old Style and a glass of red wine. He handed the wine glass to Madison on the floor and went to his record collection He picked out Neil Young's album *Everybody Knows This Is Nowhere*.

Flynn sat down next to Madison. "Music to get stoned by. You know, all those bands in the late sixties early seventies were making music for people to do just that. All those singer-songwriters like Joni Mitchell, Crosby, Stills and Nash, Jackson Browne, The Beatles, The Stones. It's all still relevant."

"I liked Zevon's rendition of 'Knocking on Heaven's Door,'" said Madison.

"Yeah, Dylan. He's probably the best writer of any of them. You want to hear *Nashville Skyline*? Or *The Basement Tapes* recorded at Big Pink with The Band? Levon Helm sings 'Yazoo Street Scandal' on one of them. Dylan really discovered the Band. They were called The Hawks back then."

Flynn gently embraced Madison and kissed her. She hungrily kissed him back. They became more and more passionate and moved over to the warm, thick rug in front of the coffee table. Flynn went into the bedroom and brought back a cozy comforter.

"Oh, that's nice," Madison said as she cuddled up under the comforter.

The fire crackled, the music filled the room and Flynn and Madison slowly made love. They were very gentle and affectionate with each other as if they had been doing this for years. When they were finished, Madison eased off of him and laid down next to him, then moved over and put her head on his chest.

"That was so nice. I've dreamed of this moment."

"It took us a long time to get here. But here is where we are."

"That makes a strange kind of sense."

"You should have told me a long time ago how you felt. You never gave me a hint."

"Well, we're here now. That's all that matters."

"You want to go again, Madison?"

She answered with a lingering kiss and they made love again.

★ ★ ★

In the morning, Flynn opened his front door and picked up the Sunday *Chicago Tribune*. Madison came out of Flynn's bedroom wearing one of his shirts and nothing else.

"You look great in my shirt. You should always wear it."

"I'll light a fire. My turn to do it. We will want to be cozy when we read the paper. I'll make some coffee. Got any eggs?"

"You can have anything in the refrigerator or cabinets. I don't keep a lot of food here, but I'm pretty sure there's bread."

"Bread and coffee. Wow. Can't wait."

A little while later the fire was blazing and Madison came in from the kitchen with two plates. Scrambled eggs and toast. She handed Flynn his plate and put hers on the coffee table. Then went back for the coffee.

"You're a genius. And I actually had eggs. You made a meal out of the Flynn-no-meals kitchen."

"I told you I was more than an assistant director."

"Can't believe what I've been missing."

Flynn grabbed Madison in a bear hug and kissed her before they dug into their breakfast.

THE YEAR THAT ROCKED

★ ★ ★

Flynn was in the booth on the set of *The Brett Adams Show*. The studio audience was getting settled. Jeremy and Isaac were camera-ready. Madison came in with a bio of that day's guest. Irene Bozman, Head of Psychiatry at the University of Chicago Hospital.

"Happy Shrink Day," she said as she read the notes out loud.

Flynn broke in, "Oh, please, let me lie down on your couch and you can solve all my problems."

The techs in the booth were laughing and on the floor Jeremy and Isaac and Zeke broke into it, too.

"I haven't told you guys. I'm starting my own show. *Rock the Town*. A talk show featuring rock musicians. The network has given me Saturday night at 10 P.M. No live audience. A very intimate format for interviewing the music elite. If any of you guys want to jump ship and come with me, let me know. I'll be hiring the crew myself."

"I've already jumped ship," said Madison. "I'm going to direct."

"Sounds intriguing," Isaac mused.

"Everybody's welcome. I'll be staffing up and I'm still working on the guest list," said Flynn.

On the stage, Brett came out of the wings and sat in his chair. "Cue the theme music," said Flynn.

The cameramen spoke in unison. "Ready."

Zeke did the countdown.

Brett took off. "Welcome to *The Brett Adams Show*. Today's guest is Irene Bozman, Head of Psychiatry at the University of Chicago Hospital."

The tall, good-looking doctor entered from stage right. She shook hands with Brett.

★ ★ ★

Madison and Flynn were at their usual table by the fireplace at Gio's. They were both eating pasta and sharing a bottle of good Cabernet Sauvignon.

"Okay, I've talked to reps from Foreigner, Journey, The Eagles and The Who. Nobody wanted to do it. This is harder than I thought," said Flynn.

"What about Tom Petty? You said he was pretty accessible," added Madison.

"Yeah, oh, and Fleetwood Mac. Stevie Nicks was pretty cool. But a lot of groups don't want to be near Chicago in January."

"Just keep at it. You'll get a great first guest. Then after that it'll be word-of-mouth."

"I'm glad you're my producer. And if you were my girlfriend, too, that would be okay."

"I don't know if we're at the girlfriend/boyfriend stage yet."

"It felt like it the other night."

"True. But I'm still a little scared. You've always had a trophy, high-maintenance type. Complete opposite of me."

"I like complete opposite. It's new and I definitely like it."

"But we'll be working together."

"That makes it even better."

Madison raised her glass. Flynn followed suit. They clinked and shared an intimate smile.

★ ★ ★

Flynn sat inside the broadcast studio at WQXA. Skye Matthews was on-the-air. "Midnight Rambler" by the Rolling Stones soared through the ceiling speakers. Skye turned down the music to talk with Flynn.

"I'm going to a commercial break after this song. Hang on a minute and we can talk." When the commercial came on, he turned down the monitor again.

Flynn jumped in, "Hey, man, Skye! How's it going? How's the new Program Director?"

"Man, he's not J.J. He's already added a bunch of punk music. And it bugs me 'cause this is a rock-and-roll station. I want it to be kept pure."

"Yeah, I know what you mean. I want my show to be pure rock-and-roll, too. Speaking of that, I wanted to ask you how to rope these musicians and bands in?"

"Free stuff. They love free stuff. Who's on your wish list for the opening show?"

"Foreigner, Journey, Fleetwood Mac, Tom Petty."

"Talk to their managers. See who will be in town."

"Do you know anybody personally?"

"Tommy Shaw from Styx. I'll talk to him."

"Thanks, man. A bunch of us are headed over to The Palm at 5. Wanna join us?"

"I'll be there. Gotta get back to my board." He turned the monitor back up and the commercial had segued to REO Speedwagon's "Ridin' the Storm Out."

★ ★ ★

Flynn and Madison walked the last stretch of sidewalk to The Palm. Across the street, the icy wind rose off of Lake Michigan to meet them. Madison pulled up her fur-lined hood the last couple of feet. When they reached the hangout they had trouble, as usual, opening the door against the wind. Finally, somebody came out the door and they scooted in while it was open.

Inside, it felt like a warm cocoon. The bar was jumping. They hung their coats on brass pegs and grabbed the last two barstools at the end of the bar. Flynn looked around and noticed Skye and Miles. He waved and they made their way over.

The bartender approached. "Hey, man, Frank! How's it going? I'm into Johnnie Walker Black today, straight up. I'm giving up my ice cube. Madison, what do you desire?"

"I'll have a glass of your best Merlot."

Miles and Skye stood next to the stools. "Buy these guys a drink, too." They gave Frank their order.

Flynn sipped his drink. "I just found out that the difference in alcohol content between Johnnie Walker Black and Johnnie Walker Red is 4%. So, it doesn't really matter which one you drink."

"You're so full of factoids, Flynn," said Miles. "Where do you find this information?"

"I read the *Tribune* and *Rolling Stone*."

A new face appeared at the bar. Miles introduced him as Bud Stanton, the new Program Director at WQXA. Everybody exchanged greetings.

"Flynn, I know that name. You're infamous at the station for getting all those All-Access Passes. 'Course it was J.J. Watts doing it, but still you were part of it. Skye told me you're starting a new music show. Let me know if I can help."

"Thanks. You'll love the music scene here. A lot of rockers come through this part of the country," said Flynn.

Suddenly, Don came up to the bar, seemingly out of nowhere. "Anybody want to go to the bathroom?"

Bud asked, "Is this the blow guy? I've heard of him, too. Yeah, I'll go."

Miles and Skye were already headed in that direction.

"Where does that guy come from all the time? He gives me the creeps," said Madison.

"He floats around on the fringes. That's his job," said Flynn.

"Weird."

"Of course, but he serves his purpose if you want some blow. And a lot of people do."

"Not me. Not tonight."

"Same for me. I'm into drinking tonight."

When Don, Miles, Skye and Bud came back, they all wanted another round of drinks. Frank was at-the-ready and took their orders.

Bud addressed Flynn. "I was thinking about your new show and I do know somebody who'd be great. Jackson Browne. I know him really well. I'll see what I can do."

"Far-out! Jackson Browne would be great. I'll call you at the station next week."

The talk turned to music and the drinking continued.

★ ★ ★

Later, when they exited the restaurant it had dropped about twenty degrees. The temperature was hovering around zero and the windchill was -12. Madison and Flynn walked up to Michigan to find a cab for the short ride to his apartment.

Back in Flynn's apartment the fire was roaring and crackling. They sat together on the couch and cuddled. Flynn lit a joint from the tray on the coffee table, took a hit and passed it to Madison.

"Something about a roaring fire and marijuana. The fire seems so alive. You can get totally mesmerized by it," said Madison.

Flynn agreed. "That's why I took this apartment. There were some in the building that were bigger, but I wanted a wood-burning fireplace."

"Good choice."

"We'll have to go to your place sometime. We don't always have to be here."

"I don't have a fireplace. But I do have a view of the lake."

"Your apartment can be our summer hangout."

"Deal."

Madison spoke hesitantly. "You sure you're not moving too fast after Stephanie? It worries me a little."

"I do everything fast. Doesn't mean it's wrong."

"True. But I guess I'm looking for something along the lines of commitment. I've dated a lot since college."

"Yeah, the period of my life where I must have been braindead not to notice you."

"You were too busy being the President of Students for a Democratic Society. To spell it out for you. SDS and trophy women."

"Forget that. We're together now."

"Some things are worth waiting for." She reached over and kissed him gently.

They fell into a passionate embrace. Then Flynn went into the bedroom and came back with the comforter. He put it on the rug as close to the fireplace as it could get without starting on fire. They stayed there all night.

★ ★ ★

Flynn was in his office on the phone. He was talking to the head of the network, Barry Sanders.

"...Yes, I know the first show is January 8th. No, I don't have a first guest yet. Yes, I know I'm out if I don't get someone. Yes, I have to schedule the other shows as well. Okay, okay. I'll talk to you on New Year's Eve."

He hung up the phone as Madison walked into his office.

"What gives?" she asked.

"Barry Sanders is calling me on New Year's Eve and I need to be buttoned up with a guest for my show."

"That's only a week away."

"Thanks for reminding me."

"Someone will come through. Street of Dreams, remember? Always keep that in mind."

"Who's on the show today?"

"Another self-help guru. Didn't you know? The seventies will be known as the decade for getting in touch with your feelings. It's almost 1980. There will be something completely different."

"I'm in touch with my feelings. I'm terrified."

"Someone will come through. Right now, we've got a show to do."

Flynn grabbed the clipboard off his desk and followed Madison out the door.

★ ★ ★

It was New Year's Eve day and Flynn was in his office trying to hit the ceiling with some sharp pencils. Madison came in and sat in one of the visitor chairs.

"The deadline is approaching."

"N.B.D. I'm becoming fatalistic about it."

Madison laughed. "Tonight will be fun at Ernie's New Year's Eve party. I've seen the infamous Mt. Everest-size mounds of cocaine. I'll even have some for a New Year's treat."

A ringing telephone could be heard from Madison's cubicle. Then a second ringing immediately following.

"Two phone calls. I'll go grab them in my space."

Flynn looked down at his phone and saw two red lights flashing. Madison was back. "You're not going to believe this!"

"What?"

"It's Tom Petty on line one. Says he wants to talk to you about being on *Rock the Town*."

"Far-fucking-out!"

"The other line is Barry Sanders, his highness of the network."

"I'll take the Petty call first. Put his highness on hold."

Madison went back to the phones. Flynn relaxed in his chair and put his feet up on the desk. He punched the first flashing button and picked up the phone.

"Hey, man, Tom!..."